PRAISE FOR

BOREAL

"Seas of green broken by white peaks. A place to forget and to be forgotten. This anthology is lovingly curated with stories of monsters and worlds that moved on. The horror shatters the door to your winter cabin to splinters or lurks among the pines. It walks into your remote mountain tavern with a different mask each night, or haunts the crumbling halls of your gingerbread home. The strength of voice in these tales is remarkable. Threaded through this disconnected Universe is an emotional resonance that holds it together beautifully. Highly recommended."

L. P. Hernandez, Author of *In the Valley of the Headless Men*

"*BOREAL: An Anthology of Taiga Horror* blurs the boundaries between reality and nightmare as characters navigate towering forests in search of meaning, redemption, safety, or escape. Survival is uncertain in this unforgiving wilderness, where even the briefest encounter leaves a lingering echo amongst the trees. Each story offers a haunting exploration of isolation and inner darkness, where the only certainty is that one will never be truly alone."

-Amanda Headlee, author of *Till We Become Monsters* and *Madness and Greatness Can Share the Same Face*

BOREAL

Collection Copyright © 2025 Strange Wilds Press
All individual stories are owned by their respective authors.
Paperback ISBN: 979-8-9923509-0-6
E-Book ISBN: 979-8-9923509-1-3

All rights reserved. No part of this book may be reproduced in any form or by any electronic or mechanical means including information storage and retrieval systems, without the permission in writing from the authors except by a reviewer, who may quote brief passages.

This book contains works of fiction. Anything that bears resemblance to real people, places, or events is coincidental and unintentional.

Content warnings are listed in the back of the book by story.

Published by Strange Wilds Press
Print first edition: February 25th, 2025
E-book first edition: February 25th, 2025

Cover design by Katherine Silva
www.katherinesilvaauthor.com
Strange Wilds Press Logo by MartaLeo
Cover photos and assets courtesy of Pexels, Unsplash, and Canva

B O R E A L

AN ANTHOLOGY OF TAIGA HORROR

edited by KATHERINE SILVA

SWP

CONTENTS

INTRODUCTION

Boreal, otherwise known as the subarctic or taiga biomes are some of the most widespread ecosystems on our planet. We often view them as cold and inhospitable, home to the hardiest of survivors, to the mysterious, the brutally fierce, and the antediluvian. Whatever appears to survive in these places does so because it has the fortitude to endure the toughest of conditions. For centuries, these forests have lain untouched by humankind, offering shelter to a variety of species, from caribou to tamarack to Siberian tiger.

But what happens when humans intersect with these ancient woods? What kind of mirror do they become for us to reflect back on ourselves? Do we try to adapt in their wake or do we conquer as humans have done for centuries? Do we destroy, do we let it destroy us or do we find some way to harmonize?

Collected here are twenty-two stories of grief, existentialism, and self-reflection all taking place within the taiga biome and amidst the boreal forests within that environment. These stories come from known authors in the horror genre as well as first-time storytellers and all have something inexplicably unique to say about how the boreal landscape has impacted them.

Trek alongside an adventurer in his quest to scale a mountain peak in J.R. Santos's *Cold White Teeth*, be carried off into the deep dark pines in *In The High Places* by Ally Wilkes and fight against the voices that try to dominate your spirit in Brian Rowe's *Desecrations*. These are only a few of the horrors awaiting within these pages. We hope you enjoy getting lost in them.

Remember to keep a light with you at all times, tell a friend where you'll be embarking. If you find yourself adrift in the verdant darkness, remember that you're not alone. There's always something lurking just beyond the light.

- Katherine Silva, editor

CABIN CREATURES

E.M. ROY

Trails are scattered throughout the wilderness all over the world. Hiking trails, game trails, paved pathways and well-worn walks. Twisting and turning like tangled veins between the trees. All trails have unique destinations. All trails lead to the cabin.

Untouched by time, the cabin seems to exist lightyears away from civilization. Gnarled wood paneling, a rickety covered porch and just two rooms: one for sleeping and one for gathering. Well-crafted, sturdy, and quaint. It smells of wood stove and pine. Nostalgia. Home, even when darkness falls at impossible hours and the days turn to minutes. Even when the cold comes to claim its forest and all the unknowable inhabitants.

Now, the cabin houses two women. Signe stands boiling a pot of water on the stove at its heart, warming herself and the surrounding walls. The light from the small contained flames caresses her hands, her face, but she is not comforted. She braids her blonde hair back and glances over her shoulder at the door for the thousandth time. It does not open. Pinpricks of stars find their way through the windows and their paths are unbroken by passing travelers. She sighs and bites at her fingernails.

Signe's wool sock-covered feet tread over to one of the cabin's few cabinets. It opens with a shrill noise on tired but willing hinges and she retrieves two tea bags from its depths. The cabin knows they are tea bags because they always make its rooms smell of lavender, lemon, and elm. Floors creak beneath Signe in anticipation of such delicious warmth.

The tea bags fall into two empty mugs as the water begins to bubble at the stove. Signe's long fingers worry at the thread of one as she stares unfocused before her.

Then, a different sound cuts through the quiet. Crunching snow beneath running, stumbling feet. Closer and closer. A weight suddenly collapses against the front door of the cabin, and the porch trembles in protest. Signe flinches and lunges for the doorknob.

"Halley?" The door swings open to reveal Signe's wife on her knees. Half-frozen, snow in her dark hair and eyelashes, blood runs down the side of her face. Halley's icy blue eyes are wide and feral. "What the fuck?!" Signe yanks her to her feet and into the cabin's embrace. Gravity, or some other force, shuts the heavy door behind them unnoticed.

"It…it saw me—I think I woke it up," Halley stutters. Her body convulses under the harsh kiss of winter, as if she carried the cold in with her like a pack on her shoulders. The thick blanket Signe drapes over her does almost nothing to lessen the burden. "I-it's coming!"

"What? What saw you, baby? You're all right, here. I'm making some tea that'll warm you up—" The water is bubbling over the rim of the pot. It stings against the stovetop.

"No! We need to hide!" Halley grips her wife's wrist in a vise. She's pushing away the hand that holds a cloth, delicately wiping the wound at her temple.

The cold weaves tendrils of night through the two rooms of the cabin. Signe and Halley's bed, its multitude of blankets, a rug-covered living room and couch, photos and artwork adorning the walls. The cabin has never felt more exposed. "Halley, there's nowhere to go—"

A thundering. Tree branches snapping like bones. The impressions in the snow of Halley's panicked boots are overtaken by something bigger.

The forest gives way to a shadow. The thing steps onto the porch and it has to duck down to fit under the overhanging roof. Boards break into splinters beneath it. Breath fogs up the windows and obscures the stars.

Halley scrambles like a cornered animal into the bedroom, while Signe tiptoes over to a chest built into the floor. She opens the lid on silent hinges and loads the shotgun waiting inside. Her heartbeat ricochets off of the wood paneling. Aims the gun at the front door and waits.

Heedless of the latch, the door bursts open and snaps from its frame, hanging limp and lopsided. An unleashed gust of winter wind extinguishes the flame within the stovetop. With lumbering effort, the thing bends down to look inside the cabin. A penetrating red glare is framed by massive, molting moose antlers. Bloody tissue falls in tendrils from the forked branches. A broad and fiendish countenance glares inside with red reflective corneas that feel too far apart. The antlers and the shape of its skull are at least remotely recognizable; but this is no moose. The cabin knows this because moose do not stand on two legs.

Signe screams and fires the shotgun directly between the creature's red eyes. The sound hurts in the enclosed space, but the creature barely falters. Instead, the shadow slowly parts below the eyes and widens into a gleaming wolf grin, full of canine teeth and bloodstained gums. Droplets of gore and saliva seem to freeze when they touch the wooden floor, joined by a string of strange tissue from its molting antlers.

It lumbers forward. The creature's antlers knock unevenly against the wooden doorframe, too wide to fit through. It snarls instead and reaches a thick-pelted forelimb inside. The appendage is padded, but with extended digits not unlike fingers topped with crooked claws and too many swollen joints. It stretches towards Signe's shaking, frozen form. She still clutches the shotgun as if it were nailed to her palms. She leans against the wall as the creature's distended claws inch towards her throat. The cabin supports her weight, as it was built to do, but it cannot shelter her from this fate.

Halley then dashes out from the bedroom and throws the pot of still-steaming hot water into the creature's face.

The limb snatches back to its owner in an instant. Its red eyes squeeze shut as the flesh sizzles and smokes. Through teeth sharper than daggers, it releases an earsplitting, window-shattering howl. Glass shards explode out into the night from the force of the eldritch screech, and Signe and Halley's ears leak blood with their own cries of pain joining the cacophony. It trudges backwards off the porch and into the snow, still emitting deadly reverberations of grief and agony. The forest parts to clear a trail wide enough to suit the creature. Its dark pelt and hulking antlers melt back into the trees' embrace.

Signe and Halley collapse onto wood floors that are powerless to cushion their fall. Their breath comes heavily, shuddering against the cold leeching into the cabin through the broken door. Gravity, or some other force, is unable to close it. Something is wrong ; the blood doesn't stop flowing. Halley crawls to her wife against the wall and allows her head to fall into her lap. They each speak comforting words that the other cannot hear. Redness pools beneath them and seeps into the wood flooring, the rug...and then they are quiet.

The cabin eventually knows they are dead because its rooms smell sickly sweet and rotten.

It stays that way for a while, until even the smell abandons the cabin.

Now, the cabin houses a fox.

Her fur is at its thickest, warding off the cruel winter months. Though, at this point, a thaw is on the horizon. She is apprehensive at first, but trusts the trails that led her here. Wind whistling through shattered windows, snow blowing in wherever it can. It's dark within the old wooden walls. As if to shut her out. As if to grieve in solitude. To rot, alone.

The fox lifts her snout to sniff the air, and finds that there is no life inside this strange den. So, she makes herself at home.

She tears up the bedsheets and shreds the rug. Rips holes in the couch with her teeth and plucks out the downy cushioning within. The cabin submits to her; that is all it can do. She collects the softest material into a sizable nest, and settles herself in it with a fluffy tail covering her chilly nose.

The fox becomes three in Signe and Halley's bedroom; two wriggling kits warmed by their mother's belly. The cabin does its job, insulating its inhabitants as the snow becomes pouring rain and the forest becomes green. The kits teethe on the femurs and ribs so eagerly discovered in the main part of their den. It smells of fur, dust, and distantly, pine. Once in a while, an uncanny scream echoes between the trees from miles and miles away, and the cabin quivers on a crumbling foundation. The fox-mother perks her ears and guards the entryway to her den intently.

It stays that way for a while, until the kits grow to mirror their mother in stature. Even this trio of foxes stops returning back to the den.

Now, the cabin remains barren. Winter arrives to greet its skeletal structure, the mismatched bones and frozen wood stove at its core. The snow is heavier than it ever has been before on the cabin's exhausted roof. But it does not cave in. It waits. It remembers.

And the night finally comes. Stars poke holes through the darkness, the trees awash in moonlight. Vibrant greens, blues, purples carve winding trails in the sky. Shifting, illuminating lights to guide lost creatures home.

The hulking creature with moose antlers and wolf teeth reappears.

The cabin creaks its floorboards. Nails fluctuating, settling, woodgrain ever-so-slightly bending of its own accord. It creates different rhythms. Mimics Signe's soft footfalls. Halley's urgent movement. Even the fox-mother's pacing and her kits' tussling. Noises of life transmitted through the longstanding wood edifices. The slightest of flames flickers among the ashes in the wood stove. Gathers strength to share any semblance of warmth. It is the phantom smell of tea that lures the murderous creature back .

Piercing red eyes gleam through the windows, the doorway, as it did so long ago. Gravity, or some other force, shuts a cabinet in the darkness. The creature lurches toward the sound. It's starving, and turns the brittle walls into splinters with its massive bloody antlers in its mad struggle to enter. Its heavy footsteps cause the cabin's weakened foundation to creak and groan. Just a bit longer. Hold on just a few moments more.

In Signe and Halley's bedroom—the fox-mother and her kits' den—the cabin shapes the wind into whispers. Lost voices, murmured declarations, yips and comforting croons.

The creature is drawn to the room like a moth to flame.

It enters, splitting wood in its wake, and finds the room, the whole cabin, is abandoned. Before the creature can turn to run, the roof collapses under the weight of snow, and the foundation sinks into the frozen ground. It howls its lethal, unearthly cry, but is cut short by the crushing beams that split its skull with their weight and send preternatural blood spilling new trails into the white of the snow. The winter-toughened ground opens to swallow the creature until snow, wood splinters, and dirt cave in on top of it. The green and blue and purple paths in the sky converge above this singular point. The forest itself quakes for miles in all directions, shuddering snow off of the most precarious and remote tree branches, until every creature on every trail knows that the cabin's revenge has been wrought.

All trails lead to the cabin. Now, in the spring, the wood ruins of the house is overgrown by innumerable, bountiful plants. Animals visit its nooks and crannies, raise their young in its shelter for a while. Hikers stumble upon it, remark upon the craftsmanship evident even in its destruction, and then they move on. Winters come and go, and certain spaces between the wood planks are able to keep the mice, squirrels, and other small critters warm. They do not know they rest upon a grave, a birthplace, memories, and forgotten, fragile lives. It smells of pine. It is home to many creatures.

The cabin loves them all.

EVERY MASK, ANOTHER CASK

AKIS LINARDOS

A stranger wearing a crow mask entered my inn. It wasn't a plague-doctor kind of mask, nor even the half-face one women wore at the masquerades of our town. It was a full-head crow mask with beady eyes, a large shiny beak, and fake—I thought, *hoped*—feathers reaching down his neck.

"It's not a crow," he corrected me, voice tobacco-raspy, when I approached his table and asked him why he looked like one. "Can't you see the glossy sheen of the feathers?"

There was indeed a bluish glimmer to the mask. "Apologies, sir, I—"

"Assumptions again. I am Madame Raven. You may sir someone else. In the meantime, I want your best ale from oakwood cask. And please tell me what a raven could eat in this place?"

I stared at her dumbstruck for a while. It was a slow day for my tavern, like any day was midwinter. People cozied up in their homes and aside from a traveling merchant seeking refuge from the cold, I had not seen a single person in five days. So, maybe my charisma was rusty. Or maybe I grew numb in the head from this person's tomfoolery.

"So?" she asked.

"Uh, yeah, right. The best ale. Oakwood helps with the aging process so it's my personal favorite. Vanilla, spice, and subtle hints of oak suffuse the ale. Excellent choice."

My smile was met with a blank beady stare. Which I suppose was the best I could expect.

When I brought her the ale some time later, I had somewhat surpassed the unsettling feeling this masked person exuded, and reverted to my flamboyant (as I like to think) personality. I hoisted the wooden pint and thumped it on her table allowing some cool foam to spill on my hand for effect.

"Here you go, ma'am. Best ale you ever had. A hearth and a pint make the heart warm and shine."

Beady-eyed stare. She did not appreciate the flamboyance. "My heart has no need for warmth. And be wary of shine, lest it give you away in the night."

"A figure of speech. But anyone needs a warm touch to the soul."

Beady eyes on the pint now. A bird-like cocking of her head, which seemed appropriate. Not natural, though.

I was curious to see the person beneath. What if the woman was severely disfigured? Or if she had an enormous mole?

Instead of sipping, she stared at me again for a long, awkward moment.

I took it as a sign: a quiet demand for privacy, so I nodded and smiled—awkwardly, I assume—and returned to the bar. I clenched my jaw against the urge to look over my back.

THE STRANGER CAME a second time wearing what I thought was a beaver mask and fur down to the belly.

Not *the* stranger. *A* stranger, because they corrected me again—this time voice heavy and bass.

"It's not a beaver; it's a bear. And what makes you think we are a she? We're man from lip to toe, can't you tell? Can't you see the slowness of our gait and the weathered fingers? Or did my eyes fool you?"

It was true, the fingers were different. Where there were colored nails black as midnight before, now there was natural pale, and grime on the tips. But although men were generally slobbier, even my mama's fingers had been dirty mid-winter. She'd smelled as bad as he, too—a mix of spoiled tomato and fresh herbs to cover the rot of our own food—although this stranger carried the tang more reminiscent of wild animals, like he'd just been gutting rabbits.

He made my spine shiver. I never believed it was a beaver, but I didn't want to accept the beastly alternative. While traveling merchants were fine with discussing about pacifist bears in distant lands, no one from this side of the world wanted to talk about such things—much less cloak themselves into them. Maybe pacifists there, in a dreamland I failed to fathom, but here? Bloodthirsty killers, hungry for bellies of men and innards full of digested meals. They were the devil's own animals.

Still, in a world of stalking shadows and prowling beasts, an inn like mine was meant to be a safe haven for all. "My mama moved slow, too, dear patron, and her fingernails were just as grimy. I should never have assumed, though. I don't mind what's your business, and I'm happy to receive the business you're willing to impart. In my inn, you can be what you want to be. Beaver, bear and all the rest. You are the second one to come to my inn all dressed. Going to a festival?"

"No one is dressed. We simply follow. Now, have you chestnut?"

"Chestnut?"

"A fine ale, stored in chestnut cask. That's our desire. Give us ale and quench our thirst."

The way he spoke, raspier, rougher, like a beast drunk in bucketfuls of alcohol, and now the eyes, in a way I could not put into words, pierced through me, punctuating his request for alcohol. Motherly eyes of a wolf seeking to feed its cubs—or one cornered to protect them. It was all wrong, so wrong, it planted an idea in my mind: there had to be something off with my own head, or something wrong with the world entirely. I couldn't shake the feeling that something worse than devil-bears stalked the forest, loomed closer, and these patrons were all masking themselves to hide their human smell from it.

Nonsense.

Might just be a wandering circus came to a nearby town, a preparation for a grand festival these people stroll from. Or got fired from—which would explain their uptightness, strangeness, and the aura of bloodthirst. Nothing like being fired to make you angry at the world.

"That is an unusual request." I forced myself to smile. Forced the bright vibrant persona to cloak my own dread. "I haven't had one asked in years! The finest ale in chestnut. Adding the slightest sweetness and nutty flavor to the brew. A depth in taste to remember."

"That we like to hear. We are thirsty for succulent, chestnut cask liquid. It wards the chill of the winter forest. Sweetness to make our bones feel right and the flesh digested settle."

I swallowed at the word *flesh*. My smile was unstable at the very least, the muscles twitching, struggling to keep it straight.

"I'll be right back."

I hurried away from this man as nonchalantly as I could muster. But as I took the second step, a guttural, hungry growl gave me pause.

My gaze strayed to the far-right wall. Beyond the barred window, the midnight wind whooshed wildly against the wooden shutters. Although I squinted, hoping to believe a beast prowled the rustling bushes past that wall, I knew the source had not come from there.

The source was the man behind my back.

At that moment I realized how isolated my inn was, in mid-winter, mid-storm, and in the middle of a barren night.

I craved to twist around and witness whatever happened behind me but I stood frozen like a rabbit before the looming predator. The more my back remained exposed, the more naked I felt, my bare chubby sides within reach for him to grab and force me to stillness. Or maybe he didn't have to grab me at all, petrified as I was by his mere presence—soon beastly fangs would dig deep holes into my neck.

"The chestnut?" the throaty voice said, still in his chair. My chest unclenched.

By some weird relief, I turned dumb-smiling at him, and nodded like a child eager to please his father and show him what a good boy he was.

NIGHTMARES PLAGUED ME of a snout digging deep into my belly, pushing inexorably with muscles iron-strong in places inside me nothing should reach. The beast shoved me powerless against the wall, and I'd awake banging my head against the rough oakwood of my bed.

Drenched in sweat, I'd trudge down from my room to the bar, and dull my mind with ale from a cask of beech. A subtle earthy, slightly smoky flavor. To quiet my buzzing mind, to quiet the wild nights I spent alone.

Until a stranger came again.

He knocked three times, times three. Three knocks upon the window, three knocks upon the oakwood walls. Then three upon my inn's main door, and with the final knock, he shoved.

This time the stranger was a man with ashen hair, and although he wore no mask upon his head, somehow his cloak of midnight feathers made him more crow-like even than Madame Raven.

His knuckles rapped upon the wooden pillars, rapped upon the elm chair back, and rapped thrice upon the table surface, banging the final rap with a demand. "Cask of ash. Your strongest ale."

His words were sugar, honey-sweet. Though it shames me to admit, they made my manhood hard as wood. Maybe that was why I acted so rashly, why I wanted him out of my inn.

Maybe I feared my masculinity assaulted by this man of poison words. A man like me should not grow hard for a man like that. What did that really speak of my own will I wondered? To crumble before the cadence of a sentence. To feel my own knees weak like a little boy in love with only a glimpse of this marble statue of an angelic face.

"Ale in ash," he repeated. "Bring to me."

Had he ignored my words? No, I must not have spoken. In my mind I had imagined a whole fight. Demanding him out of my inn. The echo of a voice within the chambers of my mind buzzed and pulsed with the craving to get him away, out of here, out into the night where he belonged.

Rap-pap-pap his knuckles rapped on the table surface punctuating three words: "Make it quick."

Three words. Three times my body throbbed. First my mind emptied of any hostile intention, second my heart rushed with warm comforting blood, and third the viscous love-liquid spilled to my trousers.

There was no real reason for him to leave.

More importantly, I didn't want him to leave.

"The finest ale," I said at last. But my voice was not my voice. It was frog-like, spider thin. I coughed. "We have—" I coughed again, struggling to find the voice of the innkeeper. "We—" What did it matter, how shrill my voice was? I had to tell him. "We have the finest rooms as well. Please, please stay for one night. It's on me."

No, one night was not enough. "Please stay forever."

"That is unnecessary." He looked at me with bloodred eyes, with cherry-red mouth. Juicy divine cherries, handpicked by heavenly maidens to shape the perfect set of lips. Ones to suckle on forevermore. "You will follow," he said. "Now, Frog, bring."

I did as he told me, my mind swollen with thoughts of the delicious tongue hidden behind his sugar words. I licked my own lips, only to realize my tongue had grown larger than I recalled it, longer, pulled back and magnetized, craving to thrust itself through cherry lips.

Happy to go wherever he pleased, envisioning the wet touch of his word-shaper upon my mouth, I rushed behind the bar. Wrong, I didn't rush——I *hopped*, so over-full with joy I was.

Under the linen covers, I pulled the finest ashen cask, and as I pulled, I bumped my head on the shelf above, clattering the bottles. Messy, messy, messy—don't be messy before his presence, I chastised myself.

But the impact had dislodged something from my cheeks. Made me itchy beneath the skin. With strange relief I wormed my fingers into my mouth, and pulled from the lower lip, squeezed my own mask out of me and dropped it to the floor.

It was my face.

It was not my face. It was the mask I wore so long, wrapped around me to imprison my true self. What a relief to have it gone. An innkeeper no more, now the Master finally found me, saved me from my own delusions. Saved me from the lies the humans said, about how I was born, about who I was. What I was called.

Now another name cloaks me in warm shadows, and I can be his Frog once more.

GATHERING OF THE DEAD

VINCENT WEST

There's a monster in the woods of my town that eats girls.

The warning itself is engrained so deeply that I can't recall the first time I heard it said. I knew about it before it was used against me as a reprimand, with the calloused fingers of my father gripping tight around my forearms.

"You can't play this far from home," he scolds. "Do you know what might happen?"

I do know because the story feels like a mantra in my head, but not everything makes sense when you're six. I cry and cry rather than make any real answer to his question, and my father's shame quiets his voice straight away.

As I'm carried home, I see the woods over his shoulder. My wet eyes look between the trees and imagine what dark creature might've snatched me away if my father hadn't found me first.

IN GROUPS, children are dangerous storytellers. Riling one another up is almost too simple a task and little lies breed into big fears.

It's an easy story to tell and a fun game to play: pretend to venture into the woods and get gobbled up as a result. We take turns playing monsters or damsels (naturally no boy ever wants to play the latter) until one day, a game ends in sobs.

No one wants the teacher to hear and scold us, so we're quick to try to soothe her, but any attempt at comfort is shot down by her tearful declaration: "It isn't funny!"

For some time, she cries without elaboration, but eventually she says more. It doesn't take much since her misery makes her explain.

"My sister is gone," she manages through trembling lips, "And if I'm not careful, I'll get eaten, too!"

At the time, it's enough to stun a group of meek children into abandoning the game for the rest of the school year. At home, however, I start to wonder.

Is that really the truth or just a story to scare a daughter from venturing too close to the woods?

Is all of it that way?

AS I GROW OLDER, cracks in the story begin to show. Curiosity leads to questions and answers are equally ominous and unconvincing.

"What kind of monster is it?" I ask my father, whose whole livelihood is involved with the woods. It's is safe for him, of course, but not for me.

"I don't know. No one knows," he explains. "No one who meets it survives."

"Then if no one has seen it, how do people know there's a monster?" I push.

Brows furrowed together, my father's tone turns short. "Where do you think all those girls disappear to?" he asks. His voice picks up volume as he continues, "What else do you think could do those awful things to them? Leave them in such horrible shape, until we find them? What do you think is capable of—"

He stops himself, eyes going wide before his expression sours.

I don't ask him about monsters again or about my absent mother.

NOW THAT I'm older, I know better.

When you're a child, no one tells you anything. The disappearances are simply that: disappearances without a trace or origin or hope to understand. When you're older, you hear whispers.

A mother loses her child and locks herself up in her room for weeks, refusing to speak to the man who should, by now, be a father. Then, she vanishes in the woods. A young girl is engaged to a man twice her age with a reputation for beating his dogs, and then she vanishes, too. A wife who is overheard arguing with her husband nearly every night doesn't need to make good on the threat of leaving him—she simply disappears as well.

So, what is this monster? A cultish beast who men pray to in order to remove troublesome women? Or is it something far more ordinary than that? Is it a kinder way to describe a suicide or an excuse to give cruel men? Is it easier to name an unfit husband a monster, rather than have people believe a violent man shares their quiet town?

But none of those men ever disappear. They simply go about their lives and the monster continues to be fed.

MY FATHER, old and bearing no sons, works himself raw. The colder the days get, the higher the demand for firewood, and my father returns looking stiffer than any tree he's ever chopped down. He shouldn't be working; there are men younger than him to take the job… But there's no work in town for an old man who needs to provide for his child.

"Let me help then," I offer. "I can do something."

A wave of his weathered hand answers me, the motion colder than he's ever given before. "You know perfectly well that you can't."

"But why not?" Frustration edges in. "What is it about me that means I can't survive in the woods and you can?"

"You're a girl," he answers. "You know what that means."

My face burns hot and my hands clench. I don't argue any further because no amount of yelling will let me anywhere near the woods.

It would only further convince him I don't belong there.

ON SOME wild, angered fit, I march from the house. I tell myself I'll step right in and I'll prove him wrong. With my father's axe, taken without his knowledge or consent, I'll either cut down a tree or cut down whatever monster might attempt to stop me.

I do stop and it's not because of some dark force.

On the edge of the woods, out in the cold, a young girl plays: picking up freshly fallen snow and throwing it up in the air. She spots me and waves her tiny mittened hand.

I wave my own in return. Relief washes over me that she greets me rather than flees into the trees at the sight of a stranger. Considering the wild state of my appearance, and the axe in my hand, that would be a reasonable response.

"What are you doing out here?" I ask as I step forward. "You shouldn't be out here. It's dangerous"

"Why?" she counters, which nauseates my stomach.

My shoulders sink. All of my righteous defiance deflates out of my chest. I can't. It's one thing to take a chance myself but the moment I see her, the reality of it all crashes in, and I immediately feed into the superstition that I was in the middle of so actively resisting.

"There's a monster in the woods," I tell her. "It eats girls."

"I'm not a girl right now," she tells me. "I'm a bird."

As she says it, she mimes wings with her arms, flapping them as she soars over the snow. I can only watch her, silent and still. I'm afraid for her and, at the same time, a stab of envy bites in: how has she lasted so long without having this mantra sung in her ear over and over?

Or does it simply not matter to her? In her head, is the simple logic that she can just become something else which makes her untouchable?

"Birds fly away for the winter," I tell her. "Should we go away? Maybe towards home?"

She nods, fully accepting, and I walk her home: one hand in hers and one on my father's axe.

ONE NIGHT, while my restlessness leaves me awake, I see movement by the woods. I can't decide if it's bravery or foolishness that draws me outside but I am rewarded with a familiar face instead of claws and teeth.

I recognize her as a runaway sooner than I see her for who she is. "Oh, it's only you," says a girl I've known for most of my life, though it takes me a moment to place her. She's bundled up in a heavy coat and has brought a basket.

"Where are you going?" I ask, though I know the answer already.

The sight of her ready to brave these woods feels surreal when not so long ago, through tears and sobs, she stopped a childish game and insisted her sister had been swallowed whole.

The runaway shuffles her feet. "It's all just stories, you know." She sounds as if she's trying to convince herself more than me. "They just do it to keep us here; keep us isolated…And they use it as an excuse for all the harm they do."

I stand very still across from her. Hearing the words I so often tell myself in my own head should feel inspiring. Instead my stomach churns with icy dread. I want to say that I agree, that I've known since I was ten, but instead fear grips my throat.

"There's other towns through the woods." The runaway pulls up her hood while her eyes scan for any other intruder who might try to intervene. "I'm going to make it there and make a good life. You can come with me if you want to."

I stay frozen to the spot. I want to take her hand; I want to go more than I've wanted anything in my entire life.

Instead, I open my mouth and ask: "What if you're wrong?"

She wets her lips and glances back towards the town. Her voice is hushed. "If I go and there's a monster in the woods, I will be swallowed whole," she says. "But it's just a chance. If I stay here… I know this place will devour me for sure."

I bow my head, wincing at my own cowardice.

She leans in to touch her lips against my cheek. "Goodbye," my runaway says.

I watch as she disappears into the dark.

"HAD SOME VISITORS today," my father announces, the statement dropping like a weight from his thinning lips. He refuses to look at me when he speaks. "Got asked if you had any suitors," he continues. "I couldn't lie."

I can already tell who came knocking on our door, and can't help the swell of bitterness in knowing they called when they knew I would not be here.

"His wife is barely in the ground," I counter. As if there was anything of her to properly bury in the first place.

Another woman foolishly wandering in the woods. Or, so it was said. I knew her as something else: a woman with a rebellious side; a woman with a loud voice and boisterous nature; a woman who didn't like to settle down. A recent accident left her dependent on a crutch, having nothing below her left knee, and I grew to know her in the aftermath. I would offer her my company when we were going the same direction, lending her a hand even when she insisted it wasn't needed. Her hurricane of energy quieted enough for me to feel truly close to her for the first time—or, at least close enough to doubt the story behind her disappearance. When even a walk around town exhausted her, it simply didn't follow that she would wander out among the trees.

It seemed more likely that her ungrateful husband did not care for the burden he thought she made, resented her boastful attitude, and made a decision for himself.

"What do you want me to say?" my father asks. "I can't take care of you forever."

A swarm of retorts, sharp as nettles, swell up in my mouth. *I didn't ask you to do that. Do you actually think this man would care for me? I can take care of myself. Who is going to take care of you?*

I say none of them and I swallow instead, feeling them sting on the way down.

A MAN BECOMES my fiancé, for lack of a good reason for him not to be. He smiles at me, compliments the length of my hair, and laughs gently at the roughness of my hands. Outwardly, he acts fond and carefree, and no one would guess that he lost his wife to the deep, dark terror of the woods.

"Do you know why she went out there?" I ask at dinner.

My father shoots me a look of warning that I pretend not to notice.

My fiancé doesn't seem to mind, and wipes his mouth on his sleeve. "I can't even guess." He shrugs his shoulders. "My darling was always very strange. You know how she was; no one could ever make her obey the rules, even if it was dangerous." He smiles then, with a glint in his eye. "But you know better than that, don't you?" he asks, his tone tender and sweet. "You wouldn't make trouble like that, would you? Knowing it would put you in danger?"

He holds my gaze like a jailer holds a prisoner, and I feel as if a noose has wound itself around my neck.

"You'll listen like a good girl should?"

AT NIGHT, I make up my mind. I bundle myself up in my thickest cloak, grabbing food and flint for fire. I try to level out my shaking breaths, wishing my courage was something I could wrap in handkerchiefs and carry with me.

I don't feel brave enough to be a runaway.

My father meets me at the door.

"I'm not going to stop you," he says, his voice ashamed. "I just wanted to see you one last time before you left."

I clench my hands to stop them from shaking, tighten my jaw, and ask a question that has hung between us, tight as a well-strung snare.

"What happened to my mother?"

He doesn't answer right away. Instead, he hangs his head, his voice quieting to barely above a whisper. "I never meant her any harm."

On my way out, I take the axe and let the forest swallow me whole.

AS IF EXPECTING to be set upon by hounds or a caravan of hunters, I run through the woods with no thought or care to my direction at first. Only when my lungs begin to burn do I think better of it. Slumping my weight against an old oak tree, I stop and gulp for breath, wiping futilely at the tears that have frozen to my cheeks.

For a moment, despair swells in my chest and I almost succumb to it. But then I remember my runaway and how her lips felt when she kissed me goodbye. Somehow, it's easy to accept my own defeat but impossible to imagine hers. She's somewhere there, on the other side of the woods; I have to believe that.

Then, I hear movement: a shambling, heavy sound and a grinding drag. Instinct drives me behind the tree trunk, crouching and clutching my cloak tighter against myself. Suddenly, I feel four years old, pulling my blankets over my head against the monsters lurking in my closet.

The men have come looking for me, I tell myself, as if that thought is abruptly a comfort. There is no monster except what evil lurks in their hearts. There is nothing else here that can touch me. Still, my hand tightens on the axe and my pulse rushes in my ears.

The noise builds: one heavy stomp after another, each accompanied by an eerie creak. It comes close enough that I clasp my hand over my mouth to mask my shaking breaths. Try as I desperately might, my mind cannot summon up any explanation. I don't want to look, but a terrible, defeated part of me admits I have no choice.

I lift my head and choke on a scream.

A hundred missing women lurk before me in a mass of bone, sinew, and twisted flesh. The creature stands on paws made up of hand after hand, layered over one another in a pattern of bone, glued together by ripe muscle. Its claws are naked fingertips spiralled together, its limbs an amalgamation of a hundred femurs. The jaw is the long sweep of extended arms, where at its center, hands are joined together like a prayer. Its face-- its terrible, naked face—turns to me and I see the gaping of two hip bones where its gaze should be, and the eye sockets of a human skull sniffing like nostrils to seek me out.

Before my eyes roll back, they fixate on one terrible part of the creature's anatomy, where one femur in the cacophony of its collection is broken with sharp precision, and I think about a bride who used to walk with a crutch.

A whine builds in my throat, my heart sets to burst from my chest, both strong enough to suffocate, but I run. I don't stop. I can't. My head swims with a rush of delirium, but I don't dare to look over my shoulder to confirm that I haven't lost my mind entirely. I keep moving, pushing back towards the town I was so desperate to escape, and find myself met halfway.

I never thought the sight of my fiancé would bring me such relief. I throw myself against him, voice strangling in my throat. "It's there," I manage hoarsely. One hand twists in a fistful of his cloak, while the other brandishes the axe to the wood at my back. "It's real; it's there. It's..."

It's not my lack of breath that stops me; it's his stiff indifference. My declaration does not strike fear in him at all. He does not embrace or soothe me. He barely even moves.

"What are you talking about?"

His voice is dull, almost irritated. I stare up at him, my grip loosens from his cloak, and I realize why he hasn't touched me. His hands are full: occupied with a shovel and a simple knife, as if he hadn't considered me worth anything greater. This isn't the arsenal one brings to defend their beloved from a beast. This is dispelling a simple inconvenience.

My heartbeat thunders, feeling loud enough to deafen, with another rhythm coming in tandem. With shuddering footfalls, that thickened maze of flesh and bone closes the gap between us, leaving one monster behind me and one in front of me—and I don't know which one is more compelled to mercy.

I hear it now: pushing past brambles and I can't bring myself to turn around. My fiancé lifts his head, his eyes wide in disbelief, and I make my choice. I bury my father's axe into his side with a sick, wet thud and he somehow looks more horrified at me than at the beast emerging from the dark.

He falls and nearly takes me with him. I untangle myself in frantic desperation, scrambling across damp earth. Despite every instinct demanding that I run, I watch as the creature looms over him, in all of its hideous grandeur, and my fiancé speaks with a mouthful of blood in quiet recognition.

"My darling?"

The creature descends on him, its teeth a mangled mess of fingers and toes—tiny as a saw blade—and my eyes clench shut at the sickening crunch that follows.

I should run, but somehow cannot muster up the strength. My muscles ache, my hands drip with blood, and some part of me fears movement will inspire the creature to seek further prey. Perhaps my fiancé will not be enough to satisfy, and it will claim me into its sick labyrinth of bone and tissue. I stay frozen to the spot as I wait, but my fiance, a mess of gore and ruin, remains. His body isn't taken into the mass. He's left as he is, undignified and defeated on the forest floor.

The beast's tangled maw drips with blood as it turns towards me. With no gullet to swallow with, torn flesh falls from between its jaws as it approaches. I stare, transfixed, at the terrible grind of bone on bone, and I don't understand.

Then the creature sets upon me. I want to run, but I stay, miserably aware of my own defeat. The back of my cloak is gripped and I succumb. I do not struggle as the creature begins to walk—and that is all the creature does. It does not thrash me back and forth to snap my neck. It doesn't tear me open with its razor teeth. It carries me and I do not know why my body won't summon up the will to fight.

I close my eyes and submit to a fate that does not come.

I STARTLE when my body hits soft earth. Gasping, I sit upright, as the creature who carried me shambles back towards the woods.

My instinct, against all odds, is to stumble back towards it, my mouth open to…do what? Say some plea? I try and the words fail, leaving me touching my forehead, as if I'd imagined it entirely.

When I look behind me, I feel almost convinced that I am dreaming.

A little village sits in a clearing close to the treeline. Carried in the creature's teeth like a child, I was brought here, and now my feet almost fail me in my hurry to rise and run towards it.

I see her, looking radiant and beautiful: my runaway. She stands in a circle of women—many of them strangers but several that I know, women who were meant to be lost and wasted among the woods, and it's a sharp, sob of relief that alerts them to my presence.

Laughing, my runaway embraces me, kissing the tears that stain my cheeks. "You made it," she says, soothing her hand through my hair. "I'm so happy you're here."

I'm happy, too, so desperately that I can't say it. I can barely express my gratitude for all of this—for her, for this sanctuary hidden from the world, and the gathering of the dead that came out across the woods to protect me.

NIGHTMARE IN KETTLE PARK

JON GAUTHIER

The car shakes like a broken carnival ride as Mark guides it across the blanket of potholes that masquerades as a parking lot. He takes the least treacherous path he can and parks next to the two fence posts that serve as the park's entrance. Beyond them, a dirt trail snakes into the trees.

"OK, sweetie, we're here," Mark says.

There's no reply from the back seat, and Mark turns to see Ava staring down at his phone. She's so engrossed in Peppa Pig that she doesn't even notice they've stopped.

"Hey, baby zombie."

Ava looks up at him and smiles. It's wide and toothy and melts Mark's heart every time he sees it.

"We're here." Mark puts out his hand. "Give me my phone please."

Ava hands him the phone, and he glances at the screen to see the battery's down to three percent. With a sigh, he stuffs it into the center console. Then, he grabs the backpack from the passenger seat and gets out of the vehicle. As he opens Ava's door, he draws in a mouthful of the pine-sweetened air.

Ava unclips her seatbelt and slides out of her booster seat. Her shoes hit the ground with a soft crunch as Mark shuts her door.

"You ready?" Mark asks.

The six-year-old shoots him another grin and a thumbs-up.

He smiles back at her. "OK, let's go."

They pass through the fence posts, and the trail leads them around the first curve where they see a large green sign that says "Kettle Park Hiking Trail" in simple white font. Next to the words is a map of the trail that shows every point where it branches off, as well as all the picnic tables, garbage cans, and outhouses along the way. The longest loop is about 15 miles, but there are more than a dozen others to choose from, including the one-mile trail that Mark and Ava plan to take.

A laminated sheet of white paper stapled into the wood sign makes Mark's heart fall. On it, in an almost mocking black font, are the words "Park closed for maintenance until October 15th."

Mark mutters, "Shit."

"Daddy, we don't say that word!"

"You're right, sorry." He sighs. "The forest is closed, sweetie."

Ava looks up at him, her brow furrowed over bright blue eyes. "Closed?"

"Yeah. They're doing work here. We have to come back next weekend."

Her lower lip begins to quiver. He can tell she's trying to be brave and not cry. "But I want to walk with you," she says.

"I know, sweetie."

"You said we would go for a walk in the forest."

Mark sighs and looks back at the parking lot. Through the trees, he sees only two cars other than his own: an old station wagon and a small black sedan. They aren't vehicles that anyone doing any kind of park maintenance would be driving. The odds of anyone being in there actually working right now are pretty slim. Plus, if they aren't worker vehicles, it meant that at least two other people were on the trail.

"OK," Mark says. "I think we're allowed to go ahead."

Ava's face brightens again. "All right! Let's go!"

"Let's go," Mark mimics, doing his best to match her enthusiasm.

The sun peeks through the tops of towering pines and thick spruces that creak and moan in the cool August breeze. All around them, creatures scurry about, unbothered by their quiet, peaceful presence. They chirp and chatter among themselves while Mark and Ava amble along in no particular hurry. Ava is swinging a branch at the weeds and juvenile trees that border the edge of the trail. They've been walking for about ten minutes and haven't crossed paths with anyone. Mark figures they're in the clear.

"Do you see any animals?" Mark asks.

"No," Ava says.

"They must all be hiding."

"Or they're all eating their dinner."

"Yeah, maybe," Mark says with a chuckle

Ava's quiet for a moment, and then, "Daddyyyyyyy?" She draws the word out in a way that Mark recognizes all too well—she wants something.

"Yeessss," Mark replies, matching her tone.

"I'm hungry."

"Well, you can have a banana or an apple."

"That's it?"

"That's it."

Mark knows what she actually wants is the Twix bar he's packed: the one he told her they would share when they stop for a break.

Ava sighs and says, "Fine, I'll have an apple."

Mark swings the back pack off, digs an apple out and hands it to her.

She immediately takes a bite.

"What do you say," Mark asks.

"Thank you," she says through a mouthful.

After another fifteen minutes, they pass a small blue sign that indicates a rest area is fifty feet ahead.

"Almost there," Mark says.

"Yay!" Ava lets go of his hand and skips ahead. Mark picks up his pace to keep up with her and, before long, they arrive at an old weather-beaten picnic table that's sitting just off the trail. A small path leads away from it, marked by a sign that features the international symbol for a bathroom.

"Do you need to go pee?" Mark asks as he slides the backpack off.

"No," Ava says. She climbs up onto the bench and swings her legs underneath.

Mark digs into the backpack and pulls out the Twix bar.

"Yum, yum!" he says with an exaggerated tone. "I can't wait to eat this whole thing by myself."

Ava smiles and rolls her eyes. "Daddy!"

"What? This is my chocolate bar. You can go find some worms to eat."

"Stop, Daddy!"

"OK, fine. Here you go." Mark opens the wrapper and pulls out the two bars and hands one to Ava.

"Thank you!"

They sit, eating quietly and looking around them. A light wind has kicked up, and the trees are creaking high above them.

"After this, we have to turn around and walk back to the car, OK, sweetie?"

Ava nods, too enraptured by the chocolate to put up a fight.

"What should we have for dinner ton–"

THACK!

Mark and Ava both turn towards the sound.

"What was that?" Ava asks.

"I dunno," Mark says. "Maybe a branch falling."

THACK!

The sound is both familiar and unsettling. It belongs somewhere, but not out here. Mark stands up.

"Where are you going, Daddy?" Ava's voice almost trembles.

"Nowhere, sweetie, it's OK"

THACK!

Mark's head snaps, almost involuntarily, towards the trail that leads to the outhouse and that helps him work out the source of the sound.

"I think it's the outhouse," Mark says.

"The what?"

"It's like a little shed that's a bathroom."

Ava grabs his hand and presses herself against him.

"Hey, it's OK," Mark says. "There's nothing to be scared of. I think the wind is just making the door bang." He begins to lead her down the trail. "Come on. Let's see if we can fix it."

After about twenty feet, the small building comes into view. It's an old wooden structure with two separate cubicles sitting on a cement pad. Mark and Ava face the building's side and Mark can see that the door to one of the cubicles is unlatched. After each gust of wind pulls it open, the spring-loaded hinges slam it shut again.

THACK!

"Someone didn't close the door properly," Mark says.

"Why?"

"Probably just an accident. Come on, I want you to try and go pee."

He grabs Ava's hand and pulls her toward the outhouse. As they come around to the front, Mark stops dead.

"What's wrong, Daddy?"

Mark doesn't answer; he just stares in equal parts shock and confusion at the blood pooled outside the unlatched door.

THACK!

"Daddy?"

Mark picks Ava up and carries her back to where they can't see the front of the outhouse.

"I want you to wait here for a second, OK?"

"Why?"

"I just need to check something."

"No, Daddy!"

"It's OK. I just want to make sure there's no spiders or anything."

THACK!

Ava nods and Mark makes his way back toward the outhouse. The blood glistens on the cement like a spilled quart of oil. It's redder than anything he's ever seen.

"Stay there, Ava." He says it too loudly; too crazily. He knows he needs to stay calm for her. No matter what he finds, he needs to stay calm.

Mark steps up onto the pad, grabs the door and slowly pulls it open.

There's a dead man in the outhouse. He's crumpled against the corner, his pants around his ankles, his head resting on the wall. Everything is soaked with blood, and from what Mark can tell, it all came from the deep black gash etched into the man's throat.

At first, Mark doesn't think it's real. He's convinced that he's on a TV show, or has stumbled onto some amateur film set. His mind screams at him to do something—to turn around, grab Ava, and run back to the car. But all he can do is stare at the carved throat.

"Daddy?"

The shock of his daughter's voice draws Mark back into the moment.

With a sudden burst of adrenaline, he dashes to her, gathers her in his arms and begins running back up to the main trail.

They reach the area with the picnic table in seconds.

"Daddy, what's wrong?"

"We've gotta go, OK? We've gotta go."

"Did you fix the door?"

Mark doesn't answer. Without putting Ava down, he rushes to the picnic table to retrieve his bag but slams his knee into the wood.

"Motherfucker!" He hisses it through tightly closed lips.

"Are you OK?" Ava asks.

"I'm fine, sweetie. Come on."

He reaches for the backpack when the sound of a snapping branch echoes from further up the main trail, just around the tight bend a few feet away.

Mark's eyes go wide.

"What, Da–"

He slams his palm over Ava's mouth. "Be quiet," he whispers. Another branch snaps and soon, there's the crunching of footsteps.

Without even realizing what he's doing, Mark dashes back down the path toward the outhouse carrying Ava with him. His knee screams at him with each footfall.

When the outhouse comes into view, he slips into the trees. He drops down behind a fallen maple, praying its tangle of branches will keep them hidden.

Ava slaps at his hand. He can hear her crying "Daddy!" under his palm.

"Listen, sweetie," Mark whispers. "I need you to be very quiet and very still, OK?"

He hears feet scraping against dirt. Whoever this person is, they're coming down the trail towards them.

"Shit." He draws a ragged breath. "Listen, Ava, I'm going to take my hand away but you need to be completely quiet. There's a bad guy coming and we have to hide from him. Do you understand?"

Ava nods.

"OK," Mark says. He pulls his hand away and Ava turns her head to look up at him. He raises a finger to his mouth and she nods again. Through the branches, Mark watches the trail.

A tall man in a black suit appears. He wears thin glasses and his jet-black hair is combed back. He walks with a slight bounce in his step, one hand buried deep in the pocket of his overcoat, the other clutching a gleaming leather briefcase. To Mark, he looks like someone you'd find on a London street or working in a funeral parlor, not in the middle of a forest on a Sunday afternoon.

"Terribly sorry to have kept you waiting," the man says.

For a terrifying moment, Mark thinks he's talking to them, but then the man steps up onto the concrete and opens the outhouse door. Holding it open with his foot, he looks down at the dead body inside. Even from this far back, Mark can see a thin and oily smile creep across the man's face.

"Wild garlic can be difficult to come by around here," the man says to the corpse. He pulls his hand out of his pocket and holds up a fistful of green and white vegetation. "But it's so much better than store-bought, wouldn't you agree?" He stuffs the garlic back in his pocket, then sets the briefcase down on the concrete and opens it.

"Right, then, shall we get started?"

The man hums quietly to himself as he pulls a small cooking stove out of the briefcase, along with a frying pan and a small bottle of olive oil. He lights the stove and pours some oil into the pan and sets it onto the flame. Then he pulls a paring knife from the briefcase and shaves some garlic into the pan.

It doesn't take long for the pan to begin sizzling. The man uses a white cloth to wipe the knife clean and then gets to his feet. Mark knows what's going to happen next and he knows he shouldn't watch, but it's impossible not to.

Kneeling there in the trees, Ava clutched against him with her face buried in his chest, Mark can do nothing but stare in horror as the man ducks into the outhouse and, after a minute, reappears holding a thin red slab of meat. He drops it into the pan, where it joins the oil and garlic and begins to hiss.

Mark covers his mouth and nose, desperate not to smell the frying meat. The man pulls a pair of tongs from the briefcase and flips the pan's ghastly contents.

"I like it rare," the man says. "There's something more authentic about it." He watches the meat for a few seconds, before raising his gaze to the surrounding trees, a sly and knowing expression on his pale face.

"You left your bag up at the picnic table, by the way," the man says. His eyes dart around, probing the forest. "I know you're close by."

Ice cold sweat explodes out of every pore in Mark's skin. His heart slams against his ribs. His stomach tumbles into oblivion.

"And I figure you found my friend here," the man continues. "Otherwise, you wouldn't be hiding from me."

Mark closes his eyes, pleading with his body to relax, for his breathing to slow and the trembling to stop. He looks down at Ava who is still nestled against him, not daring to show her face to the outside world.

The man kneels down again and opens his briefcase. He pulls out a white plate and a silver fork and sets them on the concrete pad. Then he pulls out a large steak knife and sets it next to the fork. "You're welcome to join me," he says as he prods at the meat with the tongs. "It's almost ready. Plenty to go around." After not receiving a response, the man shrugs. "It's not everyone's cup of tea. I understand that."

He sits cross-legged in front of the plate and stove. Then he grabs the meat with the tongs and drops it onto his plate with a wet splat. "Divine," he says, taking a deep and ravenous breath of the aroma. "Simply divine. Almost godly."

He picks up the fork and steak knife and begins slicing into his meal.

"I will find you," he says as he cuts. "I don't fancy traipsing into those trees but I will find you."

He puts a piece of flesh into his mouth and begins to chew.

"You know how I know you're there?" he asks after swallowing. Then he grins, revealing two rows of bright porcelain teeth. "I can smell you. It's a sort of...gift, I guess you could say."

He begins cutting off another piece of meat but is interrupted by the whining, throaty cry of a small engine. A vehicle is coming up the main trail.

Mark turns his head toward the noise. The familiar smell of exhaust soon invades the macabre picnic.

"Oh dear," the man says, setting down the knife and fork. "And here I thought this was going to be a quiet meal."

There's a crunching skid and an ATV suddenly appears on the trail. It's driven by a man wearing work overalls and a hard hat. Relief floods Mark's veins. The driver brings the machine to a stop and kills the engine.

"Good evening," the man in the suit calls, offering a small wave.

"Park's closed," the ATV driver says. "There's a sign."

"Oh, I'm terribly sorry. I must have missed it."

"Well, you've gotta go." The driver takes a step toward the outhouse, but stops when he finally notices the blood pooled at the door. He looks back at the man in the suit, who's getting to his feet.

"Of course," the man says. "Before all that, though, perhaps I can offer you some steak?" He picks up the plate and begins walking toward the ATV driver. "It's incredibly fresh."

"N—no, thanks," the driver says, his voice breaking slightly. "I just need you to go back to your car."

"Please. Indulge me," the man in the suit says. He's beside the ATV now, the plate in one hand, the fork and steak knife in the other.

The driver takes a step back. "Look, buddy, I just—"

There's a flash of sunlight on steel as the steak knife is buried into the ATV driver's neck. The man in the suit pulls the blade out, a geyser of blood coming with it. He steps out of the way as the driver, hand clawing at the wound, slides off of the seat and crumples on the forest floor.

After what seems like a lifetime, the choking and gurgling come to a stop. The man in the suit stares down at the fresh kill and shakes his head. "Such a pity."

Terror is all Mark knows. He watches helplessly as the man turns away from the ATV and carries his plate and silverware back to the cement pad. "Now then," he says. "Where were we?" He sets the plate down, sits cross-legged in front of it, and continues eating.

Mark draws Ava's face from his chest and looks at her. "Ava," he whispers. "I *need* you to run. Run back to the car as fast as you can. Can you do that?"

Ava shakes her head, her eyes wide. 'No, Daddy.'

Mark looks back at the man, who is now finishing the last forkful. He wipes his mouth with a cloth napkin and looks contentedly at the sky.

"Delicious," the man says.

Mark looks back down at his daughter's face. "Ava," he hisses. "You run. This man is very, very bad. I need you to run."

She shakes her head again. "I'm too scared, Daddy."

Mark lets out an exasperated hiss. He looks back up and his body turns to ice.

The man is staring at him. His dark gaze bores straight through the trees and branches—right into Mark's eyes.

"Ah," the man says, getting to his feet. "There you are."

Mark stands, his knee protesting the movement.

"Run, Ava!" He screams. "Run!"

"No, Daddy!" She clutches his jacket.

Mark tries to peel her off but it's impossible and he's out of time. He grabs a branch and holds it up in front of him and Ava like a sword. "Stay back!" he cries. "You stay the fuck back!"

The man doesn't respond. He just slinks toward them, hacking at the branches with the steak knife. His eyes continue to drill straight into Mark's. His smile is so wide, it seems to come off the edges of his face.

"Come on, Ava!" Mark screams. "Come on!" He picks the girl up and barrels through the trees, holding her face against his chest. He bursts back onto the main trail and hobbles back in the direction of the car. His knee screams with every step. After ten feet, he stops. He'll never make it. Not on foot.

An idea strikes him, one so obvious he's furious with himself for only thinking of it now. As the man in the suit fights his way through the trees, Mark heads back down the trail to the outhouse, trying his best to remember how to drive an ATV.

He keeps moving, looking back after every step. The man is behind them now, walking quickly, his fist wrapped around the steak knife.

Mark reaches the ATV and climbs on. With Ava still clinging to him, he can barely see any of the buttons or knobs—not that he knows what any of them do anyway. He turns the key and lights come to life on the dash panel, but the engine doesn't start. "Shit!" Mark turns the key again and again, but nothing happens. There's something he's not doing right... He looks back to see the man is almost upon them.

Mark slides off the ATV and tears Ava off of him.

"No!" Ava cries. She tries to grab hold of him again, but Mark has to fight her off. The man in the suit is only a few feet away.

"You've got to run, Ava." Mark begs. "Please. Please run."

The man raises the knife and, without thinking, Mark charges toward him, shoulder first. He collides with the man, and the two of them hit the ground. As they struggle, Mark sees the steak knife is now on the ground. He punches wildly. The man's body is thin but rock hard, and every punch hurts Mark's knuckles more than him.

Mark makes a grab for the knife, but a bony fist slams into his nose. There's a hurricane of pain. A torrent of blood. Then another punch, this one to his cheek. Mark is dazed. He claws at the dirt for the knife, but knows the man already has it.

Then he's on his back and the man is straddling him and, through a haze of tears, Mark sees the glinting metal rise… rise… rise.

There's a sickening crack and the man suddenly collapses on his side. Mark wipes his eyes to see Ava standing over him, holding a thick branch.

Mark sits up, takes the branch from Ava's hands and slams it into the man's head, again and again. Finally, the branch snaps and Mark drops the useless hilt to the ground. He forces himself to his feet while the man rolls onto his stomach with a groan. "Come on," Mark says, picking Ava up. He turns back to the ATV and sets her on it. As he does, he notices something strapped to the rear rack. He looks back to see the man is back on his feet, the knife back in his hand.

"Jesus Christ," Marks gasps. "How the fuck…" He looks down at Ava and grabs her shoulders. "You stay here, sweetie," Mark says. "You keep your eyes closed."

Mark unstraps the ax from the back of the ATV and turns to face the man. The man tilts his head and gives Mark an almost pitying look of disdain. "Such a brutish implement," he says.

Mark swings, connecting with the man's ribs. A sound like a wet slap echoes into the trees and the man howls in pain and rage. Mark yanks the ax out and slams it into the man's knee, dropping him instantly to the ground. Then, he raises it above his head and brings it down into the man's chest.

There's an explosion of blood and the man's eyes shine and he smiles wider than ever. Finally, he goes still.

Gasping, Mark drops the ax and turns back to the ATV where Ava is still perched on the seat, her eyes squeezed shut.

"Keep your eyes closed," Marks says. "Just for another few minutes, sweetie." He staggers to the ATV and opens a small tool box that's attached to the front rack. He digs through the contents, and pulls out the owner's manual.

"Where's the bad man?" Ava asks.

Mark finds the startup instructions, stuffs the manual into his pocket and gets on the ATV behind Ava.

"He's gone," Mark says.

Second later, the ATV is running and he makes a slow three-point turn and starts to head back up to the main trail.

"We don't have helmets, Daddy!" Ava shouts.

"No, I guess we don't!"

"That's not very safe!"

Mark smiles. "No, it certainly isn't! Let's get the fuck out of here, shall we?"

"Daddy!" Ava cries. "We don't say that word."

"It's OK," Marks says. "This one time, it's OK."

With one arm around Ava, and the other on the handlebar, Mark turns the ATV onto the main trail and starts the journey back to the parking lot.

High above the roaring engine, the treetops quiver, indifferent to the carnage below. Creatures flee from the noise, scampering into the safety of the roots and deadfall. When silence returns to the forest, they'll return to their roles in the great green opus—the unending struggle for survival. Always fighting for their lives. Always searching for something to eat.

ALL AFFAIRS WILL PROSPER

K.L. MASSEY

Icy kisses fluttered over Ling's body and she shivered at their touch. The cold groped past her scarf and nibbled at the crescents of her cheeks. A trace of copper was drawn from the bleached sand of her complexion.

As she trekked through an endless monochrome landscape, cocooned between blankets of cloud and snow, she tried not to dwell on the isolation that lived deep in her bones. Colossal larch trees surrounded her and extended upwards to oblivion in search of an unseen sun. She might have been the only person that existed in this desaturated world.

Tense strands of muscle advanced her forward Ling pushed onward as she always did, to a point that could be considered too far. Her focus narrowed and she walked on. She kept her camera tucked close, a constant companion and good luck charm.

Beyond her, the muskeg rippled in anticipation as it awaited her arrival; aching aeons passed since its last visitor.

ALWAYS PREPARED, Ling had researched every aspect of the unknown environment, and became consumed by it before the trek had even begun. Over fattened hours, Ling had basked in the blue light of her laptop screen as she assessed every potential step of her journey.

She had chosen this path and was trapped on it now, disconnected by the nomadic lifestyle that paid in social currency. She documented her existence, her adventures, her endless search... Displayed it online for nameless, faceless people who would never know her and would never understand she was barely a participant in her own life. She was as much a viewer as any one of her audience, detached behind the camera lens. Her true self lay disguised beneath the filtered layers that formed her imaginary world.

Ling had escaped the country that raised her but could not escape herself. She was committed to a life of escapism; determined to travel every corner of the world until she found a chosen land that satisfied her wanderlust. Nowhere felt like home, but that had always been her truth. It was safer to travel to inhospitable places where she could master the landscapes; capture their art and make its beauty her own. It was better to go alone.

The taiga would take Ling to a realm outside of time, where the sun shone at midnight. There, she would prove herself worthy to those who watched.

LING CONTINUED deeper into the arboreal void. Finding its unblemished perfection repulsive, envy clenched in her guts. Being surrounded by beauty made any imperfections more obvious, and though her scars were hidden, she could not escape their toxic embrace wrapped round her ribs.

Ling trudged forward, each footstep a seismic occurrence first dulled then dissipated through compacted snow. The impact of her tracks would soon be covered and, just as easily, she could disappear.

Pressure throbbed behind Ling's eyes. She nudged her wire-frame glasses higher up her nose and blinked. The movement stirred something and as she looked across the horizon, it was marked with vivid crimson veils. Concerned by this intrusion, she blinked again, blinked harder, and forced the colour to retreat. Reassured, Ling saw that the fallen snow was still pure, it had not been stained by her presence.

Everything continued with or without her. How much further would she have to go until she would be sated? Here, she was engulfed by untouched wilderness calling her home: a spiteful reminder she had no place of her own, no such person she was tethered to. Regret bloomed fragrant in her memory.

Ling suppressed her thoughts and softened her gaze enough to witness the veil return. Fluid crimson diffused the periphery of her vision, soaked into everything that it touched. The bleeding haze dredged up forgotten memories of wishes buried long before. She glimpsed countless possible futures that predicted vitality, fortune, sacrifice... Surrounded by wealth, accomplished in her art. Success was in her grasp. People would know her name, but they would never know her. Ling would remain closed to faith, to community, to belonging. Fate weighed heavy on her, and she ached under the burden of its mass.

Ling halted and pressed her thumb and forefinger to pinch the bridge of her nose, where her glasses perched. She sighed. The only sound for miles, or so she thought. But she was answered by an echo: a response to her rhythmic breath. The taiga lived and breathed around her. Each impossibly tall tree was a vital component within the heaving lungs of the forest. Ling and the larches exhaled in turns. Each frozen breath fed the other, their symbiotic transaction completed.

Stubborn eyes fixed ahead as she walked, a flash of scarlet jolted her vision. Red branches arced across the scenery with electric precision and reframed it into something malicious; greedy tendrils eager to consume. Ling's pulse throbbed and her scalp prickled under her beanie.

Conflicted by the familiar unwelcome sensations, she recalled the monsters of her childhood. They had names. Mother, Father, Auntie, Uncle. Confusion blurred their faces into one amorphous creature. It lashed out, tortured her tiny body with beatings she could barely endure. The pain of their words landed deeper, made wounds that stole her voice as she healed. Her trust in others had been stripped away: a safety blanket torn to shreds.

Ling's skin flashed hot with memories that spanned years of emotional torment. Her senses had been finely tuned to identify phantom dangers and vigilance returned to her in an instant. Ling prepared for an attack.

Dewdrops of dread trickled down the back of Ling's neck, streamed to her arms and flowed out to the estuaries of her gloved hands. She gripped her camera, reassured by the familiar tug of the strap around her neck. A shudder wracked her shoulders and caused the leather strap to recoil from her touch; a once-living thing that closed about her neck like a noose. Ling gasped for air, released her talisman and anxiously contemplated the tender sting of her throat. Cold could feel like fire, could burn and devour like flames. Her pain merged, inseparable and inescapable.

Stirred by shame, her heart fled and the rest of her followed. She did not want to be out here alone, fearful and expectant of a dark descent that had already proved it would not arrive. Night could not fall here yet the weight of her nightmares lingered. She walked on, bathed in midnight sunlight, radiant as the witching hour persisted around her. Bound to nothing and no one, not even time, she had finally found a place where she could outrun it.

THE VEIL TINTED the landscape red once more. She peered over the top of her glasses, but the colour expanded and nested in her mind to adorn it with daydream horrors. Feelings of loss and shame and dishonour stuffed down into the cracks.

She tried to fight this invasion, but a quiet part of her challenged her to reflect. Ling listened as it whispered, heard it say she would never overcome the shame of her past.

Fear of failure picked at Ling's patchwork ego, and she doubled over to retch. *You are fucking stupid. It's pathetic that you tried so hard, pretended that you're important. No one wanted you. Why are you here? You're worthless. An embarrassment.* Her inner voice scraped raw. She righted herself, but it was hopeless. Her only choice was to complete the final stage of the hike that taunted her endurance.

Stagnant in the eternal taiga, her spirit weakened. Her heartache conjured further visions, gifted Ling with a corona of light that danced between the jagged branches around her. Auras reflected from every snow-steeped surface and illuminated the red veins which overlaid her surroundings. The light shone throughout her, flowed to her limbs and radiated from her head.

Somewhere distant, she heard chiming sounds clear as a bell. The resonance filled her, vibrated at the very core of her being and spilt into her throat. It swam to her head and lit her like a beacon, crowned her with an energetic halo that powered the movement of her legs; form and feeling lost to function.

Her world moved on. The snow continued to fall and covered her with reassurance. Washed away fatigue and calmed Ling like a devoted new mother, who murmured gentle shushing sounds.

She contemplated how Nature was a Mother; her Mother had been a God. One that demanded Ling to obey, and enacted terrible vengeance when not appeased. She abandoned Her creation, and left Ling to her own devices. Fevered words of prayer and acts of worship went unanswered, and eventually, Ling's faith decayed. She fought to swallow the bitterness in her throat. Ling had learned disappointment in the sacred age of childhood.

Now she wished for mercy, and the muskeg yielded, ready to receive its honoured guest.

ALL WAS SILENT. The soft drone of the bell that guided her here had withered away to nothing. There was nothing natural about this new silence. Ling's skin crawled. She shook herself, but the silence remained, joined by ropes of fear that climbed and tightened around her limbs.

She stopped, exhausted, at the opening of a circular clearing edged by generations of trees. They sagged at irrational angles, sprawled on either side of her like a mouth split wide to reveal rows of jagged teeth, gleaming with frost. She felt oddly comforted. This was a lonely, inhospitable place but perhaps she belonged here, surrounded by a forest of relatives; mothers and fathers and siblings who had all grown old together.

Where life was present, death followed. Young saplings poked their mischievous fingers through crumpled snow coverlets. Miniscule particles of lichen and moss clung tight to surrogate mothers. Expired needles littered the ground, shed like an unrequited uterine lining.

The land had altered, no longer solid sheets of rock under the snow, but something spongy and giving that boiled from within; organic matter that moved and breathed: an undulating layer of skin over muscle.

SHE UNDERSTOOD that art was violence, that it was an act of brutality to wield her camera and turn it shamelessly on an exposed subject. It required patience to track a scene in her sights and take aim with a finger poised, ready to shoot. She conceded she must wait, temporarily vulnerable whilst she placed her fragile trust in something outside of her control.

She paused, unmoving and not breathing. As a vision of serenity standing before eternity; surrendering her peace to the Gods so they might bless her with a bountiful harvest. Transcending thus, she was rewarded for her offerings.

AUTOMATICALLY, Ling reached for her camera and raised it up to behold the scene before her. The shutter activated in a blaze of clicks. She checked the display screen before she released her faithful companion; it settled and found a place of rest near her heart. Ling should have been relieved, but fear limped back towards her, red and hot as it hungered for attention amongst the cold.

Ling's focus was drawn beyond the far side of the clearing toward muddy shadows that heaved and shifted, forming vast craggy shapes like broken mountains. They slowed as they observed her, and taunted her with stillness when she tried to return their stares. Ling shut her eyes tight and looked deep for inner strength as the silence weighed down on her, barely dared to breathe as the disinterested mountains ceased their movements and restored her solitude.

LING SUBMITTED to her unavoidable past and accepted her fate. She hugged frail arms around a frail body and she grieved. The air glittered around her as she released tiny shallow breaths.

Rooted in place, the red haze blurred Ling's vision. Cracks appeared in the skin of the land, torn in jagged scars, the rending of flesh as a gaping mouth opened before her and silently screamed.

The muskeg yawned wider and revealed a meaty core beneath its distended surface. It burst open, to a grave saturated with once-human bodies planted like bloated tubers. The earth was stained red, swelled with thick veins of rusted clay and disgorged bulbs of weeping viscera. Beneath her was an entire root system of networked flesh, interconnected and bound to the family of trees. She heard her elders calling to her, ringing voices that commanded attention.

Ling forgot to blink, forgot to breathe. She understood why the living mountains had turned away from her, those seeking, curious observers far removed from circumstance. She stared bleakly at their forms, unable to plead for their help.

Ling startled, became aware of movement above her. Drifts of snow shuddered down to the ground, too dense to be sent from the clouds.

Then she heard it: a high-pitched scream as the Earth delivered its child to her. Groaning, yearning for release, the chosen tree swayed. Roots bared themselves, naked before a sky they have never known, as the trunk collapsed exhausted toward her. Many arms opened wide to embrace her, Ling returned the gesture.

Taken home to rest, wrapped in safety like a comfort blanket, she surrendered to the unconditional love that she had craved her entire life.

CLOSING HER EYES, Ling glided into a slipstream of bliss and discovered freedom. Feeling the shallow expanse of her ribcage contracting, breath exited her body. Liberated from the burden of expectations, she provided an offering to her ancestors, weaving her fibrous threads of sinew into their elaborate underworld tapestry. Here they can achieve equality, entwined in folds of dirt.

Ling provided for her found family, and they loved her for it. She died in harmony so that all affairs will prosper.

TRUE NORTH

NICOLE LYNN

Dad and I lived in a tarpaper cabin in a forest north of the world's devils. I didn't know there was any other way to live. We had a working generator, a dug-out well, and a collapsing shed in the back that sheltered several generations of feral cats. He never took me down the webbing of gravel switchbacks that surrounded the home, so I don't know the way back. The bodies there will never be recovered.

Dad pointed to the Big Dipper and showed me how it swiveled around Polaris. If I knew the season, I could always orient myself.

"True North," Dad said. "It points straight to heaven. This is heaven."

I never argued.

The pinewood forest was the only paradise I knew.

My years had a rhythm. They began with the snow geese flying overhead. In autumn, we put plastic tarps on the roof so we wouldn't have leaks when spring arrived. The snowmelt turned our world into shades of mud. I counted the weeks with my filet knife, ripping sinew from hides and stretching them out to dry. In winter, we put up new sigils, scraping them along the too-tall trees.

"What are they for?" I once asked him.

"Protection," Dad said. "If you peel back the bark, the woodworms make them too. But they gotta be seen, or else they don't work. That's why we put them at eye-level."

It took a while, but eventually, they chased away the dark.

They didn't belong to one culture but many. Dad saw them in dreams, transmitted directly into his third eye by some higher power. Odin, Thoth, Saint Peter, and extraterrestrial angels. They all worked together, looking down at the earth from different angles. I used to stand on the bottom of a trunk, look up at spears of fir, and count the years we made new sigils.

I felt holy; I felt safe.

Dad left me alone a few nights a year to sell skins and fill his pickup truck with supplies: Kraft dinners and instant noodles, hardtack, blotter paper and saturated sugar cubes to open his third eye. When he came back, a stranger would ride in the cab of his truck. He found them on Craigslist, people looking for room and board. Sometimes, they were teenagers looking for a place to run off to. Sometimes, they were adults running from life.

"To be clear," Dad would write to them. "I live off-grid. It gets cold, and there's a hole in the roof. I could use some help fixing up the place."

Only the desperate answered his classified. True North was the only way to live, and they were looking for a slice of it. They didn't know how to live in such a holy place. It wasn't something Dad could teach.

When I saw them, my stomach turned because other human beings made me anxious. I was like an unsocialized dog—seeing new things made my hackles stand up. People scared me more than whatever Dad said lived in the woods.

It felt like Darkness was winning. I didn't know the earth was tilted twenty-three degrees and that the winters in the north were longer than those near the equator. We lived well above the fiftieth parallel. That was the price for stretching our fingers toward Polaris.

How could I know? I didn't speak in the same frequencies as higher beings.

I DON'T REMEMBER most of the boarders Dad brought home. They became a tangle of bones, needled through the thicket of saplings that Dad said were off-limits. My brain liquidated their faces, and they spilled through the cracks in my skull. If I tried to recall their hair color or the constellations of moles on their skin, my brain could only produce trees. Landmarks. The syllables of their names got jammed up in my stomach and made me sick, but I couldn't shape them on my tongue. Tabby, tortoiseshell, and tuxedo cat, I whispered to myself, because it was easier to recall the cats in the shed.

Their existence was a skittish one. They had a fighting chance.

But I remember Janice.

She came at the right time in my life. I was outgrowing my clothes, and my joints ached with growing pains. I had one sports bra I wore to keep my chest tight to my body so I could be streamlined. She was a pretty woman, and for the first time, I wanted to look like someone else. Someone so different from my dad.

I heard her before I saw her—the door of our pickup slamming down the driveway and the clipped end of her laughing. The cat sitting on the windowsill stiffened and scurried away. Dad walked in with a canvas backpack slung over his shoulders. He dropped it next to the door, moved aside, and there she was.

Nineteen.

We shared a spattering of freckles and honeyed, suncatcher eyes. That's where the similarities ended. Everything else on me belonged to my dad: charcoal hair, cutting features. Her face was wide, soft, and girlish. Adulthood hadn't quite caught up with her.

She, like every other tenant, was relieved to see me. I was their insurance of safety. This place couldn't be so dangerous if there's a kid around.

"Hon," Dad said as he let the backpack slip from his shoulders, and set it next to the door. "This is Janice. She's going to stay with us for a little while and help me fix the septic tank."

"Hi," she said.

My mouth was full of cereal. A bead of milk on my lips. I swallowed and said hi because Dad would be angry with me if I scowled or showed fear. My smile stiffened my cheeks.

She looked vaguely like the picture of my mother that I kept folded on my nightstand. I could see myself growing into something roughly Janice-shaped, but that could've just been wishful thinking. I wanted to be her— friendly, smiling, clean-skinned, and white-toothed.

I went into the bathroom brushed the knots from my hair; washed the pine pitch from my cheek. I searched my reflection to see if there was anything that didn't belong to my dad. Meanwhile, he went into the shed to cut rope and sharpen his hacksaw.

I WAS AFRAID to talk to Janice during the first few days of her stay. I made too many mistakes before, revealing too much of our lives and beliefs. I had rules to follow: I couldn't ask them where they came from, what it was like there, or if I could go with them to see it. They couldn't come out to the woods with me to pray where we carved the trees, and I couldn't warn them of the impending night.

"They have eyes, don't they?" Dad said. "They see it coming."

"But they don't know what will happen," I said.

"If you come on too strong, they'll think you're crazy," Dad said. "They'll think you're fucking with them."

I disobeyed him once. There was a teenage boy who was staying with us. He split firewood in the early morning hours, so I drew a protective sigil on the back of his hand in permanent marker. He must've had a shred of Darkness in him because the shape of it frightened him. Dad had to evict him because we couldn't have someone with a shadow in their heart living with us.

"I'm sorry," I said.

Dad stayed quiet. I never forgot the look on his face, wordlessly saying it was my fault that he was gone. I wish I remembered his name. His face. I carried that guilt with me, even after I learned that everything Dad told me about the world was a lie. I thought he had been brought back to town, stripped of the salvation the woods and Dad could offer him. Now I know he's with the others: ivory bones tangled up in the thicket.

Even without speaking, I knew that I liked Janice. I watched her dig up the septic tank from a hiding spot along the tree line. She sang off-tune and danced around as she worked. Sometimes, she'd pause to click at the cats, but they wouldn't come to her. They were bred by the wilderness and wary of people. True North does that to all creatures. The paradise that Dad presented to me was a cutthroat place. At night, I stared at her while she ate. She winked. Those nights, I pretended we were a family.

"Thanks again for the help," Dad would say.

"It's only fair. You're letting me stay."

I wondered why she came here. Of course, the answer was obvious. She was looking for Light, for True North. The universe brought us together.

"Have you made her feel comfortable?" Dad would ask. "Have you offered her food or helped her unpack?"

I shook my head. "I'm afraid of her."

"We want everyone to feel loved here," Dad would say. "Fear is for them. Not us."

Dad hardly talked to her beyond asking how she slept or if she wanted coffee. He didn't care whether they were afraid. It was my job to keep them calm.

THE BATHROOM DOOR didn't close, so I spied on her when I could. I watched her shave her legs with a disposable razor and dress herself in workwear. I'd never seen the shape of a woman's legs in their entirety before. Just mine, thin, and straight – I thought about my own, growing to look like hers. She bit down on an elastic and plaited her hair into two sections. They looked like trout muscles, each layer laid atop the other. I'd never seen a braid before. My hair was perpetually tangled and split.

In the mirror, we made eye contact. I flinched away.

"Can I help you?"

Her voice lilted with playfulness.

"Sorry," I said. "I just thought it was my only chance to learn to braid."

She opened the door with her foot, still twisting her hair.

"I can braid yours if you'd like," she said.

We sat on the couch, and she hummed while she interwove my hair. I was shaking, embarrassed, and excited. I wanted to say more, but what could I say? My whole world was made of spruce trees, night, and sneaking into places Dad said were off-limits. My life was like the big dipper, moving around Polaris, each season marked with different work. Dad said regular folks don't know what that's like.

"You're very pretty," I said, unable to think of anything else.

She exhaled and sounded like a laugh. "You are, too."

I was automatically distrusting, but she took me into the bathroom, and when I looked in the mirror. I believed it because we both had brown eyes.

THAT NIGHT, I crawled into Dad's bed and listened to the rhythm of his heart. It was steady. When it was fast, I knew he would kick out our tenant. That was the only time he seemed disturbed. I woke him up by kissing the salt and stubble on his cheek.

"Can we keep her?" I asked.

He blinked the exhaustion from his face. "It's never my call if we can or not," he said. "It's up to them whether they can stay."

"Can we try?"

"We can try," Dad said. "But eventually, we have to let them go."

Dad once had a family of his own. None of them were related, but they decided to love each other anyway because they knew truths that no one else seemed to understand. They traveled together along the coastline, chasing summers and sunshine.

"Why'd you leave?" I asked him.

"We had a difference in vision," Dad said. "But that's family: untrustworthy and quick to throw you away."

I nodded. I wanted to ask if that's what happened to Mom, but he never said anything about her.

ON CLEAR NIGHTS, Dad took me outside to show me the constellations. Polaris always pointed north, and the further north you were, the closer you were to heaven. The other stars were deities. I wasn't allowed outside without him to decipher the stars with me.

Some nights, I snuck out of my window and stood past the orange light from the shack. I watched the sky for UFOs, searching for beams of information they'd send to Dad as he dreamed. I watched the Darkness underneath the spruce trees to check for movement. Evils that I was protected from. I never saw any of it. Dad only saw it because he searched for it with a willing and indoctrinated mind and a bloodstream saturated with LSD.

DAD SAID JANICE was running from something. All our tenants were. It wasn't often that people ran toward the Light as much as they were running from Darkness. The distinction held an air of hopelessness. My adolescent rebellion was in my beliefs: people could be good.

Janice taught me to braid, using three strands of bailing twine. She wrapped it around her wrist like it was a friendship bracelet, even though it was itchy and ugly. She showed me the music she had on her mp3 player, and we listened to The Doors, splitting a pair of earbuds. She smelled like vanilla from the body wash she carried in her backpack. I disemboweled her belongings in front of her. Puckered on a layer of strawberry-tinted lip gloss. She had a twenty-dollar note for emergencies and a picture of her twin brother in her wallet. The two of them had a look that said they were up to something, sharing an inside joke.

"His name was Samson."

"He looks like you," I said.

"He died last year," she said. "I think he took half my soul with him. He was my best friend."

"Is that why you came here?" I asked her, while Dad was outside splitting wood. The sound of his ax cracked through the valley, hiding our conversation. "Everyone who comes here has something wrong with them."

She laughed. "Is that so?"

"Yes," I said, a matter of fact.

"Then, yes," she said. "That must be why."

She held my hand, but not for anyone else but herself. I wanted to ask her how he died. Not just how, but *why*—why is a much more interesting question anyway, and it opens up many more avenues for conversation. I didn't. She wouldn't have the answers to my whys because she wasn't Dad. She came to us, after all, looking for answers.

"It must be so lonely here," she said.

"It's not something I think about," I said. "I don't like people. Everyone is a liar and cheat."

I didn't believe what I was saying, but it came out of my mouth anyway. Quoting my dad, nearly word for word, indoctrinated into whatever church he belonged to before he was kicked out.

She laughed. "You're awfully jaded for a twelve-year-old."

"You're far too trusting," I said.

"And you're like one of those stray cats," she said. She pointed to the tabby that liked to sun himself on the windowsill.

"I swear, I'm going to get one of them to like me."

In another few days, while Dad was outside, meditating, I found the courage to ask the questions I wasn't allowed to.

"What was home like?" I asked.

"When Sam was alive?" She whispered. "Bright."

I looked at the picture of her brother, not for his face that rhymed with hers, but for the backdrop. I think it was a home garden—the greens were yellower, creamier than the blackened pine needles of True North. There was a rosary of lens flare. Bright.

I wanted to be Janice's friend. I hated her twin out of jealousy; imagine being so close to someone that you shared the womb. I looked in the mirror for so long I could trick myself into thinking I looked like her. That we were sisters. Even then, I knew I'd never replace Samson, but she would never replace a mother I never met, so we were even.

IT'S NORMAL for kids to begin questioning their parents. I lay under the grove of spruce trees we carved with our sigils and prayed. We didn't have one higher power but many, and they all belonged to the same universe, so I prayed to the universe for protection. My desire to rebel picked up momentum.

It started with trying to be Janice's friend.

I wanted to see her world, so I crossed the threshold, past our line of defense. Past a mile's worth of trees. I saw nothing. More trees.

More North.

EVERY NIGHT, I hugged Dad, for no other reason than to listen to his heart. The steady pounding of it, the rhythm promising that Janice would stay. Until one night, they became war drums.

I stood in Janice's doorway with my arms crossed as she folded her laundry. Her face was knit in concentrated worry. I was about to say something—either beg her to stay or call her a traitor for leaving, but Dad pulled me aside.

"Need you to go stack the firewood out back," he said, before leaning in and growling in my ear. "Don't bother her. Darkness spreads through words."

As I worked, I listened to them load up the truck. The engine coughed, woke up, and then they were gone.

I STOPPED TALKING to boarders after that. They didn't interest me. I made a point to forget their faces, to mix up their names. I wanted permanence. I wanted to know what it was like to swim in amniotic fluid with another person. Dad was right—people weren't worth it. I managed to get that orange tabby cat to eat out of my hands. Its ears flattened every time it did, always distrustful of me, but I didn't blame it. I was human, and humans can't be trusted.

Dad stopped hiding things from me after that. It took a few years for him to let his guard down. It started small. Coins of blood stains on his jeans that he never fizzed away with peroxide and cold water. Then, the tools on the workbench that he didn't clean right off were sticky and rusted red. I guess he got sick of me asking roundabout questions, nettling him into telling me where the blood was coming from.

"You're too old to be coddled," he said. "It's time I show you what Darkness can do to people's hearts."

He took me to a clearing beyond the sigils, where the trees were young. Bones were tangled in their limbs. They'd grown up through them. He took me to a fresh patch. A tenant, nameless, faceless in my memory – I can still see their skin dehydrated in a nearly mummified state of decomposition. It was the height of summer, when even in the north the sun can bake moisture from flesh. The smell was sweet and unpleasant, and it made me throw up in the tall grass.

I wiped my lips with the back of my sleeve.

"What did you do?" I asked.

"I didn't do nothing," he said. "They do it to themselves."

I walked out there frequently, searching for something recognizable. A braided piece of bailing twine, a pair of earbuds, or a canvas backpack. I thought of Samson—I thought of whoever was behind the camera, taking a picture of Janice. They would miss her. I only knew her for a little while, and I miss her.

I found nothing.

I DON'T KNOW how to get back home. When I hitched a ride with a trucker to town, I was disoriented by the switchbacks and the constant change of direction. I know Polaris points north, but that's a very general direction. True North isn't real. It just keeps going until you're so far north you're heading south. There's no proof of the dichotomy between Light and Dark.

I stood in front of the steps of a police station, ready to give my statement. People make me nervous, so I have a habit of rehearsing conversations so nothing I say can surprise me.

The police would ask me where the bodies were.

"I don't know," I'd answer. "Somewhere in the woods."

They'd ask me if I could identify any names or faces.

"I can't," I'd say. "I don't remember any of them."

I pictured myself breaking down into tears and reciting the colors of the different cats that I memorized. What good would I be? When they asked where they were, all I could give was a direction. I stuffed my hands in my pockets and walked away.

I don't know how to live in the south, where I rely on people. Cashiers to check out my food, workers at the homeless shelter, and drivers to take me to job interviews. Nothing here marks the seasons except the trumpeting of geese. I tried living around people, but life has been disorienting. There's no wood to split, no roofs to fix by hanging tarps. All the things I know don't matter in town, and there's no place for the homeless in the countryside.

Now, I live like Janice and survive off the kindness of strangers. It's the only other way I know. I walk out onto the highway with my thumb erect. I know I'm going in the right direction, even in daylight, because the sugar maples and white pine have turned to balsam firs and shedding tamarack. Someone like my father is bound to pull me off the asphalt, take me home, and hide me away in the pines. As I hitchhike, I come to peace with the idea of bones hooked and knotted through saplings and new growth. I'm following the stars home, searching for a higher power than mine. I'm northbound.

COLD WHITE TEETH

J.R. SANTOS

It was the farthest north they had ever been. Like in every land that ever was and ever will be: to go north was to chase dread winds and bitter cold.

Reason enough why the socialite and the two dandies had never bothered. Arthur Kincaid and his two companions arrived at the valley heralded by the winter king's breath.

Kincaid had dragged his one friend in the world, Benny, into this miserable place, and the one woman who had ever put up with him besides his own mother. Aria was a thrill seeker, willing to accept some discomfort in exchange for novelty.

They traversed lonely hills and seemingly endless woods and met a great number of fascinating people; though they did not appreciate the fact much. Natives that had adapted and survived in these climates: deadly cold in winter; surprisingly warm in summer.

Yet, all their knowledge, culture, and well-meant advice, all fell into mute ears and blind eyes. With nothing learned and little gained, the trio reached a world so removed from their own that the reflection in the icy cold water, when Kincaid washed his face every morning, felt like a parody of himself. His human satellites were nothing but the means to shield his fragile ego, so he did not bother to think how they themselves might have felt. He was the lone intelligent being in the cosmos; his pedigree placing him in a pedestal above all creation. He was no more isolated here, with these two familiar souls at his beck and call, than he was when trapezing through feasts and dancing balls.

In the only village on the valley close to the foot of the mountain, they hired three men to help carry their things. Though all three men knew the mountain and its treachery, only one of them acted as the guide. That was the one who spoke Kincaid's language, took the time to explain to him the safest routes and entertained his questions while the others barely talked except among themselves. To them, Kincaid was just another empty man with a full wallet, not the first or the last of his kind. These men had little to say to their employer, except when necessary.

The day before the mountain range expectation, the mood turned sour between the travelers.

"I'm changing my mind, Art. I'm not sure I can do this." Benny had put up with Kincaid's abuse longer than any. Him having made it this far had been quite the feat.

"I know you're a coward, but have some shame. Even Aria is going. If a woman can do it, what's your excuse?"

Neither friend nor fiancé cared for the comment.

"We'll climb this mountain, and make a name for ourselves by simply coming back after finding whatever's at the top."

"Ice, I presume," Aira put forth. "At the top, I mean."

"Yes, darling. Very clever of you."

Benny began to comment when Aria interrupted. "But not as clever as you. Quite the genius, our dear Arthur."

"I get the impression you're being sarcastic."

"I was promised adventure, not frostbite. I'm all for exploring the trails, and hiking, but certainly not to the top of that!" She pointed out of the window of their room. The cold, white teeth of the world stood, one fang standing jagged, higher and broader than the others. An ocean of clouds was pieced by that lone bucktooth. A gum speared by an unruly canine.

"I'll go as high as is safe to go," she continued. "Take in the sights, then right back down. God's sake, you can't even ski here. We could have been on the French alps having a lovely time!"

Benny tried to say something again, but this time, Kincaid interrupted him. "Arthur Kincaid doesn't settle for mediocrity. We go all the way to the top, or not at all."

BLUE SKIES and slow drifting clouds kissed the mountain sides and seemed to melt into each other. Despite himself, these visions provided Kincaid with the painted world wonder he could never hope to find in the everyday life he knew.

The effort of climbing and the warm clothes shielded him from the ice and snow enough that the fire of adventure burned bright in his chest and filled his lungs with sunlight. Above him, everything was impossibly blue and went on forever. Below, at the foot of the icy maw of the world, spread great forests. These were a sea unto themselves from which echoed the cries of strange giants. Crystal clear and beautiful to the point of making him tearful.

What stories he would bring back! Let others know how much better he was! Arthur Kincaid had taken the trip. He would reach the summit and look down on creation. He would touch and see all.

This high lasted him a day. After that, the First Nation guides would find their work made a hundred times more difficult, their progress slowing down to the point the guide asked Kincaid if he wanted to go back. Kincaid refused, and the guides exchanged looks between themselves knowingly.

Two days of dragging their feet and of being miserable, concluded with the signs of a storm heading their way. Kincaid's guides knew the best shelters, when there were any, but something made Arthur act out, contradicting their advice seemingly at random. In his arrogance, deaf to the pleas of the men who accepted the job of keeping him alive, he made the party push on, and up the mountain.

I CAN'T TELL when I'm dreaming or when I'm awake. There's the white, the howl, the cold ... and sometimes, I remember things. I'm sitting next to one of the guides, the only one of the three who speaks my language with a heavy accent and long pauses. There's a light, a golden aura and burning orange center: a little sun in the ocean of clouds we rest upon.

"We can't help you."

"Why?"

The guide looks at me with the saddest eyes I've ever seen on another human; eyelids heavy with the weight of the lifetimes, the pupils carved with the memories of horrors that have been nothing to me but tales.

Meaningless suffering, as I read about it with indifference from the newspapers and shielded by the safety distance, my home an ocean away. Always assured of the comforts of my privilege, safe from this man's world by staying out of it. In my world, nothing gained felt worth having.

I'm a man who had only known minor inconveniences: never the cold sting of strife. Boredom, bothersome relatives and so on. What were these compared to starving and freezing to death?

HE COULDN'T help himself. Kincaid had pushed his guides away much in the same fashion he had pushed everyone else away in his life. All who dared to worry about him.

Having cut off all his friends and relatives, only Benny and Aria were left. "Where's Benny?"

"He's gone. He couldn't face you, so he left this morning, quite early."

"Coward. Useless." Kincaid breathed deeply. "Well, I still have you. Get ready."

"No. I'm waiting for the next convoy to get away in some comfort, hard as it may be to find any." Aria indicated her things all packed up, with a nod of her head. "They'll drop me at the nearest place resembling civilization, then it's the next train home for me."

"Leave me then! I don't need anyone! Get out!"

She didn't cry or raise her voice which had made him all the angrier. Kincaid shouted, and felt even more of a fool.

Aria, always a practical soul, cut anchor and sailed to happier shores, leaving him to his self-destruction.

A dark sea it was, and every lighthouse that tried guiding Kincaid away from dangerously close shores had instead the opposite effect. Lured as a moth to flame, Kincaid not only wanted the fire, but hungered for the light of conquest. At least, so long he could use the trials ahead to prove himself the better man.

But for what? Better than who? No one was foolish enough to believe they could survive such things unscathed, as if they were immune to fire. Who had he meant to impress?

I CALL FOR the guide and he doesn't answer. He's not here. I don't remember his name, so I just cry for help. I can see myself outside my body, looking back at the hunched, miserable form that is trying to shield himself from the cold that cuts.

"You wanted this," is what I want to shout at myself. "You did this to yourself and no one else is to blame. You fool, you complete idiot."

Why did you tell them to go?

THE STORM was close, and to be caught any higher was death. Yet, Kincaid refused to go back, or at least wait out the storm somewhere safer.

"You will die," said the guide, discarding all subtly.

"I don't need you. I'm carrying my own things. I'm taking a pack mule with me and you can all go back to Hell for all I care."

Though two of the party members didn't speak the stranger's language, Kincaid's meaning was clear enough from his tone alone. They tensed, knowing how these mad idiots who came to the mountain to conquer it, to know it and mark it, often came to be consumed by it. Many such people would become impossible to reason with at some point or another. As if there was a pleasure to it, a sport of committing suicide in the most horrific way possible and attempting to drag others with them.

Outsiders called it mountain madness, but only they did. The people of the valley knew these fools were mad long before reaching the mountain, and the mountain wasn't to blame. All the mountain did—their protector and greatest villain, this heavenly sword—was simply cut the skin to peel it back, revealing what people really were like underneath.

Their own people were shown their true faces when climbing the mountain, both their kindness and their cruelty displayed for all to see in ways they had never known possible. Both sword and mirror, the mountain judged all.

The guide, who spoke the foreign language, was patient. He had known his patience to be his greatest strength, and that virtue had been revealed in full in this limbo. It was a great gift which had brought him wisdom as well as allowed him to reach an old age, older than most in the village could brag of. This foreigner was, however, making that precious hard-shell start to crack.

"If we continue, we will die. If we leave you, you will die alone. I cannot help you if you won't let me."

"Damn you, and damn your help! Go back and leave me with my things."

The guide did not speak or even move. His silence was only interrupted by the wind which became stronger the longer they waited.

"Take them then." The guide handed him the rolled-up tent and a second backpack with tools and food. "Your things are all here. The mule and the rest are ours; our lives are not for sale. Goodbye."

"Wait! Don't you turn your back on me! I need at least one of the mules; I can't carry all of this!"

"You said you don't need us." The guide replied without turning back, gesturing to the others to start the track down the mountain. "You don't need the mules either, big man. Bigger than a mountain: you can carry your own things, you said."

Kincaid would have shouted at them but he realized the danger of an avalanche. He would have run in pursuit, but the snow slowed him to a crawl, especially with the added weight of all he had to carry. His guides walked at a steady pace. They made it look like a mild jaunt back down the mountain while he stared at them in anger.

"I need no one."

If the guide or the others heard the whisper, they did not look back to acknowledge it. The valley men had family to go back to and did not spare this traveler another thought. After all, it was just part of the ritual. In the end, their lives always revolved around this sacred monster. Harsh daylight as well as the rituals of feeding it. In due time, the mountain had become its own country, and its citizens were the dead.

I THINK the blizzard is calming down, though I'm not sure. Could be I'm dreaming it's ending. I can hear myself at least, even if the wind doesn't stop. I think at this height, it goes on forever because everything does. That somehow, the higher you climb, the closer you are to infinity.

Sometimes, I see things in the blizzard. Shapes: I can't tell if they are rocks or people. They can't be animals, not at this height. Nothing lives at this height.

Nothing. Whatever I saw moving had to be made up. I imagined it. I imagined everything. I'm outside my body looking at myself. I know I'm delusional, running a fever…

I'm sure it's all in my head.

HE CLIMBED ONWARDS, somehow, all on his own and carrying twice the weight now. He would stop to camp at one point and bask in the glorious view as the sun set, and for some moments all the world was painted gold and red, pink and purple.

He watched as he prepared his meal over a tiny gas stool, cooked canned food, and warmed himself. He could tell great clouds were coming close and the storm would catch him soon. But that would be then and he had a knowledge, a sixth sense that made him absolutely sure that it would pass like a breeze. He would find a place to wait out the coming storm, make it to the top on his own and later make it all the way back down.

Night took over the day. Stars were a million jewels on a great dark-purple mantle. The biggest full moon he had ever seen in his life rose up to join them.

Once night had conquered the day in full, Kincaid saw great lights manifest. A cosmic aurora ran through that same heavenly fields, like a curtain of lights of green that hypnotized him.

Everything was perfect and he had no regrets.

I FELL ASLEEP again. I can't remember what I dreamt about. It's all white out there.

It doesn't seem as bad as before, but it's hard to see. It hurts my eyes.

Looking down at my hands I realize I'm holding something, two little white things that have a yellow tinge to them. It's two of my teeth. I coughed them up and don't even remember when it happened.

There's only a little blood. I think it's freezing in my veins.

God, help me God, I'm sorry. I'm sorry I was a fool. My hands won't stop shaking. I dropped them, they're lost to me. They're followed by a third tooth. I spit the latter after I felt something being pried loose by my tongue.

I'm inside some kind of cavern but I don't remember how I got here. I need to warm myself.

HE COULD ONLY keep going up; he could only keep going up by never turning back. As he progressed through the storm, it became harder to see what was happening around him or where he was heading.

If he got turned around, he could easily walk off a cliff and only realize it as he was falling to his death, so his entire focus turned inwards on the compass of his mind to direct him forward and up.

He remembered his first hike; with friends he had long severed ties with. People who he had loved once, yet he could hardly remember their voices anymore.

"Don't look down. Never look down, and you'll be alright."

Escaping the city to climb and camp, walk nature trails in green forests away from home. The place was different but the rules of nature would apply, he reasoned. If he kept his cool, he would make it. He knew he could, so he kept going.

Once he had planted his little flag on the top of the mountain, he could forget any of this had happened. He had no words to describe his astonishment when he found himself back in the forest ground. Arthur laughed, his ego rejecting the reality of his tired eyes. He was atop of the world. Trees didn't grow on teeth.

The storm got so bad, Arthur felt the cold and the wind cut his skin even under all the clothes, and saw the tops of the surrounding mountains, the ones dwarfed by this one.

Sometimes, the fever made him see things. Everything grew darker as he became surrounded by trees. He hears a moose, or some other monster, but knows it's just the wind.

I'M CLOSE to the top. So close.

My body tells me to stop and I refuse, despite everything. Worst right now is this horrid hunger: it's become a wolf in my stomach. It's eating me from the inside out.

I trip again and again, not even realizing in the process I lost a spare backpack to the white void erasing everything around me. I saw the summit and simply pushed forward. I know I saw it, it has to be there, it has to be real.

Can't help but laugh. On that summit of mine I find only a cave entrance, and above me the mountain keeps going up. The wind rises higher and higher as the world becomes a blur of blinding white and I crawl miserably into the cavern. If this endless mountain was, or is to be my Olympus, then this cavern is the mouth of Tartarus. I plunge from the highest top to the deepest low.

Inside, I find only more darkness and depths I would not dare face, despite the death waiting for me outside. It smells damp and earthy; the darkness looks like trees covered in snow. It almost seems to glow in the dark, populated with animal eyes. Howls, wolves, God knows what else. But they can't be real.

I stay close enough to the entrance of the cave that I can find my way out— then understand, to my horror, how little food I have. How most of the things I need for the climb back down are lost to me somewhere along the way.

I'm both freezing and burning up. I crave it more than life itself: alcohol. Even just one drop, while repeating to myself constantly, "but alcohol will dry you up".

Water, water is what I need and the snow had not been like this at the start. Whatever water we melted from the snow was the purest liquid to ever grace my lips. Since I got to this cavern or cave or whatever damned hole this is, the water tastes like mud.

I wash down what little food I have with it. Down you go! Have keep myself from drying up from the cold. Oh, yes, yes.

I can't let myself become like you, huh?

HAVING LOST track of time, Kincaid did what he could to stay warm and sane. Though he would not explore too deeply, he wanted to avoid wasting what little fuel he had for light; heat was far more vital. He walked down the darkness in search of something, anything that could breathe hope back into him.

He found a mummified corpse, robed in clothes that were frozen solid to the shriveled body. It could have been tucked away here for months, years or millennia.

He spoke to the dead body in a feverish pitch, but the body did not reply.

Perhaps just one of a million bodies, carried up the teeth of the world and frozen in time until Judgment Day. Sometimes, between his feverish delusions, the human corpse resembled some sort of dead elk.

Kincaid returned to his impoverished camp: his sad little shelter in range of the blinding white lights of the storm, snowflakes drifting in like star showers. He sat down, rolled up in his sleeping bag and began to speak to himself.

IT'S OVER. It's over.

Not a dream or a memory. It really ended, and I can see it now. A great blue sky that goes on forever. I made it through the storm but I can't move. At least I don't feel it: the cold or the hunger. The rock feels like bark, the ground is soft like dirt.

All that light pouring in, it makes me so happy.

I've never seen a bluer sky.

BLACKENED, as if he had been charred by flame. Black, and purple skin, eyes eaten by the crows. Naked but for a mantle over the wizened shoulders, his body sat crossed legged under the shadow of a sequoia.

A pack of wolves smelled his sparse, frostbitten flesh. Despite the temptation they thought better of it, and moved on. Spring grew nearer, and brought with it a promise of better meat and fewer fools.

THE FAMILY AXE

NEIL WILLIAMSON

*M*am *went to the Wood too soon*, Haw thinks as he climbs up among the watchful trees. That sour recrimination has never been far from his thoughts this summer. And it's true, despite what people say to their faces, him and Rowan.

Everyone knows when it's their time, lads.

She's still doing her bit, just in a different way.

And Uncle Alder: She's with the ancestors. *You'll respect it, or you can find another roof to sleep under.* Haw's never done wishing for Uncle Alder to hurry up and go be with the ancestors too so Haw can respect him at a bearable distance. But Uncle Alder isn't the problem, not really. It's Mam just going like that. Without a word.

Striding on through the evening stillness, calves protesting at the steepening gradient, Haw swings Mam's tool bag by its strap, the weathered leather deadheading the harebells. Every so often, he pauses to scrutinise the ground beneath the tumbled blue blossoms. There's piss all here. They're going to have nothing but twigs to offer for the Burn. First year without Mam and everyone will see how ill-favoured her boys are.

Everyone will know what's in Haw's heart.

You're either part of it or you're not. Another of Alder's favourites.

"Found her!" Rowan's reedy voice pierces the swaddled silence. "Haw, look! I've found her!"

Haw's been so wrapped up in his thoughts, he's surprised to see his wee brother dawdling a hundred yards back down the slope in a dapple of shadow and cooling light. The wavy chestnut hair that the kids at school tease Ro about—Kin and normal alike—curtains his pink face. His lurid Incredible Hulk t-shirt looks muted and artificial amid the natural hues that surround them, leaf and moss in all High Summer's saturated vibrance. He's set down the family barrow so that he can place his palms against a craggy Scots pine.

Haw loves his brother, but he can't half be a tiresome wee wank sometimes.

"No, Rowan," Haw whisper-calls back, because anything louder in this place feels as wrong as laughter at a funeral. *It attracts attention*, Mam always said, *and you dinna want to attract attention on Burnday, son.* "That's not her, mate."

"Is so!" Rowan reaches for a slim branch and tries to bend it back. "See, she—"

"Shoosh, Ro! It's not her." Sighing, Haw retraces his path down through the flowers and slow-swaying bracken. The loamy aroma here is so heady, it's making him a little dizzy; the piney air heavy in his lungs. "Think about it, man. That tree's a hundred-year-old, easy. Mam only went last year. She'd be in a sapling or something, right?"

Haw hates the way the hope in Rowan's open, trusting face so visibly curdles. He's only nine and he still totally believes everything he's been told since he was a wean. It's a big thing coming to the Wood for the first time, let alone when you've lost your mam. Of course he'd be looking for her. Of course he'd gravitate to something strong, something solid. Dependable.

Haw, fifteen now and suddenly saddled with his brother's care—Uncle Alder might be their guardian on paper but, beyond providing meals and the box bedroom the brothers share, they only ever see him when he wants to bitch about how much they're costing him—wishes life really was that simple. Stories are one thing, but he's been doing a lot of thinking lately and he's halfway to convincing himself that when Mam went, she just went. Out there, somewhere. Like the boys' dads did, six years apart. Maybe she even went to find one of them? To make a normal life away from the Wood.

And maybe Haw even understands wanting that a bit. But to not say anything? To not sit him down and explain? If she had, he knows he'd have kicked up a fuss, yelled the house down like it's him who's only nine, not Rowan. He knows he'd have done anything to stop her going. And, aye, obviously Mam would've anticipated that, so maybe that's why. But even so. Not even a note? Mam could be snippy at times, but it would be a cruelty Haw can't get his head around to just...*go* like that.

So, maybe she went to the Wood after all. Was simply called in the night and couldn't resist, exactly as the stories say. How would Haw know? He's never seen a shred of proof beyond what his imagination sometimes conjures within the tree shadow when the Kin perform their quiet rituals at the high and low ends of the year. It never mattered before because Mam was there. Mam and Haw and Rowan were a family of the Kin, all together on Burnday. Whatever he imagined, they were safe because Mam said so. But Mam isn't here anymore.

How is it fair? People just vanishing like that.

Haw doesn't remember his own dad, but he has clear memories of Rowan's. Alex was a tall, bearded man, with that same long, brown hair. Quiet, mostly, but besotted enough with Mam to resent Haw being around almost as much as Haw had resented the interloper in their small house. At the kitchen table for breakfast every morning. Choosing what to watch on TV, always football. Coming out of the bathroom in nothing but a towel, the tattoos on his arms and chest glistening from the shower. Like he was the king of the house. Not to mention that Alex was a normal. They'd had to tip-toe around him when it came to Kin stuff. *Taking the boys to Alder's* was Mum's excuse whenever they went up the hill. Alex must have noticed this always happened at dawn and dusk, but Haw never heard him say anything about it.

The intrusion of Alex lasted what felt like forever, but really it was less than a year. A winter, a summer, and then one morning he was gone, and it was just Mam and Haw again, until Rowan joined them the following spring. Haw's old enough now to do the arithmetic. Alex hadn't been the first or last of Mam's boyfriends, but he was the one who left his mark.

When Haw once asked Mam why she needed men around, she'd laughed and replied, "Ach, pet, the only men I need is you two. You're my Kin." She'd said it a little sadly but, at the time, her response had satisfied him. Made him feel wanted. Loved. He'd been young, though. The age Rowan is now, and every bit as gullible.

Mam didn't take anything with her when she went. You didn't need clothes or make up or a phone when you went to the Wood, but that wasn't proof. All it meant was that no one would go looking for her. She was smart, was Mam.

Rowan is still trying to bend the branch, break it off, his cheeks red from the exertion.

"Ro, we can only take what's freely given," Haw says. "You know that."

"But Mam—"

"Mam'd give us her wood freely. All of it." Haw tries to infuse his words with conviction. "Doesn't that prove this isn't her?"

Reluctantly, Rowan lets the branch spring back and then flicks a strand of hair off his cheek, an out-of-place, grown-up gesture that takes Haw by surprise. Alex used to do that.

As Haw turns away, the shadows shift in the corners of his vision. Coalesce, clot. "Bring the barrow," he barks, scolding himself mentally. It's only his imagination. This is just a normal wood, full of normal trees. Even unspoken, the words sound flimsy, not defiant like he'd hoped.

"C'mon, Ro," he says. "We're going to look somewhere else."

Stomping back up the hill, Haw can hear Rowan labouring behind him. All the creaks and jolts as the barrow bumps over roots and hidden rocks. He could help, but Rowan's old enough now to learn to do his bit. The wee guy should want to help if he believes the stories. He has to help, because Haw can't do this on his own.

On the other side of the rise, the Wood's edge comes into view. Haw wanders down to where the trees peter out and looks out over the wild meadow and the glen beyond. Below the summer night's sky, milky and stretched-out as teased cotton, Haw can make out the top of the silage tower marking Uncle Alder's farm, where he and Rowan live now; and, directly in line, the church spire in the village of Uig where they used to live with Mam. Further on lies the green and gold patchwork of the fields. The villagers are harvesting the first barley, while the late crop, dense and lush, waits its turn to ripen. Between the fields, trout streams tumble down into the glittering loch. A single-track road skirts the waterside, passing through several more villages before reaching Lochend and the main road that, if you're driving—or hitching, maybe—would eventually take you eastwards out of the glen and then all the way on down to Glasgow.

From there, Haw thinks, who knows how far you could go?

The air is fresher out here in the meadow, the breeze stirring the poppy and blawort, nettle, thistle and loosestrife in a chaotic dance, and Haw can hear mavises and yellowhammers yelling their evening chorus from the brambles. It's a riot. But it's better than the judgemental silence of the Wood. He breathes easier.

"But this isn't the trees, Haw," Rowan whines, catching up. "There won't be anything out here!"

"Aye, well, there wasn't much of anything back there either."

Haw regrets snapping. It's not Rowan's fault that this isn't fun like it was when Mam was here. That they're not laughing and joking even as their muscles ache from the weight of all the branches they've collected. Ro doesn't know because he's never done this before. Maybe bringing him was a mistake, but what choice did Haw have? They're Kin.

"Anyway…" Haw pins the word to the air like a piton, clings on to it while he calms himself. "This is still the Wood, technically, Ro. Right down as far as the gorse, see?" He points at the bushes that fringe the meadow and guard the rocky drop down into the glen, their golden blossoms bright as watchnight candles. "Come on, mate. You start looking around up here and I'll start down there. Let's be quick though. The day'll be dying soon."

Although the summer days here are gloriously long, it is properly getting late now, the clouds above the trees already starting to bronze. The Burn starts at nightfall and they need to have *something* to contribute to it.

"Okay." Rowan's small voice is all but drowned out by the birdsong at first but then, with a subtle shift like a gentle popping of the ears, it seems to Haw more like it's plaited into the frantic tapestry of trills and chirrups, bedded in with the bee drone and the impatient, rhythmic rush of the wind through the stems. Natural. Part of it all in a way that evokes in Haw both envy and the urge to run, just run, as fast and far as he can.

"Okay," Haw says. He sounds like Mam, he realises, and out of the blue wonders… had she been scared too? It's a shocking thought. Mam was an adult, not a fifteen-year-old who doesn't have a clue what he's doing.

Then again, Mam left them.

Rowan is looking expectantly up at him,

"Let's have a competition," Haw says desperately. "Whoever finds the most branches gets a whole afternoon on the Xbox."

He is rewarded with Rowan's gleeful grin. "Deal," his brother says, but then, "Haw?"

"What?"

"Can I have Mam's axe? For when the branches are too big for the barrow."

It's so unexpected that Haw can only laugh. The family axe isn't large, but that solid lump of oak and steel is way too heavy for Rowan to wield yet. He can't fault the wee man's ambition though.

"Aw, come on," he says, making it into a joke. "You've got the barrow. I've got to carry all my branches myself!" More gently, he adds, "If you find a muckle one, give me a shout and I'll come and chop it up for you."

His brother still doesn't look happy. Mam wouldn't have sent him off on his own like this. She never had with Haw, always kept him close by when they walked among the ancestors at High Summer. But as Rowan said himself, they're not really in the Wood anymore. It'll be all right.

"Hey." Haw puts a hand on his brother's narrow shoulder. "You've got your amulet, haven't you?"

Rowan nods, laying his hand over Hulk's fierce grimace. Beneath the cotton hangs a twist of silver birch bark on a thong. Rough on one side, inscribed with the Kin's Prayer on the other.

"And you know the words to the Leid of Protection, don't you?"

Again, his brother nods.

"So, you're going to be fine. I promise. Now let's get on, eh?"

"All right."

"All right."

As Haw turns away and starts quartering the meadow, it's not Rowan's asking for the axe that sticks in his mind so much as the way Haw himself had instinctively tightened his grip on the strap of the tool bag. When he was twelve, Mam had heated the tip of a bradawl on the hob and then helped him burn his name into the axe's haft. His *Hawthorn* beneath her *Briar* beneath his gran's *Rose* beneath another *Hawthorn* and so on all the way up to the head, which was a dark and serious thing with the singular exception of its keen, bright edge.

You're either part of it, or you're not.

Which is he? Which does he want to be?

Haw looks over his shoulder and, seeing Rowan still watching, waves. Then he turns away and gets on with scanning the ground. *Come on,* he thinks. He used to be so good at this, finding the hidden sticks and branches for Mam. Keen to prove his worth, even as he held his breath and kept half an eye out for *them,* coming to snatch him away to be tested by the Wood. It was the promised fate of all who fall out of favour for not doing their bit.

Now, he shuffles through the undergrowth, exploring as much by feel as by sight. And there *is* something, under the thin sole of his Converse. He eases aside a profusion of wild garlic to reveal a dead branch. It's a couple of inches in diameter and barely as long as his forearm but, at last, it's a start.

Using the branch to push and probe, Haw soon finds several sticks of varying sizes. Still not much, but they're at least dry and free of rot. Old wood, freely given. He's feeling more upbeat as he approaches the wall of gorse at the meadow's edge, making a plan to follow the bushes for a bit before climbing back up to see how Rowan's getting on. He's really starting to feel guilty about bringing his brother all the way up here just to leave him unattended, but Haw rationalises that he learned plenty by cutting about on his tod when Mam and Alex wanted to be alone. A little independence will do the wee guy some good.

All the same, Haw decides to donate his collection to Rowan's barrow. He can have all the time on the Xbox that he wants. Mam's going has been hardest on him.

He's feeling pleased with himself when he hears a shout.

"Hey!"

It is not Rowan's voice, but Haw's head snaps around to look that way anyway. There's no sign of his brother. Just the meadow, and the thickening darkness of the trees above it. A bubble of fear forms in his gut before Rowan's tousled head reappears. He must have been crouching to pick something up.

Perhaps he won't need Haw's charity after all.

"Hey! Can you give me a hand?"

A momentary dip in the meadow's clamour allows Haw to work out where the voice is coming from. Approaching the gorse thicket, he glimpses a checked sleeve and a tanned arm among the thorny branches. Higher up, a blue eye, a toothy smile.

Haw blinks, unable to think for a minute. He hears himself say, "What the actual fuck?"

"I...*ow!*" The voice has a rounded warmth to it. English, maybe the South West? Bristol, Haw decides, though he only knows accents from TV shows and TikTok. "I've got myself stuck. Can you help?"

Whoever this is, wherever they're from, they shouldn't be here, Haw thinks. Not because there's no path up to the high meadow from the other side of the gorse—there is, he uses it himself sometimes though it's treacherously steep—but because it shouldn't be *possible* to get up here. Not at this time of year. Not if you're not Kin.

At least, according to the stories.

So, what does that mean? Logically... that he could be right about Mam? Right about all of it? Try telling that to his body. His jangling nerves and rabbit-racing heart.

Haw finds himself seized by the compulsion to tell this lad to *piss off, just piss off for your own good*, but the impossibility of the boy's presence stills his tongue. Instead, he lays the tool bag and sticks down and then uses his branch to ease the gorse aside, straining against the spry, stubborn branches. He manages to hold them just long enough for the owner of the voice to find their way out.

"Woo! Thanks!" The visitor is laughing and rubbing a forearm covered with scratches. Under the blue flannel shirt, he's wearing a t-shirt with a pink cartoon heart over the breast. Tiny writing underneath says "Christine And The Queens," one of Haw's favourite bands. He's wearing long shorts and a pair of black and white Converse not unlike Haw's own. His hair is blond, floppy on top and under-shaved at the sides. It looks really cool.

The visitor is, Haw reckons, a year older than he is. Not tall, but wiry and leanly muscled in a way that suggests he's into sports, though Haw wouldn't necessarily hold that against him. The lad's sweat-sheened face is the first Haw has seen in ages that doesn't belong to someone from the glen. It is beautiful.

Haw looks at his feet. "That's okay."

"It's amazing up here." The lad is staring out over the glen, grinning like he's won a prize or something. "You can see everything."

Haw doesn't care about the view. Raising his head shyly, he confirms that there are better things to look at.

His pulse has settled after that first adrenaline spike, but now he feels like he's about to start shivering. He tells himself it's stupid nerves. He tells himself to get a grip and say something to make this lad look at him instead of the stupid view. Haw wonders what his name is. Reckons he looks like a Ryan, or a Josh. Maybe an Olly.

"You visiting long?" Haw says and immediately wants to die. It's like something they'd say to the tourists in the village shop. Politely prickly. Haw doesn't want to be polite or prickly. He wants to be cool. He wants to be hot. But he doesn't know how.

"Just until Saturday," maybe Olly says easily. If he notices Haw's discomfort, he doesn't let on. "The parents are on a foodie odyssey up here. They're at the shellfish farm tonight for some ridiculously expensive champagne and oysters extravaganza." He draws the last word out into a posh boy piss-take and then turns his grin on Haw. It's dazzling. "I got fish and chips and came up here."

"Why?" Haw manages. He means how? He still needs to know.

The lad shrugs. "Just wanted to get away. You know?"

Haw does. Again, the urgent impulse to yell at this boy to leave wells up inside him, but how is he supposed to manage that without saying the words that all year have been burrowing within his heart like slugs through a potato?

I want to go too.

To wherever boys like this are. To wherever Haw can be a normal fifteen-year-old. Hanging out, getting stoned, having fun. Free. Unshackled from his responsibilities to Rowan, to Mam, to the ancestors. To the Wood.

How can he say any of that *here*? At the edge of the Wood in the last hour of Burnday.

Haw feels like he's caught between two overlapping versions of the world and unable to untangle them. It's like one of those pictures that looks like two things at once. The girl or the crone. The rabbit or the duck. Then in a rush of clarity, he understands that it's on him; the only way to see the picture he wants to see is to force the issue. Ask the outsider's name, ask if he wants to stay for a while. Long enough to prove that the stories are just stories. That Mam never went to the Wood, because nobody does, do they? When they've had enough of this place, they *fucking go*.

To prove that Haw is normal, and he can do what he wants with his life. He only needs to say the words.

But the sky is deepening now, the wind tugging at Haw's shirt, the grasses beating against his shins. He feels an energy in the earth through his thin soles, and understands that it's riddled with old roots. Older than him by a long, long way. He feels sick, his skin goose-fleshing as the shivering begins in earnest.

Haw stammers, "You should probably think about getting back, mate." His words hum, his lips tingling.

"What?"

"It gets, um, dark real fast here." He tries to raise his voice over the meadow's resurgent clamour, but he hasn't enough breath. "You don't want to get stuck up here at night."

The shiver meets the hum meets the thrum in the earth, becoming a violent vibration that jangles Haw's bones until it slips into phase with the meadow's cacophony. Becomes the start of a slowly building pulse, a coming wave and a rush of shadows that cannot be dismissed as imagination.

There isn't a *them*. There is only an *us*.

The lad looks confused but tries again with that grin that has clearly got him most of the things he wants in life.

"Figured maybe you were going to show me the scenic route back…"

The words dwindle, drowned out by the swell. The grin falls away as the confusion froths into fear.

"Go!" Haw hears only the buzzing edges of his own shout. "Run! Get away!" He shoves the boy, who bends but doesn't move even a step. It's like he's rooted.

All his life, Haw has been warned what is supposed to happen when someone is tested—be it called or, it is whispered, sometimes *taken*—by the Wood. All the kids know, even Ro, but as long as Haw had never seen it with his own eyes… *Couldn't* it have been a story? Couldn't Mam still be out there, somewhere?

Deep down, though, he knew. He has needed it not to be true for a little while. But it is, it really is and accepting that makes the most sense out of everything in the end. It explains why his dad never once came back to visit and his birthday cards were all in Mam's handwriting. It explains all the junk Alex left behind too, before Mam binned it all.

Haw's always known that Mam really did go to the Wood. He knows because he's Kin. Part of it, even though right now he doesn't want to be.

And he doesn't want *this* to happen but is powerless to prevent it. Clutching the twist of bark under his shirt, he finds himself rooted too as he watches the violent transformation sweep up the boy's slender trunk. Supple to stiff, smooth to rough. Freezing those wiry limbs in agonized torsion. Twigging fingers. Knotting orifices. Shredding flannel and cotton into leaves that quiver in the aftermath.

The testing is over in seconds. The wave collapsing, its noise ebbing. The realisation dawns that this lad, who only came up here on a holiday whim, has gone to the Wood. An outsider without favour. As Haw watches, the leaves shiver and wither and fall, and the young wood dries and turns grey.

Dead wood, now, for the taking; if far from freely given.

He hears a rustle behind him, and Rowan is there, grim wonder illuminating his face. He has extracted the family axe from the tool bag Haw had discarded among the grasses and doesn't hesitate to step up.

"No," says Haw, too eagerly snatching the axe from his brother. "Let me."

SOFT FIRE

MARISCA PICHETTE

Inside my gingerbread house, there dwells a candy floss ghost.

They are pale like clotted cream, invisible by the windows but painfully there when they linger by my stove, searching for the warmth they've lost. I shoo them back with my broom, bristles tangling in their softness. I'm not sure if it is ignorance or childishness that drives them again and again to the heat. Don't they know they will melt into strings of sugar, caramelize on the iron and fill my house with the tang of their burning?

But they drift back when I'm not looking, my head bent over the loom, black licorice wrapped around my fingers. I have some minutes of peace—time to craft a blanket, a rug, a mat to delay this house's collapse another day. Sugar works its way into the creases of my cuticles, the wrinkles of my hands. Only smoke filling the house alerts me of the ghost's latest attempt. I untangle myself and rush into the kitchen, waving them away from the stove that sizzles with blackened floss and fades into new scars.

They retreat but never go far, waiting for me to turn my back again. I can't manage to keep them away—no matter how much damage the flames cause.

I think they want to burn.

I SWEEP my gingerbread house twice a day. I wipe the windows with handfuls of caster sugar, beat the rugs with rock candy. At the end of the day, sticky callouses are all I have to show for my efforts. My tools melt and crack.

My feet sink into a doughy floor. Everything I make is unmade overnight.

The path to my house is lined with chocolate pebbles, candy canes curling from my ribbon-shingle roof. Beyond: the leering trees, the darkling woods.

Shadows pick at the fringes. Roots disturb foundations. Clouds gather while I sleep, finding the weakest spots and pressing their advantage.

With each rain, every snow, I fill a mixing bowl with frosting and set to work repairing the damage. My knees ache and my muscles tire, but I will not let this last refuge fall.

Even so, the house tries every day to melt, to sink into the earth and forget what it is. Is the pressure from the trees too much for it? I hear their branches at night. I dodge their leaves in the day, edges hard and sharp. I'm used to not being wanted. The house, though, is different. It cannot move on like I have; it's trapped in the place it was made.

I think it's sympathetic to the ghost. I wonder sometimes if the ghost made it. I wonder if the ghost was here before, and found the house like I did. The three of us huddle in a clearing that shrinks each night and try to hold onto ourselves.

The house would burn, too, if it could. Peppermint bark walls heat up and melt in pools on the floor. I shore up the beams with graham crackers, but I'm running out of supplies. There's no magic in something this unnatural. The pantry doesn't replenish, but steadily empties. In a few months, a year—I will have to eat my way out or sink into the softening floor.

I watch the stove carefully. It is unique, inedible. Iron radiates heat as cinnamon burns. I stand in the kitchen contemplating the only piece of the house made of something enduring. The only piece that will outlast me when trouble comes and I'm forced to move on again. When I turn, the ghost is there, waiting.

IN THE EVENINGS, I sit by the stove guarding its heat from the ghost, which lingers in my peripheral vision. When I'm not looking at them directly, they seem almost human. I can almost imagine they're me: wearing white instead of black, young instead of old. They drift closer, and I see them as they are: wispy, insubstantial, vulnerable to fire and rain, ready to be dispersed by a strong wind… Just like this house.

I lean forward and stoke the fire, remembering the flames that scarred my hands, the smoke that took my breath away. I know when it's time to move on. I've survived pyres and riverbeds.

This house may be failing but I can keep it alive. In the corner of my eye, the ghost turns.

I will not burn again.

THE GHOST LIVED in the kitchen before I knew the gingerbread house existed. Their candy floss fluttered in drafts I had yet to plug, dripped onto floors I had yet to clean. When I moved in, they didn't try to hide from me. I think they were lonely, lingering by the popsicle-cold stove I had yet to light.

They are mostly white with the slightest blue tinge, like the sky gasping between cluttered trees. They are shaped like a gum drop, amorphous yet I know once they were human. Once, they may have been a child. Once, they may have been a witch.

Now they are my shadow, waiting for a chance to destroy themselves completely. If I let them.

I refuse, holding them back while I cultivate fire to keep myself alive another day. I plug all the leaks I can find when the weather washes sugar away and exposes us to the world. Every day, I work to keep the house and the ghost as dry as possible—but more rains come. More trees grow, shrinking this clearing to nothing.

Living here is a constant war against all that is natural.

I WONDER SOMETIMES how the ghost died, turned to candy floss that withers in the rain and crumples in heat. Did they burn, like me? Were they drowned, cooked, beheaded? All I escaped from, proving my guilt through survival. Giving my persecutors only more reason to hunt me.

The forest is quiet today. I look out the window, the trees shadowy and still. When I first came under them, I thought this silence peaceful. I thought, without people, I would be safe.

Now I see the silence as an intake of breath. Something is brewing. A fresh assault on this house, on me.

Leaving my room, I find the ghost in the hallway. It turns—towards me, away, I don't know. Is this how they died? Did they retreat into loneliness until at last they faded entirely, becoming one with the house?

I think we are not so different. Except they have given up.

THIS MORNING, I bake pies to replace my broken bathroom tiles. I use molasses to grout them in place, my hands sticky and shining brown. When I turn, the ghost is hanging in the doorway.

I don't know if they're watching me or looking out at the stairs. I don't know which side is their face or if they even have sides. The floss that faces me is melted near the bottom, where I was too slow and they drifted too close to the stove.

We look at each other—maybe. Before I can wonder how to skirt around them to go back downstairs, they slide away, silent and smelling of sugar.

I follow them out of the bathroom. They lurch at an angle, crookedly drifting to the second-floor window. Cinnamon bark beams snag fibers of floss, tugging bits of them away. If they notice or feel pain, they don't show it. I walk after them, plucking the pieces down and wrapping them into a sticky ball in my molasses hands.

The ghost stops at the window. Are they looking out or at me still? Through their body and the crème brûlée crust pane, I see the woods.

Nature exists outside of my gingerbread house. Silent still, leaning in. Waiting for the next attempt to pull my world apart.

I wonder if the ghost has ever been out there. Looking through them, I feel the hatred of the trees. I'm glad the ghost is in front of me, their floss a screen between us. The woods will never welcome me, no more than villages.

I back away down the hall, leaving the ghost hanging in the soft light. There is much to be done to preserve this latest refuge I've found. I turn away, putting the memories out of my mind.

I refuse to become a ghost.

IN THE EVENING, as the moon rises behind the tilting, naked trees, I gather materials to light my fire. Chocolate-covered pretzels leave salt depressions in my forearms, stacked up to my chin. My feet ache with cold and memory.

I carry my load up from the cellar and into the gingerbread house I did not build. I stack impossible things and load the fireplace, sugar-coated embers spitting smoke into my eyes. The candy-floss ghost hovers in my peripheral vision, slowly turning like a chocolatier's display.

I talk to them when there's nothing to do but wait for the woods to pull down my house and the people to find me, force me to search for another home.

"I didn't choose to live here away from everything," I tell them. Flames warm my sticky fingers. "That choice was made for me."

The ghost hangs behind me, revealing nothing.

SOME NIGHTS, I read to the ghost. Some nights, I read through them, cookbook propped open on the counter when they drift past, diaphanous.

Whoever they were, whatever they are now, they never reply to my voice.

Maybe they don't speak my language. Maybe they don't speak any language. Maybe they never spoke. Maybe they never...

Stoking my candy fire, I wonder how long they've been dead. They drift through the living room, over licorice carpet and into the kitchen. I get up and follow them.

The stove is cold. The ghost hangs before it, floss so thin, I can read the casting marks on their other side. I wait for them to realize that there's nothing to hurt them, nothing to end whatever existence they inhabit. But they don't leave the stove. They hang there, blocking the huge iron door and shedding sugar fibers on my fresh-swept floor.

We stand, observing each other or facing different ways. I'm still trying to think of something to say when I hear the trees laughing, and it begins to rain.

IT TAKES DAYS to repair the damage after the storm. If I could, I'd move somewhere else—away from candy and crumbs.

I tried once to build a house of wood. When I'm inside, the trees move close to the house, stuffing the chocolate chimney with leaves. When I go outside, they retreat, always out of my reach. They know my desire and they crush it flat.

I should build a house of stone, but every rock I touch turns to gravel and sinks into the earth. The woods have never welcomed me.

I would move back to a village, but villagers drove me here to the gingerbread house. From fire and steel and curses, I fled and found myself only one temporary ally: a ghost.

Muscles sore, I smear a final dollop of frosting in the cracks between gingerbread boards. I carry my mixing bowl inside, glancing at the innocent-feigning blue sky. The trees are silent once more, holding their insults for an overcast day.

The ghost is spinning in the corner. I nod to them, washing out my bowl and wiping the sugar from my spoon. I keep an eye on the ghost while I search the cupboards for food.

Since coming to the gingerbread house, all my teeth have fallen out. I was missing some already from encounters with villagers and huntsmen. My nose, once flat and smooth, has been broken four times. I see its crookedness wherever I look.

The people have shaved me, tarred me, burned me, drowned me… But I do not die. I never become candy floss.

In the back of the highest cupboard, with the aid of a soft brownie stool, I find a candied apple.

Actually, I find two. One is green and rotten. One is red, a single bite missing from its perfect shape.

I take both and cut them to pieces, removing the seeds and rolling flour into dough. As I make my pie, I keep an eye on my ghost. They have drifted away from the corner, turning lazily in the middle of the living room. I have no fire burning today, having spent all my hours repairing the house.

I fill the pie crust with rotten and perfect apples and paint over them with honey. I break some cinnamon from the wall and grate it on top. It snaps and I slice my finger on the grater, adding one drop of blood to my pie.

The ghost continues spinning as I load the stove with chocolate truffles. I light it with a fondue ring. My pie begins to cook.

Drawn to the heat, the ghost drifts into the kitchen. I block the stove with my body.

"I won't let you."

They hang before me, floss and air. I wonder sometimes if they wanted me to come here, wanted me to light a fire so they could burn themselves to sweet residue.

"I have burned," I tell them. "I won't let you."

They tilt, drifting out of the kitchen and up the stairs. I can no longer see them and they make no noise, but I know as I turn back to my pie that they're directly above me at the window.

THE GHOST STAYS at the window for a week. I eat my pie and wait for rain. Outside, the woods grow cold. Frost turns even the fruit leather shutters brittle. I knit myself a scarf from all the tufts my ghost has dropped, but it doesn't last long. Sugar melts on my skin.

When the ghost comes down the stairs at last, they are moving faster than I've ever seen. They fly past me, straight into the roaring stove as I remove another pie.

I scream, my fingers burning. I drop my pie and tangle my hands in melting floss, dragging what I can away. I have no choice but to slam the stove shut, locking the rest inside.

What remains of the ghost is hardly bigger than my ruined pie, broken pan melting into the chocolate floor.

Their floss is curled and brown, sticking to my throbbing hands. I back away from the stove and try to peel them off while there's still some left.

Can a ghost die?

I sit for two hours picking floss from my skin. When I've finished, the ghost hangs close to the floor, a calico of singed sugar. I worry that they feel pain even though they're dead, even though they're made of candy floss and air.

I search the kitchen until I find a rock candy jar. It's the right size. I carry it back to the living room, where the ghost has barely moved. As carefully as I can, I move them into the jar, securing the crystalline lid.

"No more," I say to them.

Outside, it begins to snow.

I MISS my ghost. Hidden in the jar, it's like they're no longer in the gingerbread house. I am alone again.

While the ghost can no longer move like I can, I carry the jar with me from room to room, always ensuring the lid is firmly in place before I light a fire. When the stove is cold, I open the jar and look at them. They hardly move, stuck to the rock candy bottom.

I should let them burn away. I know that is what they want.

But I am selfish. I tried not to be. I used to help everyone, give pieces of my time away until seconds were minutes and minutes were hours and I was old and aching. I used to give advice and medicine until the people returned my love with hatred and my care with torture.

I used to be a beautiful person. I am not anymore.

The woods know. The trees hate me, like the villages before. The sky pours snow onto my gingerbread house, burying it until I have to peel the very walls back to burn for warmth, my ghost cradled in my lap.

We both watch the flames, yearning for escape.

I have burned. I have sunk. I haven't died.

I vowed a long time ago to never die.

THE WOODS try to kill me. Winter is long, and I go hungry. But I last. I always last.

Spring comes with broken candy canes and cracked gingerbread. I am hardly strong enough, but I can't let this last shelter fall apart. I plug the holes with caramel, wedge gum in the cracks. I eat and rest and do as much as I need to and gradually, I become stronger. The clouds try to stay but they are driven off by the sun, and the woods fail again to force me out.

Us out.

I carry my ghost outside with me, repairing the roof with fresh ribbon candy I found in the corner of the emptying cellar. I close the shutters where windows have broken or melted with the thaw. I shake sugar drops onto the path, pressing them into the mud with my bare feet.

It looks okay, my gingerbread house I did not build. I wonder what might have happened to it if I had never come, fleeing knives and tongues. Would it have sunk into the mud, been overcome by trees and chewed by raccoons? I wonder where my ghost would have gone then. Perhaps they would have been eaten along with the rest.

That is no end for us. I tuck their jar under my arm and walk inside.

IN SUMMER, the roof melts. I am too tired to fold it back into place. Sun reaches into the living room. Rain fills the bedroom. I run out of flour for pies.

Our house is dissolving around us. My hands grow sticky around my ghost's jar.

"Where do we go now?"

The trees are victorious. I hear them jeering as I walk away from the gingerbread house, caving in taffy folds behind us. I stand with my ghost for a day and a night, watching the woods reclaim our candy walls.

At the end, only the stove remains.

I pick my way through the rubble and rest one sticky hand at last on cool iron. I open the door.

The stove is cold, dead. I bend over and put the jar with my ghost inside. Hunching my shoulders, I follow, closing the door behind us.

We never wanted to burn.

There is more room than there should be. More than my pies had. I crawl deeper into the stove, pushing my ghost ahead of me. My fingers tangle in ashes and children's bones. I push us on until we come to another door.

It's stuck. I pivot myself so my feet are first. Holding my ghost in their jar, I stomp against the door.

Stomp.

Stomp.

Stomp.

It flies open in a spray of ash. Wriggling free of the stove, I look around.

We are not in the woods. Nor is it a house of candy and gingerbread that surrounds me.

No, the walls are waddle and daub. The roof is thatch and moss. The floor is dirt. I know the smell. I know the feel.

This house is more impossible than the one I left behind.

"They burned it down," I tell my ghost, cradling them in my weary arms. I inhale but I smell no smoke. The only ash is on my hands.

This is it: my home. Herbs bound to nails on the walls. Straw woven into mats by my hands before fire scarred them. Everything is as it was before the people changed their minds, before they decided I wasn't helping them enough. Before.

I set down my ghost and walk to the door.

It doesn't open. I slide my hand across the bolts that hold it in place, the chain buried in the floor. It doesn't open.

"Nothing can get in."

No wind, no rain, no vengeful snow. No people. No trees or raccoons.

I hurry back across the floor and slam closed the door through which we came. I turn to my ghost, charred and incomplete.

We have everything we need. We have medicine and blankets and eternity. My house is gone, so maybe I am too. But I haven't burned.

I'll never burn.

"Nothing can get in," I say again, the words sweeter than anything at the gingerbread house. I pick up my ghost, unscrewing the candy lid.

Their floss drifts free. I watch them sink to hover just above the floor. My floor, my home on the other side of the flames. They knew it was here. All this time, they've been trying to lead me through, make me see.

I touch the iron door, my fingers leaving a trail of ghostly ash. It's cold. The fire has been dead for a long time.

THE BANNIK

REN GRAHAM

Even though it was cold outside that morning, Pavel preferred his outdoor chores to cleaning the hearth where his father rested. His father was often in a foul mood, but with the dismal winter weather, he was even more brutal than usual. It was far better to let his father sleep when he was in these moods, even though the sun had been up for a few hours already. Just as one didn't disturb a bear as he lay hibernating in his den.

If he didn't…

The welts hurt more in the winter: stinging and stinging and never seeming to heal up. Maybe the warmth of the banya would have alleviated the bruises. The slosh of cool stream water on the heated stones. Swatting the birch branches gently against his skin to calm the inflammation. Eucalyptus, linden and juniper all tied up in aromatic *venik*. But Pavel wasn't allowed in the banya. It was a luxury reserved only for his father. His grandmother had once told him that the banya was a house of spirits, that it was unclean by its nature. He always figured this was just a way to ward him away from the place, and also, in her own rough way, to comfort him so he did not feel like he was missing out.

The light across the snow was dim and frosted, and made the forest meadow appear as though viewed through a piece of blue stained glass. Pavel liked this quality of light, even sometimes relished the winter chill on his face. Sound seemed to travel faster in the cold. He could wander among the firs and cup his hands to his mouth and chirp up to the orioles and the jackdaws high in the forest canopy. Sometimes they would respond with quiet inquiring trills.

Gathering up armfuls of chopped pine logs, Pavel traversed back and forth between the homestead gate and the forest clearing, transporting the wood into neat stacks by the chicken coop. It was tedious work and the fresh pine rubbing against his arms made his skin itch, but it offered Pavel an opportunity to stay far away from home.

The chickens were curious about the wood stack. They paused their picking at the frosty soil, heads tilted as they watched the wood grow higher and higher. A wheat-colored hen approached him as he returned with the last bundle of logs. She gave a quiet whine in her throat, eyes unblinking. Pavel set down the wood, then reached to gather the friendly hen up in his arms. She immediately sunk her head down into her plumage, eyes blinking slowly closed, as if at ease.

Pavel had always wanted a cat, but chickens could be companion animals, too, in their own way. His father was allergic to cats and he was cantankerous enough to throw bottles at the wandering barn cats in the summer. Over the years, they kept a wide berth around their property. Pavel would only see one or two hunting field mice on the edge of the meadow: just a shadow and a flash of mirror-like eyes in the tall summer grasses. Cats could bask on a sunny stone all day and not be chastised for their laziness. Cats had the freedom to leave their acre and wander the woods. They could subsist on wild pheasants and rodents and could make a new home for themselves among the moss and tall larches. It was easy to envy their freedom.

Pavel returned the hen to the coop, where it roused in his arms, excited, and clucked as it wiggled free and jumped to the coop floor. The coop was surprisingly warm, scattered down feathers and hay serving as decent insulation, and it smelled dense and avian. It wasn't an entirely pleasant smell, but to Pavel, it smelled like home.

There was a crash from the kitchen patio.

The flock of chickens fluttered at the sound, heads bobbing and eyes wide as they gathered back against the outer wall of the coop. The forest, which had been alive with birdsong only a moment before, had gone completely quiet, as if the trees themselves were holding their breaths.

Pavel rose to his feet, shoulders hunched instinctively. His father was awake. As he approached the patio, he knew it was best to appear as small and compliant as possible.

A wooden banya tub was tossed out into the snow where it rolled, lopsided and dented, to a standstill against a bush. His father stood in the doorway, wolfish brown hair damp and disorderly.

Pavel held his hands behind his back.

"It's dirty," his father said. "Take it down to the river and wash it."

Pavel nodded and knelt to grab the wooden tub. He applied pressure to the wood, his knuckles firm as he worked the panels back into place. His father had a habit of damaging things.

"Pavel," his father continued, and his voice had taken on a sharp, uncompromising edge. "I want it back in the banya before the sun sets."

The heat of fear rising in his cheeks, Pavel met his father's hazel eyes. They smoldered like cooling ash. A pretense of violence. But he turned away and stumbled back through the doorway; his silhouette broad and stooped and bear-shaped. Pavel felt his chest deflate as he watched his father disappear beyond the radius of the dim yellow of the oil lamp on the kitchen table. Into the dark depths of their home.

Banya tub in hand, Pavel wasted no time jogging down the icy path towards the stream. He knew all of the twists in the walking path and half-buried stones and patches of black frost to avoid. Running through the spruces as fast as he could almost felt like flying. This is what the songbirds felt when they flitted between dense evergreen branches. This is what the cats felt when they crept along deadwood logs and old brush, concealed in shadow. Freedom wrapped in pine.

The stream was alive with snowmelt. The moment Pavel touched the water, his hands grew pink from the cold. He dipped the banya tub into the stream and watched as currents swirled through the wooden basin. The banya tub wasn't particularly dirty. Of course, it only ever held warm water; it was just a task his father had given him to create work and an opportunity to punish him if that work wasn't done to his satisfaction.

There was a flash of scales in the river.

A small bluegill had accidentally flopped over the wooden edge of the tub and became trapped. It spun round and round in confusion, its belly the color of springtime peonies. Pavel watched it probe at its wooden confines for a moment with a sad fascination. He dipped the lip of the tub low, down to the sediment and stones, and the bluegill quickly streaked out, disappearing immediately into the silver river current.

Pavel shimmied the tub back and forth several times in the water before lifting it back onto the stony shore to dry. The wood had a wonderful smell when it was wet. He sat back. Twisted on his side to paint fading shapes on a rock with his wet fingertip. The patterns started dark before drying, invisible. Transient, secret pictograms.

At the edge of the forest, Pavel noticed two glowing feline eyes watching him. He sat cross-legged before the cat. Respectful. He dropped his hand, palm up, and made a slight gesture with his fingers.

"Here, kitty," he tried.

The cat blinked in a slow, gentle acknowledgment before it pushed through the bush, tail raised high in greeting. Its fur was as dark as a moonless night—darker even, like a pile of coal chipped straight from a vein in the rock. It was a subtle thing, and probably complicated by the dappled light through the trees, but it almost appeared as if this cat cast no shadow on the ground at all. But Pavel didn't have a chance to investigate that curiosity further because the cat did something else miraculous.

It spoke.

"You let that fish get away," the cat said. It sat down and raised one paw to clean its face.

Pavel glanced at the banya tub at the edge of the stream. "Of course," he stammered, "why wouldn't I?" Sure, he'd had plenty of conversations with cats before, but they had all been one-sided. Cats didn't typically possess the ability to reply.

"You clearly don't appreciate a good smoked bluegill then," the cat replied. It gave a small sigh of irritation at this lost opportunity.

Pavel continued to stare at the cat, perplexed.

"I don't mind the staring," the cat said, after a moment. "It's better than having a bottle thrown at you, after all."

Pavel held his breath. "My father," he started.

"Yes," the cat answered. "Quite a troublesome fellow. I gather you're not fond of him either. You're almost old enough to be on your own, aren't you?"

"Yes, but…" Pavel bit his lip. "…I have nowhere else to go. I've been living in this little valley my entire life."

The cat did not respond to this, only raised up off its haunches and investigated the drying banya tub. It sniffed around the rim, placing one paw in the wooden tub.

"Don't," Pavel cried. "You'll get hair all over it and I just cleaned it!"

The cat's tail twitched, likely in irritation at being scolded, but it removed its paw from the wooden tub.

"You're going in the banya tonight," the cat said. There was a strange, inquisitive quality to its voice, a twitch of its whiskers.

"Not me," Pavel corrected. "My father." He glanced down at his hands. They were chapped from the cold stream water. "I'm not allowed in the banya."

The cat's tail swished back and forth as it seemed to consider this. Its claws pulsed in and out, raking the soft soil. "And you leave out an offering for the bannik, don't you?" the cat asked.

"The bannik?" Pavel repeated. He wrinkled his nose in skeptical surprise. "That's a superstition."

"Oh," the cat quipped, "and a talking cat is perfectly within reason."

Pavel shook his head. "I *do* think you're strange. But it's not the same as a spirit that haunts the bathhouse. That's just a story you tell children."

The cat padded over and set one intent paw on Pavel's knee. Its eyes glimmered like liquid metal.

"I think you ought to leave something for the bannik," the cat said. "A pine branch, rose petals, and a bowl of warm milk."

Pavel chewed at the dry skin on his lips. "My father will be upset with me," he said. "We only have a little milk left and I don't think I should waste it."

"It won't be a waste," the cat said. The paw resting on Pavel's leg was now sharp, toes tipped with unsheathed claws. The cat stared up at Pavel, its irises cavernous. "You want your freedom, don't you? Leave those items by the banya door this evening before your father has gone inside."

Pavel stood then, spooked by the cat's sudden intensity. He reached down for the banya tub and held it tight against his chest like a shield. "I should go," he said.

Distracted by the rustle in the bush, the cat turned with its tail low and head flat against the ground. A bird swooped up from the bush into the high boughs of the pine tree, decidedly out of pouncing range. The cat flicked its ears back and refocused its attention on Pavel again.

"Fine, go," the cat said, disaffected. "But remember what I said. Think about how nice it would be to finally have your freedom."

It thrashed its tail and padded off through a shaft of white sunlight. Its black fur glowed a cinnamon hue in the light.

Pavel frowned and watched as the cat stalked off. He saw now that it did have a shadow. But the shape of it was strange. The shadow was in the contour of a small, hunched person with gangly limbs and a long, messy beard. Before Pavel could get a better look at the bizarre silhouette, the cat had ducked out of sight beneath a dark, prickly bush.

THE SUN had nearly set. There was a thin gold band on the horizon, barely visible above the dark treetops.

Pavel crouched outside the wooden banya and placed a porcelain bowl at the base of the door. He'd fished a handful of rose petals out of the black tea in the kitchen cabinet and arranged them around the edge of the porcelain bowl. Once they were placed, he poured milk from the glass bottle into the bowl. There wasn't much left: it was mostly perspiration on the inside of the glass container. Pavel could only hope the bathhouse spirit wouldn't mind the meager offering. After the milk and the rose petals had been set, he placed the final offering across the bowl: a small pine branch, its green needles dense and sharp.

Was that all?

Looking down at the offering bowl now, Pavel felt silly. He'd let a cat talk him into some superstitious nonsense, all on the slim chance that his life might improve. That he would no longer be afraid of the night. That his father would no longer spend the afternoon doused in liquor. That he could someday venture out beyond the meadow gate where the cats roamed the wildflowers. And what would the bannik even do for him, assuming it existed?

A long time ago, his grandmother had shared the old stories with him. The bannik ensured a clean, safe banya. As safe as a house of errant spirits could be. There was always a chance of mischief in a bathhouse. It was a sacred space, his grandmother had explained to him, but sacred in ways both holy and profane, the duality of which must never be forgotten. Spirits were drawn to these dark and intimate spaces, drawn in like condensation on the wooden walls, and the bannik was their shadow host. Even with this responsibility, at the end of the day, the bannik was a simple bathhouse spirit. Not a granter of miracles.

Pavel heard the squeak of the patio door on its old hinges. He abandoned his post next to the banya door then, darting for the chicken coop to conceal himself behind it. His father was coming. His heart pounded in his throat as he pressed himself against the wooden structure. Pavel closed his eyes.

The sounds of the evening forest took over.

Boots cracking on stiff frosted soil. The wooden reverberation of the slammed banya door. The sound of wind, far off in the valley pines. Birds in the trees, branches creaking with their weight as the flock gathered. But it was as if they were all holding their breath. Watching. Waiting. The hens had gone silent in their coop.

There was a towel draped over an empty barrel for when Pavel's father finished up in the banya. It waved plainly in the breeze. The sun was gone now. The meadow was blue and dark, the hilltop in the distance extinguished of birdsong.

Pavel rose from his crouching position, hands braced on the wooden coop. He craned his neck to see over the livestock fence. There was something odd about the way the stream filtered up from the banya roof. It was a profuse amount of steam, like a kettle's screaming spout. And the quality of the steam itself was different, too. There was something almost…glimmering about the way it dissipated out into the cold air.

A familiar black cat padded along the patio path. It made eye-contact with Pavel. Beads of milk lined the tips of its whiskers. But it didn't stop to chat as it had before at the river clearing. Instead, it slunk along the edge of the house, tail raised high and proud. Pavel couldn't help but worry that his father would catch sight of the cat if it made a habit of crossing their property so flagrantly in the future.

His father, though… That was the strange thing.

It was long past his father's usual time spent in the banya, but he was nowhere to be found. There were no clomping, heavy footsteps. As Pavel approached the banya around the back of their home, he could see the wide-open door. White clouds of humid air issued out. The milk dish was cracked in half, a jagged red line through the ceramic. But the milk itself was gone. In fact, there was no white residue or moisture at all in either the dish or the soil around it. Inside the banya, it was gloomy with steam. All he could make out was a hazy, unmoving shape towards the back bench.

Pavel held his hands to his chest and bit the flesh of his cheek inside his mouth.

"Father?" he ventured.

No answer.

Pavel took another step inside the banya. The floorboards creaked under his weight. The shape on the back banya bench did not resolve itself, too obscured by clinging steam. There was an unusual smell, though, different from the moist, hot wood. It was a very bodily odor, as if sweat and raw meat were squeezed through a fine sieve to produce a heady, unfortunate broth. Yet there was a kind of perfume in the air too. The smell of a fresh garden rose. It was deeply unnatural, and Pavel found himself taking another step toward the figure, eyes wide.

And then it all became clear.

The figure was his father, but not like he'd ever seen him. His skin was plump, puffed away from the bone with saturated moisture. The skin itself was red like a boiled lobster and split and peeling in places, weeping with steam. His eyes had sunk deep into his skull, pushed down by the inflated, wet skin of his cheeks. In the corpse's lap was the pine branch Pavel had placed in the bannik's milk bowl. A ghoulish ornament, its needles tipped with dew.

Pavel choked back the rising nausea and stumbled away from the banya.

He pitched back against the cobblestone patio as his knees buckled under him and he clutched at his face in abject horror.

Dead. His father was dead. Boiled alive.

What would he do? Where would he go? Pavel shuddered at the sudden existential freedom that stretched in all directions. A cold, expansive steppe. A silver fish no longer trapped in a banya tub. He shivered even as he clutched his arms tight around his body.

Up above, in the shadows cast by the ornate wood of the home's carved gables, there was a gold flash of feline eyes.

HALLOWED GROUND

J.S. BETULA

The fairytale color palette of Briar's childhood, as vibrant and rich as it had been two decades ago, sprawled out languidly before them. Intermingling against the forget-me-not-blue sky were budding ferns in inchworm-green, bright teal lichens, and bone-white shrubby dogwoods. Briar's other senses were awash, too: the smell of new fungi emerging through decaying pine needles, the arguments of warblers and adulations of hawks, the clean taste of cool mountain air, the gentle tug of pricker bushes on their bootlaces... They took a slow breath through their nose, sighed, and walked across one of the enormous fallen trees that had served as the Bridge of Khazad-Dûm when they were seven and things were infinitely simpler.

They'd walked for about two hours and hadn't seen anyone else at the preserve, even though it was such a sunny day. Maybe it was still too cold for other hikers, but this was Briar's favorite time of year in the forest. They sat down on a big, flat rock and took a swig of water. Then, they snapped a picture of the view—both down the mountain from their perch, and up toward the distant, snow-dusted peak—and texted it to their sister with a little sunshine emoji. She was a lot of the reason they were here today. When Briar was agonizing over dropping out last month, she'd told them, "just saying… if you leave college, you'll be able to see springtime at the preserve while it lasts."

A little reluctantly, they tugged out their new journal from their backpack to see if maybe being surrounded by trees would help them write. It was the least aesthetically offensive bullet journal they could find, and it still had a criminal number of Papyrus-font headings about setting goals and believing in oneself. Maybe there actually was a spiral-bound book out there for what to do after you spent finals week in the psych ward instead of the library, but Briar wasn't able to find it at the local book store. They took another deep breath and touched their pen to the top of the page, wondering if maybe the wind could guide their hand and scribble out something they wanted to do with their life. Just as the ballpoint began to roll, a strange noise whisked Briar's attention to the left, off past the trail marker.

While someone who was less familiar with the area would probably describe it as the caw of a crow with a respiratory infection, Briar identified it instantly: distress call, white-tailed deer, adult. Some poor, leggy thing must have gotten stuck somewhere, maybe in all the fallen branches left behind by last week's storm. The gasping cry sounded again, and Briar stood up. They probably couldn't do much for something as large as a deer, but they had successfully gotten a rabbit out from under the porch that one time, so maybe they could at least calm the creature down. Briar had a way with animals.

They adjusted their backpack and walked over towards the noise, not realizing until they were calf-deep in a pit of leaves and pinecones how tangled the storm detritus really was. Briar made their way thoughtfully through a crowded gap between two building-sized rocks and there, in front of a palisade of birch trees, was the source of the noise.

It wasn't one buck, but two, and they weren't stuck in branches and stones. They were stuck on each other's antlers, literally locked in combat. One of them had lost the fight a long time ago.

The living deer was nosing around by the dead one's hooves, and he was in awful shape. His ribs stuck out an inch from his sides, his stomach was distended, his nose was dry, and his eyes were crusty. He had been hurt in the fight, or maybe after—a sickly pink gash on his flank buzzed with flies. His breath clouded in the early morning air, each exhalation racking his body like a deep, painful cough.

Nausea sloshed in Briar's stomach. They tried to convince themself to assess the other animal as they fought the childish impulse to squeeze their eyes closed and cover their ears. The smell of rot and fear yanked a wet retch out of them, but they shook their head and forced their eyes down to the dead buck.

Its head, once so strong and proud, wobbled on its neck fluidly as the other deer searched the leaves, its chin forced up to the sky like it was trying to stargaze through its milky, vacant eyes. Its body was sprawled on the ground with its legs bent underneath it; its chest was hideously concave from the bloat and release process…

A long trail of disturbed leaves and unidentifiable muck extended fifty or sixty feet behind the two—the living deer must have dragged them both all this way, maybe in search of more to eat. Briar's body flooded with anxious sympathy. Maybe if the deer stayed calm, Briar could help him untangle and he could recover. Maybe.

"H-hey there, big guy," Briar attempted, their voice cracking with nerves and the start of tears. The poor animal must have been so confused, and in so much pain. "Hi, handsome. Let's, um…"

The buck didn't even look at them. Usually just the smell of a person would send a deer bolting off into invisibility, but he didn't blink.

A black shape dove suddenly through the trees a few feet from Briar's face, and they squeaked.

The regal vulture landed on the dead buck's spine, and it clacked its beak a few times, tasting the decay in the air. The bird tilted its naked red head as it scanned the corpse, and the buck sobbed out his distress.

He was trying to protect the body, Briar realized. However absurd it seemed, the dead buck was remarkably undisturbed—there weren't any bite marks or missing pieces. The living one had defended it so far. Ridiculous justifications frantically wove together in Briar's head: they were brothers, they were lovers, they were just playing…

The vulture bent its head low, toward the deer's chest, and Briar jolted. "Hey!" they yelled. Then, summoning their mother's voice from their belly, they added, "Go on, get out of here! Get!"

The bird looked up, asking Briar with its intelligent, beady eyes what—exactly—they were going to do about it. Meanwhile, the surviving buck tried to nudge the vulture, but the angle of the stretch was tough for him: his entanglement with the body tugged him downwards, so he was straining his neck to the point that his eyes bugged out of his head.

What could scare the bird away without hurting it? Briar's aim wasn't good enough for a rock, and there weren't any big sticks in reach to wave around. They grabbed a handful of leaves and tossed them towards the vulture, but it only reared back and continued to glare. Somehow, the buck twisted impossibly further and nabbed one of the vulture's tailfeathers with his teeth—the bird ruffled, disgruntled, and finally flapped off.

The buck let out a low moan of relief, stumbling down to his knees, and Briar's heart ached. In all the time they'd spent in this forest over the years, they'd never seen as much as a bird with a broken wing or a skinny ermine. They'd barely even seen a cloud. This phenomenally painful tableau, this unbearable cosmic compensation, hit them like a sledgehammer to the solar plexus.

A selfish, pathetic little thought surfaced in Briar's head: even here wasn't safe anymore. Even here, there was terror, violation, impotence. It all felt like their fault, as though this wouldn't be happening if there wasn't someone to witness it, as though they had infected the whole forest with their personal failures, as though this place that they loved so much was holding them down and drilling its rejection into their skull. If Briar stood still for another second, the existential weight was going to pulverize their bones.

Tripping on their way over to the buck, they pleaded, "Let me help you."

But the deer grunted angrily as they approached, rising up on his wavering, atrophied legs and flattening his ears against his head. He was nearly eye-level with Briar when he stood, and broad enough, even in this weakened state, that Briar swallowed nervously.

"I can try to get you out," they said as a warm tear rolled down their face. "You have to let somebody help you."

They took another step closer to him, reaching towards his antlers.

The buck stomped loudly in the leaves, his whole body shaking with the effort of refusing help. God, was this what Briar had looked like to those EMTs?

Swallowing the hot shame of the memory, Briar shot out a hand and gripped a point of the buck's antler.

The animal threw them off instantly, sending a little shock of pain through their wrist as he wrenched himself around and away from Briar. His muscles twitched randomly—like he was deterring flies, like he was freshly dead—and he dragged himself inch by agonizing inch closer to a nearby gap in the thick wall of trees. His eyes remained fixed forward as he hauled himself under a skeletal white branch, as he trawled the husk-corpse jerkily behind him until they both disappeared beyond the partition of birches.

Briar took a few hesitant steps as a sense of wrongness solidified on their shoulders like a jacket made of lead. They stopped for a second, instinctively, but when the deer called out in pain again, Briar rushed after him. They passed beneath the archway, curls of the white paper-bark lightly scratching their cheeks, and spotted the buck a few paces away. They tried to call out again, but the animal was captivated: his eyes were locked on the creature standing atop the large, flat stone in the center of the sun-soaked clearing.

And now, so were Briar's.

The Piebald Doe was perfect. Briar had never seen an animal like her before, definitely not in these woods. As they walked closer, it got harder and harder for them to remember to breathe.

Her soft belly was swollen with what had to be twins or triplets. Her small, delicate, ice-white antlers seemed to cradle the sun within them even as she turned, to split and double it behind her head like twin haloes. The mottle on her coat shifted kaleidoscopically before Briar's eyes, sliding from tawny and white to black and grey, and sometimes to pale yellow with a Rorschach assortment of brown spots surrounded by black. And those eyes… Pure black like an ocean trench, like the untouched spaces that rumbled beneath the earth.

Her divinity was as clear as the sky above her—no, nothing was above Her. Seeing The Piebald Doe was loving Her, was dying for Her on an altar of intertwined branches with a mouth full of violets.

Briar trembled, and started to overheat. They shrugged off their backpack and thick jacket at once and both tumbled to the ground behind them soundlessly.

The Doe sniffed the air, clicked Her hoof lightly on the rock, and Briar's heart leapt into their mouth: Her movements were so fluid and perfect, they'd drive a ballet dancer to spectacular jealous suicide. It was all Briar wanted to look at for the rest of their life—their eyes hurt from their refusal to blink. The stone split where The Doe had touched it, leaking glistening honey in lazy spurts. Briar could practically feel it coating their tongue and trickling down their throat, sweet as the smell of death.

Tears blurred their vision, and they rubbed at their eyes furiously with their palms to see Her more clearly. It was only then, when their stare was dragged forcibly away from Her, that Briar noticed the variety of plants that rambled through the clearing. There were familiar ones like fir saplings, tiny nearly-black wild blueberries, and foot-high ghostly mushrooms, but also an assortment of flora that shouldn't be able to grow here. Straining their eyes and credulity, Briar spotted grapevines, ivy, and strange, spindly trees with peeling bark that revealed clementine-orange wood. The plants tangled around each other so thickly, and were so delicately interlaced with fungi, that there was barely any room to move between them.

And on the ground beneath every single sprout, there were little nests of bone. Even with their heart pounding and their dizziness getting worse by the moment, Briar still discerned whisper-thin mole ribs, yellow-toothed rabbit skulls, innumerable antlers, and what must have been a grizzly bear's gigantic jaw.

She had made such a beautiful garden.

The Doe must have heard their thought, because She bowed Her head demurely. Her dark eyes finally met Briar's and She blinked once at them.

She may as well have speared them through the heart.

They fell to their knees, crunching more skeletons under their shins. It was as if the entire forest, the entire mountain range, was channeled through the voids between those long, curling lashes. Her gaze was ancient, all-knowing—the many-eyed surveillance of the spider perching on this whole ecosystem's web. Briar's mouth watered, their hands shook, sweat prickled on their forehead, and desire clenched suddenly in their stomach. They were stripped down to their base needs, pried apart to reveal a twisting thicket of raw nerves.

They had been wrong before: the forest wasn't rejecting them. It was only trying to guide Briar to The Doe, to the encompassing warmth of Her attention and Her wisdom. Briar's hopelessness and obsession over failure felt so distant and petty as they gazed upon Her; their mountainous pain was swiftly eroded down to pebbles, the way that tears on a toddler's face evaporated the moment they stood up from a fall. The emptiness inside Briar, which had ballooned out uncontrollably with helplessness and shame for months, was suddenly overfilled with incandescent joy: The Doe would give them purpose. All at once, Briar was blessed with so much clarity and such gratefulness to Her that if they were sliced open, they would bleed pure, honey-golden love.

They had to—they didn't know, they had to do something to prove themself to Her, to show Her that Her time looking at them wasn't wasted, to keep Her all-seeing eyes on them so She could show them what was next, they had to—

She broke their eye contact, and Briar's heart shattered. Her divine gaze was back on the buck, who groaned when Her eyes met his: guttural and keening and needy.

Briar had forgotten he was there. Seeing him again, smelling his acrid adrenaline, all their nervous pity from earlier was blessedly dissolved. They didn't need any fear or desperation anymore; Her love had graciously wicked it away from them. How profoundly ungrateful to display a feeling like that, to turn their back on The Doe and embody who they'd been before Her.

The buck stumbled suddenly, and an unwelcome memory tried to invade Briar's peace—the icy impact of hospital tiles on their knees when they half-fainted during intake, the struggle to stand. But that, too, disappeared as sunshine refracted off The Doe's antler-halo, warming Briar down to the soles of their feet. It was all different now. The buck may still be fumbling and lost, but Briar was found.

The Doe's gaze shifted again: She was looking at the dead buck now, to the living one's vocal dismay. Her nostrils flaring out, She examined the tangle of the body, and then She turned Her elegant head pointedly away from all three of them. The buck cried out and managed another quavering step, smearing the blackened viscera from the dead deer all over The Doe's cultivated mushrooms.

Unprecedented, preternatural wrath flash-froze Briar to the ground. He had made Her look away. Him and his putrid burden.

The dead buck was much too old to be an offering to Her anyway. Only fresh death begat life. How did he stomp through Her entire garden and still not understand that? Why did he bother spending so much time and effort protecting the corpse when it was so worthless to Her that it was an insult, practically a violation? Approaching Her like this, bringing miasmic rot to Her altar, it was unforgivable.

A proper offering, Briar realized—something for The Doe's garden that displayed Briar's understanding—yes, that would get Her to look at them again so She could guide them forth, it had to. It had to.

A feeling that Briar thought they'd never have again surged through their body: pure, enthralling ambition.

Briar licked their lips, they snatched a broken rib from the forest floor, and they advanced on the buck.

IN THE HIGH PLACES

ALLY WILKES

"It's in the trees! It's coming!"

THE BOYS ARE mucking around outside on snowmobiles when Shannon feels the trailer start to move. The floor shudders, its rag rug worn smooth from hundreds of pairs of hiking boots, and she wonders whether there are earthquakes in this part of Scandinavia; she hasn't read the guidebook.

There's the gurgling roar of an engine, and Shannon looks out of the window to see a flash of luminous colour whip past. Jonno and Eric are doing doughnuts around their Tiny Mountain Settlement, which consists of a central brick cabin, a firepit and sauna, and three small wheeled trailers. With the contents of her rucksack strewn across the bed, and Eric's wet towel lying on the floor, their trailer is definitely shabby rather than shabby chic.

Another vibration. The boys must be shaking it on its foundations.

"Come on, you're holding us up!" Christobel's voice is needling.

Shannon balls her hands into fists, continues searching for the blister plasters. Her brand-new boots have worn both her heels into soft seeping meat.

Each day of their holiday has been the same: they set off from their trailers into the snow and the cold and the relentless negative beauty of the terrain. They break for lunch. They continue along the trail towards the next Tiny Mountain Settlement, which contains—as if by magic—their own trailers, moved ten or twenty or however many miles down the path by invisible elves. Local guides meet them at the evening campsite, stoking their sauna and building up their fire and staying long enough to tell stories over pine-needle vodka.

Shannon hadn't known it was possible to be so tired, sore, or bored.

She'd only come along because Eric insisted, and Eric always got his way. Shannon had begun fooling around with Jonno simply because she'd thought it would be less predictable. Or maybe she'd wanted to stick it to Christobel, who's started making eyes at Eric—with his outdoor gear and square jaw—like he's some sort of misunderstood Viking prince.

Pursing her lips, Shannon discovers the blister plasters, nestled in her wash-bag next to the open packet of condoms. They'd had sex in the sauna the night before, her and Jonno, listening out for the others, giggling at their own wickedness.

Shannon thinks there's nothing wrong with being a little wicked from time to time.

There's another tremor, a big one, and the trailer actually rocks from side to side, making the wine-glasses clink and clatter. "Hey!" she yells. "Stop mucking about, I'll be out in a minute!" But the glasses continue to chime, and the thunder gets louder and louder, and she scrambles to her feet to see that she's moving.

"Hey!"

The boys have stopped to stare at her trailer. Eric's goggles are pushed up over his hat, his eyes big and confused as he shouts something she can't make out. Jonno is unreadable behind sunglasses, but he's scrambling off his snowmobile in her direction. Christobel, who's doing some sort of obnoxious stretching by the fire-pit ("I grew up not far from here," she likes to remind them, tossing back her long white-blonde hair), gives her a glance – then a second glance, eyes widening.

A laugh bubbles up inside Shannon, and she throws herself across the bed, bouncing, to open the wide panoramic rear window. The cold air hits her with a snap. She's moving faster now, the trailer rocking from side to side, picking up speed as she's towed away from them.

"See you, losers!" she yells. She'll end up at the next Tiny Mountain

Settlement without having to get a single blister or eat another bloody Clif bar on the way. It feels like all her prayers have been answered.

Good elves, she thinks.

A drawer slides open, and the box of firewood swings across the floor. Whoever's towing her is driving as if there's no one in the trailer, and she realises some sort of mistake is being made. But she refuses to look alarmed. No; the last thing her friends will see of her is a happy smiling face, waving out that window.

They're a small group of paint-splash colours now, receding into the distance: red and orange and cerulean blue against that stark black and white landscape. The trailer hits a bump in the road and keeps on going.

SOMEONE IS whispering outside.

It's summer in the far north, daylight relentless, although Shannon had pulled down the black-out blinds. The swaying motion of the trailer made her faintly nauseous, and she'd crawled under the heavy patchwork quilt, intending to sleep her way to the next destination.

The trailer isn't moving anymore. Shannon can't hear an engine, or any traffic sounds. But someone is whispering outside the door, the other side of the skin—sheep? goat?—tacked up by its flayed-out hooves.

There's something furtive about the sound. Whoever it is, they're not speaking to Shannon; they're communicating with someone out there in the snow and sunshine. It's all hissing sounds, rising and falling. The low sounds are like the hooting bass note of an amplifier with no input; the high sounds are like a snowstorm: sibilant, with no identifiable gaps between words.

Shannon swallows, her throat dry from the cold air. She thinks about calling out. But she remembers, dimly, dream-like, a truck driving past the rear window playing pop music loud enough to rattle the frame. Mistake or not, whoever had driven her here hadn't been the sort of person to stand outside and *whisper*.

And a group of them (she's sure) are clustered around the trailer. One by the stove and one by the door, like in a nursery rhyme.

Something taps on the window.

Shannon shrieks, and the whispering stops.

She stares up at the blinds. The single tap had come from the top corner of the window frame. Standing slowly, the covers slip off her, and the cold creeps in; the trailers don't have electricity. When she stands, her head isn't as high as the top of that window. Someone must have reached up, stretched out its hand.

A bony hand, she thinks, and doesn't know why.

Silence.

The tap comes again, making her leap back.

Shannon exhales. *It's a tree*, she realises. A branch tapping on the window. And the whispering must have been the wind in the trees. She's obviously been deposited in a wood, that evening's designated campsite: there are stands of trees all around this area, quivering against the sky. When the others arrive, they'll toast marshmallows and drink fragrant vodka and joke about the *Blair Witch Project*.

There's no more whispering. The wind must have died down.

"Okay," she says out loud, still a little shaky. There'd been something horrible about the sensation of being surrounded. Her mind supplies her with vivid images:

Tall thin women with papery skin and crowns.

"Stop it," she says to herself. "Stop it."

Finger-combing her hair, Shannon takes a deep breath, and opens the trailer door. She's confident this is where she's meant to be. So confident that she falls, in a panicked windmill of arms and legs, face-first into the snow; whoever left her trailer there hadn't folded down the little kick-step. She dusts herself off, sitting damp and uncomfortable on her arse, and looks around.

The landscape is a succession of lines: the snowy curve of the hills, the low-hanging clouds, and one of those stands of dark trees clustered at the bottom of the slope, like a group of unwanted guests.

There's no road. No other buildings in sight.

Shannon feels a flicker of unease. It looks desolate. The air is very crisp, as if she's standing on an invisible shore. *The high places,* she remembers.

One of their guides had used the phrase. "You have to be careful not to leave the trail. There are witches still here," he'd said, staring off into the darkness. "In the high places."

Eric had poked Christobel; Shannon had rolled her eyes at Christobel's thrilled squeal.

"A witch-cult from the old days. Every now and then." The guide had stared at them with hard blue eyes, leaving gaps in his sentences to be filled by the watching wide-open sky. "Someone has to be sacrificed."

Eric had laughed. "That's funny."

"It's not funny. It's not funny at all!"

He'd stared at them as if they were stupid children. His skidoo had let out a single twang of cooling metal, and he'd left them beside the flickering fire. The memory of his vanishing engine gives Shannon an idea, and she stands up, examining the tracks of the truck that left her here. They peel off into the distance without stopping, over the brow of the hill and away.

She looks quickly around the sides of the trailer.

There aren't any trees near here: just that distant stand of pines, swarming together like ants on sugar. It couldn't have been tree branches tapping on the window. The air is lifeless, no wind at all.

There are no footprints in the snow except her own.

WHEN SHE TRIES to turn her phone on, hands still a little shaky, a single red eye appears and the screen stays dark. There's no Tiny Mountain Settlement, no other trailers, no cabin with power sockets. Shannon paces the handkerchief square of the rag-rug, staring at the unforgiving wooden walls.

It's starting to get cold, and she can see her breath: the black-out blinds do little to keep out the chill. A cast-iron stove crouches in the corner, flue disappearing out the roof like a single crooked finger, and she kneels reluctantly to examine it. There are logs, matches, but nothing she could use as kindling, unless she wants to burn her own clothes. She knows kindling is important, because Eric rarely misses an opportunity to lecture.

She wonders what they're all doing now. The sun is eight fingers off the horizon, pale and overcast. It still doesn't seem possible that she's been abandoned in the middle of nowhere. Eric should be yelling blue murder at the tour company, Jonno commandeering a skidoo to follow in her tracks.

Now who's believing in fairytales?

She can manage until this is sorted out.

It's not far to the start of the forest. Shannon tucks her trousers into her boots and pulls on her parka, toggling the hood around her head. She's careful to climb down from the trailer slowly this time, boots wet on snow, and close the door properly to keep in the last vestiges of heat.

Going downhill towards the treeline, swinging the tote bag she's brought to carry sticks, she decides this will be a funny story someday. But the sun is white and leaden behind the clouds, and when she looks back, the continuing absence of footprints around the trailer makes her take in a chilly breath. There's no-one out here but her; the whisperers have all vanished, but she knows she heard them. She thinks of their breathy voices, the resonance of that deep note.

The trees start suddenly: tall evergreens with trunks the size of a torso, brambles coiled like barbed wire, as if the forest is trying to keep her out. There's no obvious trail. Shannon pushes through the thorns, and it's so quiet she can hear her own breathing. There's something about the watchfulness of the trees she doesn't like.

Ahead of her, there's an enormously wide tree stump; she sees that it's been sawn through, teeth-marks visible. The signs of human activity, then absence, make the silence more unsettling. Every step she takes sounds like an explosion in the underbrush. When she bends down, what she's walking on is far too wet and sodden to be any use for kindling.

She glances back to the trailer, sitting on its hill like a sentinel.

She goes further in.

She passes another stump, much like the first, and there are still no branches within reach, the trunks surrounding her straight and tall and naked. A thicket of thorn-bushes seems to quiver with suppressed movement, and she pauses to look, but nothing comes out.

Shannon exhales. She keeps moving.

She thinks of Eric, who'd bought an actual hatchet at the airport, even though all their trails so far have been well-marked with discreet little signs. And Christobel, who's technically engaged to Jonno (although they don't act it) who'd suggested the trip in the first place. Getting back to nature.

Shannon thinks longingly of that hatchet, because she's having to wade through the undergrowth, flailing around, and a shiver runs through her when she catches sight of a fallen tree lying in the gloaming like a dead body.

She can't see the trailer any more, or the forest's edge.

On the other side of the fallen tree there's still no path, just the ground sloping downwards towards a creek. The splashing of water sounds like something laughing. Shannon climbs down, hoping to find some branches, but it's just the same bloody damp thorn-bushes. Frustrated, she peels off her gloves and starts applying her nails to the bark of the nearest tree, wrinkled and corrugated as an old man's skin.

The air suddenly feels like a held breath.

She manages to pry off a few chunks of bark and *honestly*, she thinks, *it'll have to do*. The light under the trees is very dim and flickering, although there's no obvious wind. The sound of a bird above makes her look up with a start.

It's the first sign of life she's heard for a while. Maybe that's what turns her around. Sends her back up the slope, whimpering when her boots catch the raw places on the back of her ankles, where she can't see the fallen tree at all. It should be a few feet in front of her, broken roots like fingers, but there's just another snarl of brambles. She fights her way through with a huff, thinking she must be mistaken.

She wishes for that hatchet; wishes for Eric, although she and Jonno had been making fun of him that night in the sauna. Making jokes about elves. About witches.

She crashes through the pines as the sun goes down, and the fallen tree looms on her left. Shannon stops in her tracks.

No, she thinks, *it wasn't there before.*

There's no sign of the forest's edge. She keeps walking, fast, and can't find any trace that she's been there before. There's not a branch or thorn out of place. Just the landmarks moving around her, and past the fallen tree — she's back at the creek again.

Its sides are steep and undisturbed.

"All right," she says under her breath. It's darker now. She sets off up the little valley in the opposite direction, boots squelching. There's an echo to this place, something generated by the steep walls on each side. It sounds like she's being followed.

The fallen tree peers over the edge of the creek at her, and she wraps her arms around herself and stares back at it. A bird sings somewhere far-off, but it doesn't sound like any bird she's ever heard before. She starts to run.

Around the bend of the riverbed behind her, something crashes through the underbrush, large and snuffling.

She runs until her feet scream and she's dropped the bag of kindling. She scrambles up the steep slope on hands and knees. It's too dark under the trees.

She sees the tree stump—one of the tree stumps, it doesn't matter which—and throws herself towards it, sobbing.

The edge of the forest is only a couple more steps away; she can't work out how she'd got so badly lost. When she looks back, she sees the suggestion of antlers, jagged and branching, in the thick velvety blackness.

Whatever it is, it stays behind the treeline.

She wipes her face. There's still no truck up by the trailer, no lights; no-one has come to rescue her. As she toils upwards, it starts to snow, little pinprick kisses from the granite sky. The sun is a lemon wedge on the horizon, fast disappearing.

The snow will erase my tracks, she thinks, *and they'll never find me.*

She stops and looks up at the trailer door, checking that it's still shut. Tears prickle behind her eyes, and she draws in a shuddering breath.

A circle of bent twigs hangs from the latch, like a crown.

SHE GETS THE FIRE going easily enough. "I'm not as helpless as you think," she tells the darkness, or maybe Eric.

Whatever had followed her in the woods, massive and ponderous, surely won't drag its carcass up the slope towards her. The trailers had seemed so charming at first: bleached white-pine walls, flimsy little windows, the way they'd creaked as the wind blew around them at four in the morning, Shannon lying awake and furious despite herself, wondering what was going on in Jonno and Christobel's bed.

It all feels very precarious now. The window is large enough that anything could crawl through, and Shannon dislikes the gap between the black-out blind and the wall: a gap exactly wide enough to admit a finger. She keeps reminding herself she's closed the windows, latched the pathetic door. She pulls the quilt off the bed and wraps it around herself where she sits on the floor, shivering a little, staring at the fire.

Through the stove's stained and weathered pane of glass, she can make out the last thin sticks from that circlet of twigs. It had gone up quickly: very dry, almost insubstantial.

A howl pierces the silence outside. She hugs her knees, pressing her nose into the blanket.

She thinks it's a fox: that plaintive, shivers-in-your-marrow cry, as if something young and female is being tortured. But when the howl comes again, it's very different. This has a hooting quality, low and melodic, like a giant owl. She can imagine it flying around outside in the snow that's been falling steadily since the sun went down. The snow that's erased all traces of her arrival here.

In the high places.

"Stop it," she mutters, and crawls onto the bed to slide a finger behind the black-out blind and lift it, just an inch, so she can see out. At first, it's only her own face, pale and frightened, that hovers in the glass. Then, she can make out the thick carpet of white, the moonlight making the curves of the land luminous and violet. The snow might as well be endless, and she's alone for the night.

There's a crack of burning wood from the stove, and she whirls around, heart in her mouth.

A witch's crown.

She doesn't know how she recognised the thin circlet of twigs for what it was. But something in her marrow knows: just like she knows she was followed in the woods, and that she'd heard branches tapping at the trailer windows.

"A witch-cult from the old days," the guide had said; he'd seemed genuinely uncomfortable to be sitting around their fire. But there was nothing to justify that discomfort: four English tourists, despite Christobel's white-blonde hair. They'd had power and light and the skidoo.

When she turns back to the window, there's a wavering pin-prick of light in the distance. In the woods. Shannon swallows.

The fluting sound comes again, melancholy and wild, then…

Boom.

Something deep and loud. She can almost feel the trailer shaking. It's a drum, being beaten amongst those snowy trees.

Shannon screams, and backs away from the window, needing to put as much space as possible between her and that horrible sound. As sparks fly up the chimney, she realises she's only succeeded in making the trailer visible. The wavering light of the stove might as well be a beacon to whatever's outside.

She stays low. *Shouldn't you stay low?* She's not good at these things. She uses the last of the water, in a crackled blue pitcher with painted tulips, to douse the fire, and sits there in near-perfect darkness listening to the sounds outside.

The drum-beats continue. Sometimes two or three together; sometimes long pauses. There's no pattern she can understand, and the thought of that tiny light in the forest is nagging at her, a horrifying fascination.

There's something outside, she thinks. The oldest of human fears.

She'd planned to wait until morning, follow the direction of the vanishing tracks, carry on until she hit a road. But those tracks go too close to the forest. There's no way she's running out into the darkness with the trees on her left-hand side, watching her, waiting to swallow her up.

The drums go on.

She sits with her back against the door, and waits.

MASSIVE WINGS beat. Shannon feels a tapping at her trailer door through her spine. Hours have passed, and she's lit a candle after checking obsessively, again and again, that the blinds are all the way down. The candle smells of tree-sap, sharp and clean; it flickers with her shaky intake of breath.

She knows now that she wasn't brought here by accident, some mix-up with the guides and the touring company.

Every now and then. Someone has to be sacrificed.

The tapping comes again, sharp and resonant. Someone is using the very tips of their knuckles, bone hitting wood. It can't be mistaken for the trees.

"Shannon!" someone hisses. "Open the door!"

She draws her knees even further towards her chest, shakes her head.

Something rattles the door-frame, tries the latch, shockingly loud. She thinks about the sensation that something massive was following her: something with antlers and hooves, capable of displacing the trees around it. If it wants to come in, it will.

"Shannon!"

"Leave me alone!"

It bursts out of her. She hadn't meant to speak.

There's a pause.

Then the voice comes again. "Shannon, *please*."

Her head comes up so fast it slams against the door. Because now the voice is coming from the window, that panoramic rear window over the bed. The bed with the patchwork quilt and the creaky frame, where last night she'd slept with Eric and wondered about Jonno.

She knows whose voice this is. At least, she thinks she does.

But she hasn't heard an engine outside, or footsteps; not even footsteps trudging around the trailer from the door to the window. She tries to tell herself it's because the snow is still coming down hard. Tomorrow morning might be fine in the valleys, but in the high places there's nothing but snow and silence and the watchful trees. Her nails are making little half-moons in her palms.

"Please," the voice begs. "Let me in. Or come to the window."

She thinks about a long night, the voice cajoling and begging and threatening outside. She thinks about a night without heat or light, and doesn't think she can bear it. So, she crawls over to the bed, squeaking under her weight, and—slowly—raises the blind a few inches. Puts her face to the sliver of dark glass. The snow reflects an eerie purple light, and she was right: it's coming down hard. Thick flakes whirl under the moon, like ash falling from the sky.

For a long moment, there's nothing.

Then Christobel appears.

Shannon can only see a letter-box width of her. Scared eyes, a little unfocused without her contact lenses, white-blonde hair hidden under her hood. She isn't wearing mittens; she presses her bare hand to the window with a thump, and her nails are bluish. "Let me in," she says, her voice cracking. "I had to come through the woods. Please."

"Where are the others?"

"I don't know." Christobel glances behind her. "There's something… wrong…with the trees."

That does it.

Shannon lets Christobel in. The sound of giant wings accompanies her, and when she turns around in the dim light, she's taller than Shannon remembers.

The candle flickers.

"You should put that light out," Christobel says. Something gleams in her hand, poking out from under her parka, and Shannon realises, under the flickering, guttering candlelight, that Christobel is carrying Eric's hatchet.

She can't take her eyes off it. *This*, she thinks dimly, *is what a rabbit feels like.*

Christobel sees her looking. "I came through the woods," she says, screwing up her face as if she's in pain. Sharp eyebrows, pointed nose. "Hell, do you have anything to drink in here?"

Shannon shakes her head.

The hatchet is very sharp, brand new and unused. Eric had wanted a GPS and flare-guns too. Jonno had got bored, wanting to get out of the small two-gate airport terminal and into the snow beyond. As usual, Shannon hadn't known whose side to take.

Christobel, who'd played both sides expertly, makes a small noise and bends over.

"Are you okay?"

Christobel waves the hatchet at her. "No. I'll be okay. Just stay over there."

Shannon sits on the edge of the bed, watching the other girl struggle. The drumming has stopped. She thinks she can hear the hiss of the snow. Everything is *waiting*.

"Christo, where are the others?"

Christobel shakes her head. "I told you: I don't know." She's still clutching the hatchet, one fist buried in her abdomen. There's a rippling movement, and she clutches the dresser to stay upright, hisses out a breath from between clenched teeth.

The motion dislodges her hood. Her hair may be untidy, but on her head, she's wearing a circlet of twigs just like the one on the trailer door.

The candlelight falters.

From outside, there's a rushing wind. Roaring in the distance. Crashing branches. The wood sounds like the ocean in the middle of a gale, and once again, Shannon knows: she's standing on the shores of something distant and unknowable. If she looked outside, right now, she'd see trees all around the trailer, bending in. Watching. Waiting.

"Is this about Jonno?" Shannon tries to keep her voice very calm.

"No!" Christobel gestures with the hatchet.

Shannon fists her hands in the quilt. She's weaponless. Something is tapping at the door, quiet and steady. Something is scratching at the windows.

The forest is all around them.

"Or Eric? I know you like him. I'm sorry, I didn't mean to—"

This time Shannon's voice cracks.

"Don't—don't be stupid. The boys? As if it's about the boys."

Christobel nearly laughs, but it comes out like a hoot, a deeply non-human sound. She presses her hands to her abdomen as if she's having bad period cramps; as if she's trying to expel something.

"I didn't even know which one of you would be taken," Christobel gasps.

The twigs on her head glimmer in the candlelight, a crown of bleached gold and silver. The shadow cast on the wooden trailer walls is—antlers, Shannon realises.

Antlers.

Shannon gets up, hearing the bed make its asthmatic squeak. Her heels are killing her, but there's no time for that now, is there? She crouches on the balls of her feet and watches Christobel, waiting for the moment to make her move.

"You won't get far. Not here."

The other girl is holding herself up with wavering dignity, her eyes hard and green and shiny. Shannon moves: running to the door, to the forest, to the high places as Christobel starts vomiting pine needles.

PATRIMONY

DAPHNE FAUBER

Evren ran her hands over the cheap envelope postmarked a month late for her birthday and ripe with the acrid perfume of her childhood. Her name smeared across the page as tear-drenched fingers rubbed the letters, each written in the practiced script of a father whose address book fit onto a sticky note.

For three months, she'd avoided the Pandora's Box of mutual disappointment now scrunched in her shaky hands. His last letter had contained coupons for 24-packs of his favorite beer neatly paperclipped to a two-word note, "Send whenever". She dreamed of a letter, text, or phone call that didn't end with a request—implicit or not. Usually he asked for money, sometimes favors, and only once forgiveness. Until she read his letter, she could continue to hope her father's love was unconditional, but this was his last chance to prove her wrong.

Her phone lay on the floor, the new cracks distorting a half-composed text to Evren's most recent ex, "I know…didn't end…great terms, but… know who else…". Sputters of synthetic xylophone reverberated through the studio apartment, eclipsing the message with an unknown caller ID. The hospital was trying to reconnect the call, again. Evren paid little attention to anything but the letter in her hands and the doctor's words. They still hung in the infinity that had passed since she'd dropped her phone, pulsing in time with her ringtone.

Dad. Dead. Cancer. Peaceful supposedly, in the same way dropped bombs breed armistice. It was the same battle her mother had lost ten years ago. The two weeks spent alone at her mother's bedside was the only action for which Evren's father had sought amnesty. Evren still couldn't watch CSI reruns without smelling chemical sanitizers and hearing her mother's gasps of surprise as the mysteries unfolded. Evren smiled despite herself, but quickly the memories were torn away by claws of guilt. Her mother's death had been their happiest memories together. Her dad hadn't visited once. Evren had quit her job so that her mom didn't have to die alone, her father couldn't even bother to leave the house. Fitting his life would end unaccompanied. Cancer. Dead. Dad.

The phone fell into a silence far more deafening than the ringing. Whichever intern stuck calling families had satisfied their obligations and was now finding someone else's world to collapse.

Evren gathered her phone, intent on finding some form of distraction from the letter she still held in one hand. She deleted the message she'd been composing, before scrolling through her other messages—mostly ignored hook-up requests and delivery notifications. She paused. Her last text sent to her father had been "Happy Father's Day". He hadn't responded, just like everyone else in her phone. Millions of questions, marinating in decades of guilt and self-contempt rushed through her ears. What letter had he sent her, and what mundane pleasantries would be his final goodbye?

With a dry mouth and clammy palms, Evren set her phone down on the sliver of kitchen counter uncompromised by crusty dishes and half-finished takeout. She tore the envelope open, her fingers trembling on the precipice of no return.

On the card, a cartoon cat painted with pink glitter implored her to have a "Purr-fect" thirty-sixth birthday. It had previously said sixth birthday, with a distinctive three prepended in permanent marker. Evren snorted despite herself, a flicker of hope steadying her vertigo. Maybe this could be the final memory—a laugh projected as what they had, instead of what they could have been. She opened the card to a small key and a photo of the last happy moment she had with her father, when they'd first inherited the property in the mountains. The remnants of her smile fell into disgust. "If you ever loved me, you'll spread my ashes at the observatory," the card read.

Evren shook her head. Even in death, her father could disappoint her.

AFTER AN EIGHT-HOUR DRIVE and three long days of paperwork, Evren arrived in her hometown of Caldwell, Washington. Nestled in Cascadian peaks, Caldwell was fortified against blusters by its engulfing, ancient pines. Now, in the early winter air, ice hung from the needles like teeth, threatening to consume anyone who still managed to be blown off course. Not that there was anywhere to go for those foolish enough to brave the pines.

The only landmark between Caldwell and the next town were the rotting remains of abandoned logging equipment and the fifty miles of twisting forest that had bested them. The descendants of those original loggers, the current inhabitants of the town, fared no better. They too were left to fade away, slowly suffocating on the hubris of their progenitors. Evren had escaped before she could rust into place like every other person in town. Her parents, and their parents before them, were petrified long before Evren could have convinced them there was any other way to live.

A single road slid through the trees to compose the majority of town, maneuvering past the handful of businesses that barely turned a profit despite the propensity for funerals over any other social event. As Evren drove past the gas station, she saw a familiar card peeking from the display next to the register. It was half off, bringing the price to 50 cents for the pink glitter-encrusted cat. Is that all she was worth to her father?

Her high school class valedictorian worked the counter, absently flicking a lighter as if testing the resolve of the Smokey Bear cut-out on the wall next to him. Evren chewed on her cheek. He had so much potential. Did he deserve to be stuck in place? She wasn't convinced anyone did. She spared a glance at her father's remains, gently packaged in the cheapest urn the funeral home would allow. Maybe her father had deserved it.

The encroaching sunset and lurking pines blanketed Caldwell in the grim hues of a bloodied burial procession. Only a handful of people, easily mistaken for spooked carrion feeders, stalked the street. Their coats flapped against their brittle frames as they retreated just enough to leer at the interloper.

A single crone remained, whom Evren recognized as her eighth-grade teacher. Skin melted from her wiry muscles and her back stooped as if she had lost a war against gravity. With much effort, she held up a hand in greeting from the side of the road, the other hand absently sliding a letter into the town's post collection box. "Welcome home," she mouthed, her eyes dull with weariness from the simple gesture. Evren offered a smiling nod, but her former teacher didn't make eye contact. The teacher's eyes stayed affixed to the passenger's seat, where the ashes of Evren's father sat nestled in a blanket.

AT THE HIGHEST POINT in town, peeking from the trees as the road spidered ever upward, was an observatory. More accurately it was an heirloom, with Evren representing the third generation cursed by its preservation. As an elementary schooler, she'd been pulled from class by her parents, who were frenzied with heated whispers. "Hey kiddo, Grandma is really sick, so we're going to all go on a short visit to say goodbye," her father had explained, pulling down her suitcase and helping her choose a few stuffed animals. Evren had never met her grandmother, and never got the chance to. She was dead before they made it to the mountains, yet the short trip to say goodbye lasted the rest of Evren's childhood.

Evren was snapped from her reverie by the protests of her truck's rusted suspension as pavement eroded into dirt. Before long, the path widened into a muddy lot encircled by forest and littered with discarded trash. Evren squelched to a standstill, as the tires fought for traction. Her throat tightened. Drowning in the sea of muck were the two buildings Evren had promised herself she'd never see again.

Her childhood home was a single-story prefab with rusting aluminum siding that spread like a rash across its face. The only break in the ruptured, peeling skin was a pair of clouded windows that flanked a plastic door green with mold. A tarp fastened to one of the windows jerked in the wind as if preparing to jump over the broken glass pockmarking the ground. Cigarette smoke hung in the air, like her father was just out of sight nursing his favorite before-dinner appetizer.

A shroud of guilt smothered Evren as she surveyed the squalor. Her father had requested money to fix the window two years ago. The door request came seven months ago. Both requests had been bookended by demands she provide for his booze and cigarette addiction. She had not responded. Maybe if she had, he wouldn't have lived like this. Or maybe she would have just been dragged into the filth too.

Despite the state of the house, the observatory was as immaculate as ever. It soared above everything else: a three-story wooden column capped with an oxidized copper dome. The walls of the observatory were painstakingly fabricated from the same pines that had once stood on the hill—a memorial to the casualties and built in their likeness. The observatory was as pristine as she'd ever seen it, the building having repulsed whatever sickness was rotting the house from the inside. A collection of cherubs watched her from the embossed dome, smug looks of contempt across their pudgy faces. Evren had always longed to pluck their wings and burn the building into ash. The tower was backlit from the setting sun, enveloping Evren in its shadow as it was embraced by the final rays of warmth. As grand and beautiful as it was, it had stolen her parents from her, a sin she could never forgive. Since she couldn't provide forgiveness, she set her sights on retribution.

THE GROUND TUGGED at Evren's feet as she trudged toward the observatory, her father's gleaming silver urn tucked under one arm and a sloshing gas can under the other. Her work boots, which had at one point been her dad's, struggled to escape the grasping muck. They had been a parting gift from her parents, an homage to her childhood tendency to mimic her hero however she could. Despite her hindsight, Evren relished these rose-tinted memories and the boots she never quite grew into. Evren took one unsteady step after another, each sinking her deeper into the earth. The mud that had initially seemed like a minor inconvenience, squelched over her shoes, threatening to steal them from her feet.

There was only fifty feet of mud-covered path from the truck to the observatory, but each step was more difficult than the last. She shivered in the shadow cast by the tower, the ground before her only visible as an inky blackness.

Her next step connected with unsolid ground that shifted beneath her feet. She fell to her knees. Evren was up to her elbows in mud, the frigid sludge numbing her fingers and seeping into her jeans. The urn. It had slipped into the mess. Evren clawed through the expanse, grasping desperately for the metallic remnants of her father. Beer cans, cigarette butts, and fast-food containers flowed past her as she dug, now up to her shoulders in sodden dregs. The numbness in her extremities began to burn. She realized with horror that the mud, solid before, was now indistinguishable from quicksand.

Every motion transmuted the solid mud around her into fluid. Her own thrashing in the liquid marsh pulled her further under. She made contact with the familiar round body of the urn, gripped it in one hand and tried to keep her grasp on the gas can with the other. Evren's head bobbed under the surface and filled her mouth and nose with grave dirt from her own burial.

With a cry of rage, muffled by the waste seeping into her lungs, Evren let go of her father and shot a grasping hand out of the muck. Her hand connected with something hard. She flung her body toward the sturdy surface. With the ground still grabbing at her clothes, she heaved herself and the gas can onto the concrete steps of the observatory.

Evren coughed, black spittle scouring the pristine steps. She looked back the way she came, but only found a shallow set of footprints leading from her car to the door. The earth had claimed the urn, with no hint of what she'd left behind. Despite the barely disturbed earth, her clothes were black with slime. Evren shivered, the icy drippings stinging her skin.

Was she losing her mind, just like her parents had? No—exhaustion was playing tricks on her. She'd fulfilled her obligation to her father, now was time for her promise to herself. With one last glance at the parked truck sinking into twilight, she turned and faced her destiny—the metal mouth of the observatory. As she turned the key in the lock, the cherubs smiled in derision.

AS EVREN STEPPED inside, hot air brushed past her like a long-held breath, carrying with it the tangy stench of corrosion. For a moment, she was sure she stood in a gaping maw, the air still iron-tinged from a recent meal. She gripped the gas can tighter.

This was her first time in the observatory. Even as she became an adult, entry was forbidden, a rule that had shattered any illusion that things would ever change. Evren buckled under the weight of years of solitary dinners, as her parents spent every night locked away in this building. Evren had pleaded to be let inside, desperate to not feel like a guest in her own home. Yet, every night, her parents would turn away from her sobbing pleas and lock themselves in their watchtower. A pang of jealousy swept through her, momentarily letting her forget her aching, waterlogged form and replacing it with the warmth of resentment.

The interior was grand, more fit for a baroque cathedral than a shack in the mountains. Immediately, Evren was washed in an awe that she pushed down like bile. She refused to give the observatory the satisfaction. A bronze telescope consumed most of the room, naked in its exposed clockwork. Where there were no gears, she noticed gilded wings, that gave the impression all the angels in Heaven had been crushed by the machinery and left only feathered reminders stuck between teeth. The telescope stared at the ornate dome, painted by a mural which depicted the cherubs peering from in-between pines to witness the machinations of celestial bodies. A spiral staircase rested next to the telescope, daring Evren to descend into the unknown depths of her parent's obsession.

As she turned her head to take in the room, her father's eyes met hers, the surrounding face flecked with grave dirt. Evren nearly fell over, slamming her head against the closed door behind her as she stepped back. Her mother's gasping mouth mid-death rattle flashed around her. Evren closed her eyes and steadied herself. She opened them again.

Mirrors lined the walls, nearly obscured by the star charts that slathered them like wallpaper. Bits and pieces of her showed between the cracks. Evren traced the sharp arc of her nose with a dirty finger, struck by how much she resembled both her parents. Evren considered her muck-covered form and was ashamed of how her very presence tarnished the opulence—once again made small and pathetic by the damned observatory.

She approached the nearest wall, her skull still stinging from the impact. Upon first inspection, the star charts were relatively normal. But Evren had spent her childhood studying star charts, desperate to prove to her parents she was worthy enough to be a part of their secret. It had never made a difference. As she searched the maps for signs of how she could've been better, she knew these charts were wrong. They certainly didn't display any skies in the Northern hemisphere. Sporadic dots were connected and circled with marker, like homemade constellations of troubled minds. The rage bubbled within her as she realized she never had a chance. She could have studied every constellation in the universe and her parents would have still been living in an impenetrable mirage.

The circled stars all had the names of long-deceased family members on them, including a constellation with her parents' names. The addition of her father looked recent, the paper less yellowed. The constellation reminded her of Gemini: two people holding hands for eternity. She counted the hundreds of stars in a single constellation. The longer she looked, the more stars she found, appearing, moving, and reaching out toward her. She thought it must be a trick of the eye.

Evren pulled flakes of mud from her eyelashes and they dissolved in her hands. The constellations remained stoic sentinels on the wall, all illusion of movement gone.

Evren set the gas can down and fiddled with the cap. She paused for a moment and considered what she was doing. What did she owe her father? Herself? At every opportunity they had prioritized this observatory over her, making it more of their child than she was. Would finding out what was so important soothe her rage or fuel it? Was lighting it on fire another form of running away? Evren thought of all the birthdays spent making cakes alone in the kitchen. Of all the school plays missed. She had to know what made this observatory so meaningful to her parents and she had to know if it had been worth it.

Picking up her gas can, Evren began her descent down the spiral staircase, stepping gingerly into the dark. Progress was slow and she felt along the wall for a light switch as she moved. She could feel the wall change from wood to damp stone. She continued down and down, one step at a time. The stench of rot drifted around her and intensified with each step.

She traversed the staircase for ages before reaching the last stair. The air was frigid. Pinpricks of light floated from dark depths like a flurry, aimless in their journeys but headed resolutely downwards. The longer she stared, the more lights appeared, illuminating her fogging breath. Evren took a tentative step off the top stair, the gas can sloshing in reminder. She forgot it for a moment. Evren held out a hand, letting the speck caress her. She yelped as burning cold touched her skin, sinking into her flesh as an icy ember.

The light burrowed into her marrow and she screamed as it left a smoking hole of viscera in her hand. Through the pain, Evren heard voices. She was kissing a woman as a child blew out their birthday candles. As a particle drifted lazily into her calf, Evren stumbled to the ground, spilling gas all over the floor. The child called to her again, this time sobbing. She was leaving them for the observatory.

No, she would never repeat the mistakes of her parents. These had to be possible futures, not certainties. She grasped for another mote of light, desperate for more evidence her visions were wrong. Her dad tried to calm her as she birthed the child that didn't exist. Yet? Or ever?

Wind ripped past her, flinging memories of events that hadn't happened and might never happen into her body. The atmosphere grew rank with breath tinged in iron and decaying flesh. In a possible past, she lit a match and smiled at the trail of gasoline around the observatory .

The floor underneath her convulsed as the stone moved like muscle, contracting and releasing in deliberate patterns. She was alone in her filthy studio apartment, hands shaking as she downed a bottle of pills. Light continued to collide with Evren's stumbling movements, stabbing new barbs into her flesh. She sloshed in a pool of gasoline, as she said her vows to a woman she hadn't met. A child once more, Evren followed her parents into the observatory as a blood moon filled the sky. She had to look into the telescope. She had to know.

Then, Evren was falling. She shot a look of betrayal where the ground had fallen away beneath her. A desperate instinct urged her to keep looking up. As her brain shouted and pulled at her nerves, her eyes were yanked downwards, threatening to leave her skull behind if her head disobeyed. She gazed upon a raging hellscape. A giant fiery landscape of explosions and energy. Evren screamed and it echoed back at her as a million screams of every living soul adrift in the cosmos. As she fell closer, she could barely make out writhing faces in the flames, screaming with her. Her brain conjured up the thought that this was Hell, but she knew that what she fell toward was far more ancient and sinister.

The heat pressed into her. Her father's letter tumbled out of her jacket pocket and flew upwards on a wave of air, singed at the corners. Where it had coated her hands, the gasoline ignited in vindication. At this moment, the mass beneath her shifted, and a great pupil blinked back at her. She closed her eyes, but the great eye had already burned itself into her vision. Even with her eyes closed, she could see the black hole on a burning sun, beyond a purple, orange, and red miasma.

The screaming had released oxygen, and she tried to suck in breath but found none to be had. She gasped for air, as the heat entered her body through her choking mouth and scorched her lungs. Her clothes steamed and then burned and her father's boots fused with her skin. She and the star collided, ashes to ashes and stardust to stardust.

EVREN OPENED her eyes and she was in her truck parked in front of the house. She still burned. Every nerve ending fired like she'd pulled away from a hot stove too late. Deep in her bones pockets of coals still simmered. She knew then that she was dying, just like her parents, just like all things must. Her entropy engine, buried deep inside her, fired on all cylinders, and for once she knew what she owed her father. Ashes.

ROADSIDE CROSS

BRYAN HOLM

The buck came out of nowhere. By the time Sabrina saw it: an auburn flash behind the wall of heavy snowflakes pelting her windshield, it was too late. She cranked on the steering wheel and her truck drifted to the right, the deer smashing into the passenger side door as she spun into a snowbank.

"Shit!" Sabrina punched the steering wheel. She knew she was going too fast. It was hard not to. She had just moved into a house on the outskirts of town, and she rarely saw another car as she followed the winding county road through the dense woods at night.

She flipped on her cherries, the red lights spinning off the snow. As Sabrina stepped out of the truck; the arctic air rushing through the valley took her breath away. She pulled up the hood of her parka. The truck seemed to be fine. A scratch on the bumper but that was it. She was thankful for that.

Sabrina was the new Sheriff of Granite Falls, a small Minnesota town three miles below the Canadian border. She was four decades younger than her predecessor, and the old-timers at the station still treated her like a rookie deputy. The fact that she was a woman, and Ojibwe, didn't help matters. Now, she had to get herself unstuck before anyone else came along.

It was eerily quiet in the middle of the sprawling woodland, and stunningly beautiful. The Lost River Forest straddled the border between the two countries, and Sabrina stood in the heart of it, surrounded by a sea of pungent pines, rolling hills of Black Spruce and Tamarack, all coated with a layer of fresh snow. She stuck her hands in her pockets and closed her eyes, listening to the forest sleep.

Behind her, a whimper. Sabrina's stomach dropped. She searched the road and found the deer lying on the ground beyond the shoulder. She had nearly knocked it into the woods. A thin layer of snow already blanketed its cooling body. It looked at her with wide, fearful eyes.

Sabrina held back tears. She was raised in Gichi-Onigamiing by parents who hunted, but she could never understand the desire for such blood sport. Why would you want to hunt and kill something so beautiful? She had declined all invites to go hunting without raising suspicion so far, but she dreaded the day her new co-workers found out she was a vegetarian.

Sabrina removed her gun from her belt. Despite her convictions, this was a necessary exception. She had to put the poor thing out of its misery. She raised the gun and cocked it, aiming at the deer's temple. After several seconds, she lowered the gun, chastising herself for her cowardice.

There was movement in the trees, and Sabrina whirled around, nearly firing. There was a child, no more than ten years old, standing at the edge of the woods. He wasn't dressed for winter: only a t-shirt and corduroys with patches over the knees. His eyes were two pools of night staring at her. Sabrina's breath caught in her throat.

The child ignored Sabrina and knelt down beside the deer. The animal relaxed in the boy's presence, its muscles no longer twitching. The boy caressed the deer's back with one hand, and brushed the snow from its head with the other.

The boy placed a hand on the soft part of the deer's belly and pressed against the fur. His hand pierced the flesh, his fingers effortlessly opening a bloodless wound as his arm disappeared behind its ribcage. The boy leaned in closer and kissed the deer lightly on its forehead. The deer stiffened for an instant, and went still. Sabrina could see urine pooling in the snow, the animal's bladder emptying as it died.

The boy shuddered. He grimaced as he pulled his arm from the deer's belly. In his tiny hand, he held the deer's heart.

Viscous black tears streamed down his cheeks. Sabrina staggered backwards as the boy stood up. "Who are you?"

The boy stared at the night sky with his obsidian eyes, letting the snowflakes hit his face. They didn't melt and the boy's breath produced no vapor. He turned and walked into the forest.

"Wait!" Sabrina stumbled after him through the deepening snow. She holstered her gun and pulled a flashlight from her belt. There was no sign of the child anywhere. Sabrina scanned the ground. There were no footprints either.

Sabrina hiked back to her truck. As she left the woods, she nearly tripped over something buried against a large pine. Sabrina brushed away the snowfall, revealing a crude cross, three feet tall, made of twigs. The twigs were wrapped in thick strands of birch bark.

Sabrina grabbed a shovel from her truck bed. She was able to dig out her front tire, and was back on the road within an hour. It was after midnight by the time her head hit the pillow. She was exhausted, but it was hours before sleep found her. When it finally did, the child from the forest joined her, Sabrina's beating heart in his hand.

SIX INCHES OF SNOW had fallen overnight, and Sabrina drove to work slowly, still shaken from the night before. By the time she pulled into the station, Bonnie was nearly done shoveling the sidewalk.

"You should have saved some for me."

Bonnie took a break, leaning on her shovel. She eyed the bags under Sabrina's eyes. "You look like shit, Sheriff."

"Morning to you too."

Bonnie never pulled a punch, and Sabrina loved her for it. She'd worked for Sabrina's predecessor for over thirty years, and Sabrina had a feeling she knew more about Granite Falls than anyone.

"I wanted to ask you about something. Do you remember a fatal accident out on 61?"

Bonnie pulled a pack of smokes from her jacket and lit one up. "On 61? I can't think of any, nothing deadly anyway. Why you ask?"

"I saw a cross on the side of the road last night… Wondered what happened."

"Like a shrine?"

"By mile marker two."

Bonnie studied her, exhaling a plume of smoke from her lungs. "Oh. Out there."

"What's that mean?"

"You saw something, didn't you?"

Sabrina felt her cheeks flush.

"You did, didn't you?" Bonnie chuckled, a raspy growl. "I've heard some strange stories about that stretch over the years."

"Like what?"

"What did you see? Tell me."

"Nothing. Just curious, that's all."

Bonnie shook her head. "Fine, keep your secrets. It's mostly the town drunks, mostly a bunch of horseshit if you ask me, but some locals refuse to drive 61 at night."

"Why?"

"Who knows, but I do remember a few years back, some canned up tourist came into the station, white as a sheet, blubbering nonsense after making that drive. Sheriff Rivers had to lock him up for the night."

"What'd he say?"

"Sheriff wouldn't talk about it."

Sabrina nodded.

"That's it? You're not going to give me anything?"

"It was nothing. Forget I asked."

"Okay, Sheriff. Whatever you say." Bonnie chucked her butt in the snow and went inside, laughing to herself.

IT WAS FRIDAY, and Sabrina left the station early. One of the perks of working in a small town in the middle of nowhere. As she rounded the curve on 61, she came across a pick-up truck on the shoulder. Sabrina parked ahead of it.

It was Roger, the local highway worker, or Road-Kill Roger, as he was known around town. He was loading the deer carcass into his truck bed.

"How you doing, Roger?"

"Almost happy hour. That's how I'm doing."

Sabrina peeked in his truck bed. "What'd the day bring?"

"Shit. Got a whole buffet for you here. We got deer, fox, bear, something that might have been a beaver at one point. What else?" Reggie poked the pile of matted fur and feathers with a shovel.

A smell wafted up that singed Sabrina's nostrils. She turned away, coughing.

"Shit Sheriff, you should find me come August. That cologne will drop you to your knees!"

"This is all from today?"

"This here's one unforgiving road." Roger hawked a glob of chew into the snow to emphasize this fact. "Animals avoid the woods out here; stick mostly to the road. Must be the terrain. I scrape up more here than damn near anywhere else."

"You mind if I check something?" Sabrina grabbed the shovel and poked at the deer.

"What the hell you doing?"

Sabrina prodded the deer's belly. Nothing looked out of the ordinary. There was no incision that she could see. "You ever come across any strange wounds? Animals missing organs?"

"Missing organs?"

A muffler-less pick-up truck came roaring around the bend. The truck was a relic from the eighties, its body half sickly-green paint, half rust. Roger gave a wave as it flew by. "Poor woman."

"Who was that?"

"You haven't met Rose yet? Makes sense. She rarely comes to town."

"She live out by me?"

"Probably ten miles past your place. A little trailer in the middle of nowhere."

"Just her?"

"Yep. Ever since she lost her boy."

Sabrina's heart quickened. "Her boy?"

"Henry. He went missing damn near twenty years ago now. A terrible thing around here."

"I bet." Sabrina pointed at the cross against the tree. "You know who that's for?"

Roger stared at it, puzzled. "Can't say that I do. Not sure I ever noticed it before."

"Well, I'll let you go. Thanks for humoring me."

"Sure thing, Sheriff."

"Hey, what's Rose's last name?"

"Callahan." Roger made a Y-turn and headed back towards town.

Sabrina pulled out her phone. It didn't take long to find a news article on the case. Within seconds, she was staring at a school photo of Henry Callahan. His eyes were a pale blue in the photo, but there was no doubt he was the boy she had seen.

Sabrina stared at the pines in front of her. The sun was setting, the trees casting long shadows across the fresh powder. She trudged through the snow and into the woods. The shadows grew longer as she made her way between the towering pines. She finally stopped to catch her breath fifty yards from the road.

It was dark beneath the canopy, and there were no tracks that she could see other than her own, not even animal prints. Sabrina realized she was standing in complete silence. There were no birds, squirrels, anything that she could see or hear. It was as if the forest had been completely abandoned by anything with a pulse.

A shadow moved across the snow. Sabrina looked up, expecting a hawk or a crow. Instead, she found a pair of piercing, inky black eyes staring down at her. Henry was crouched on a narrow branch, high up in a swaying pine.

Sabrina stumbled backwards, fleeing for her truck. She staggered into the road and was nearly struck by a semi rounding the bend.

The driver swerved into the oncoming lane and gave her a long, angry honk.

Sabrina hurried to her truck and sped home.

AFTER A SLEEPLESS NIGHT, Sabrina made her way slowly down a winding driveway deep in the woods. It hadn't been plowed all winter. After nearly getting stuck twice, she reached a large log cabin home nestled into a hillside. Wispy smoke billowed from its stone chimney. A black lab, greying in his old age, leapt off the wraparound porch, wagging his tail frantically and getting snow on Sabrina's jacket as he jumped up to greet her.

"Easy, boy!" Sabrina knelt down and scratched the pup's ears. He rolled onto his back in the snow, eager for a belly scritch.

Sabrina knocked on the front door and waited. After a few seconds, she peeked in a window, cupping her hands around her eyes to see through the grime. Her predecessor, Beau, was passed out on the couch, a bottle of whiskey on the coffee table. Sabrina went back to the door and pounded on it three times, hard and fast.

"Go away!" Beau growled.

"It's Sabrina. You have a minute?" Sabrina heard a heavy sigh.

A few minutes later, Sabrina sat on a threadbare recliner in Beau's cluttered living room. The place hadn't been cleaned in at least a decade. Beau came in carrying two mugs of coffee. Sabrina thanked him, trying not to choke as she sipped the instant coffee grounds floating in lukewarm water.

Beau was in his seventies, but he looked closer to ninety, bone-thin, his face pummeled by whiskey. They exchanged awkward pleasantries, and Sabrina apologized for not visiting him sooner. The handover had been contentious with the former Sheriff, but there was no bad blood between them, at least in Sabrina's mind.

"I wanted to get your thoughts on an old missing person's case: Henry Callahan."

Beau sighed again. "Did Rose pay you a visit? She refuses to let it go." Beau grabbed the whiskey and topped off his coffee. "Want some?"

"I'm good, and no, she didn't. Just curious is all. An unsolved case in my town."

"Your town, huh?"

"Are we doing this again?"

Beau waved his hand. "Just giving you shit." He took a long swig from his mug. "Not much to tell, really. The kid missed his bus, and instead of telling his teacher, he decided to walk home. Somewhere between school and his trailer, he vanished."

"And that would have been on 61, right?"

"Most of the way, yep."

"That's a long way for a kid."

"Yeah, it was stupid. But, you know, he was just a little tike."

"So, no witnesses, no leads?"

Beau leaned forward. "Nothing. And I worked it. I really did. His mother may feel differently, but I left no stone unturned."

"What do you think happened?"

"I think some trucker grabbed him. You know how many roll through town on their way up north. I think that kid was probably a hundred miles away before anyone even knew he was missing." Beau finished his mug and refilled it.

"Do you remember any fatal accidents on 61 when you were working?"

"Why?"

"I saw a cross on the road, one of those roadside memorials, but no one seems to remember anything happening there."

"Nothing comes to mind."

They sat in awkward silence. Beau made a show of checking his watch.

Sabrina stood up. "I won't take up anymore of your time."

THE GRAVEL ROAD narrowed as Sabrina drove up the steep hill. By the time she reached the top, the tamarack branches clawed at her windows. She parked in a clearing a few yards from an old trailer, all dark yellow siding and cracked wood paneling.

As Sabrina stepped out of her truck, the trailer door opened. Rose Callahan eyed her suspiciously. She was a true northerner, her skin hardened by the elements. She wore a flannel shirt tucked into snow pants, which were tucked into snow boots.

"Ms. Callahan? I'm the new Sheriff. Wondering if we could talk?"

"What about?"

"Your son."

Rose's shoulders sagged. She nodded and went inside.

The inside of the trailer was not what Sabrina expected, and the opposite of Beau's cabin. It was very clean, and very charming. The walls were covered in beautiful watercolors, striking images of the northern woods and rivers. A gas fireplace burned in the corner of the living room, making it feel extra cozy. Rose brought out a plate of homemade cookies and coffee. Sabrina sipped the coffee apprehensively, but it was fantastic: a freshly ground dark roast.

Rose sat across from her, drinking from her mug. "Why are you here? My son's dead."

"You know that?"

"I knew it the day he disappeared. I could feel it."

"Do you think Beau dropped the ball? With the case?"

"I don't think he dropped the ball so much as I think he's a useless drunk. He was partly right, though."

"About what?"

"Henry was a sweet boy, sensitive. He would find injured animals in the woods, bring them home, nurse them back to health. Cry if he couldn't save them. He didn't belong in a place like this." Tears streamed down Rose's cheeks. "I could see someone taking advantage of him, is what I'm saying. If somebody offered him a ride, he'd take it."

Sabrina grabbed a box of tissues from a bookcase and offered her one. "It's not your fault."

"I let him grow up soft. That's a death sentence up here."

"So, do you think it was a trucker?"

"That trucker theory's a load of shit if you ask me. I mean, we know those guys. They've been running this route for years. They get gas here, they eat dinner here, they stay in the motel if they get caught in a storm..."

"You think it was a local, then?"

"More than likely, yes."

Sabrina wasn't sure how to proceed. She had never believed in any kind of world beyond our own, even as a child. Despite her life-long skepticism, it became harder and harder to reconcile that conviction with what she had experienced.

Sabrina decided to go for it. "This is gonna sound crazy..."

"You saw him, didn't you? That's why you're here."

Sabrina told her what happened. Rose didn't interrupt, just listened, nodding her head.

When Sabrina was done, Rose stood up. "I want to show you something."

Rose tugged on a parka and Sabrina followed her outside to an old shed behind the trailer. "My boy was a collector. Anything he could get his hands on." She opened the door. "This was his makeshift fort." The shelves inside were covered with agates, beach glass, pale blue robin eggshells, and piles of skipping stones. "When he was alive, there were jars of insects too. I had to force him to empty his pockets every night when he got home." Rose smiled at the memory. "Come on."

She led Sabrina to the woods. There was a narrow path between towering pines that led to a small clearing. At its center was an old well, now only a crumbling circle of weathered stones. A ring of mummified hearts lined the rim. Dozens of them in various sizes. Some were tiny, likely from squirrels. One was so massive that it must have come from a moose. One was fresh, still oozing congealed blood: the deer Sabrina hit.

Sabrina's own heart was a hammer in her chest. "Do you see him?"

"No. He won't reveal himself to me."

"Why?"

"I don't know. I've heard the stories over the years, locals that have claimed to." Rose wiped away more tears. "But I don't know why he hides from me."

Snow began to fall. Dense flakes made their way between the pines, alighting on the hearts. Sabrina realized the heavy silence she felt out at mile marker two was there as well. It was like they were standing inside a tomb.

AFTER HOURS OF mindless channel surfing, Sabrina tried to go to bed. An hour later, she was back up and dressed. She couldn't get the boy out of her mind. What had happened to him out there? What had he become?

The frigid wind hammered her face as she flew through the untouched powder on her snowmobile, weaving up and down the walls of the shallow ditch that ran alongside county road 61. As she descended the hill ahead of the curve, she saw lights, a truck pulled over on the shoulder. Sabrina eased up on the throttle and shut off her headlight.

Sabrina crept ahead on foot, staying in the ditch. Beau stumbled back to his truck, carrying the wooden cross. He was drunk, muttering to himself, falling in the snow twice. He got behind the wheel and made a U-turn, nearly driving into the ditch on the other side before fishtailing into the darkness. Sabrina raced back to her snowmobile and followed.

All the lights at Beau's place, inside and out, were on. The dog was at the porch window, barking at Sabrina. Beau's truck was half in a snowbank, still running, the driver side door open. Sabrina shut it off.

There was smoke billowing from a fire around back. Sabrina crept around the house, staying in the shadows. She found Beau, sitting before a fire pit, burning the cross.

"There she is, the woman in charge," Beau slurred, his eyes glass.

It was a miracle he had made it home alive.

"Hey there, Beau. You okay?"

Beau pointed at the cross. "You know how many of these goddamn things I've burned? They keep coming back!"

Beau tried to stand and nearly fell into the fire. Sabrina caught him by the shoulder and Beau shook her off. "Get your fucking hands off me!"

Sabrina gripped his shoulders tightly with both hands. "Let's get you inside. You're gonna get frostbite out here."

Sabrina steered Beau back to the house and up the porch steps. "That boy. He won't stop!" Beau stared at Sabrina, piteous. "Why?"

Sabrina guided him to his couch. Beau guzzled from the bottle of whiskey before collapsing onto his side.

Sabrina sat across from him. "What really happened? With Henry?"

"He came outta nowhere. I didn't see him."

Sabrina shook her head. "It was you."

Beau started crying. "That goddamn curve in the road."

"Were you drunk?"

"Fuck you."

"Where's his body?"

Beau turned away; his face buried in the couch cushions. "I'm tired."

"It's not too late you know, to make this right."

He didn't respond. Sabrina thought he passed out. Then, softly, "The cave."

Sabrina leaned closer. "What?"

Beau shot up from the couch and took a swing at Sabrina, grazing her cheek with a weak fist. "Nothing! I didn't say nothing! Now get the hell outta my house!"

He swung at Sabrina again, but instead fell forward, right through the middle of the coffee table. His deadweight smashed it to bits, sending glassware everywhere. He was passed out now, and Sabrina left the old bastard where he was, face down on his dirty carpet.

SABRINA PARKED on the shoulder next to mile marker two. Rose sat in the passenger seat. It was still dark, the sun only a faint orange glow on the horizon.

Sabrina stared at the shadowy woods. "Do you know of any caves out here?"

Rose shook her head. "There's a ridgeline pretty far back on the other side of the valley. Lots of exposed rock. If there's a cave, that's where it'd be."

"Let's start there, then."

"You know, the only caves I've ever come across out here were bear dens."

"Great."

They ducked under the eaves of a black spruce and entered the Lost River forest. Sabrina led the way, a camping headlamp strapped around her winter hat. After a hundred yards, they took a break. The air was ice in Sabrina's lungs.

"You hear that?" Sabrina asked.

"What?"

"That's just it. Nothing. These are the quietest woods I've ever been in."

The terrain was easier than Sabrina thought it'd be. The trees were virtually impenetrable, and little snow had made it all the way to the ground. A blanket of pine needles and knotty roots were still visible beneath their boots. After another hundred yards, they descended a stony hillside into a narrow valley; an ocean of ancient, undulating pines surrounded them.

Rose was huffing now too. They reached the other side of the valley, and slowly worked their way across the base of the ridge. A towering wall of craggy granite rose above them. Within minutes, they found an entrance to a cave. It was small, only about three feet wide and three feet high.

The pines grew right up to the ridge, their branches flush with the granite wall. Rank air bellowed forth from the heart of the cave. The air around them felt thick and heavy. It was so quiet, Sabrina heard ringing in her ears.

Rose crouched down, ready to venture inside. Sabrina stopped her. "Let me. If he's in there, you don't need to see it."

Sabrina knelt down and peered into the darkness. With a deep breath, she crawled inside the tight space. Her headlamp revealed an open cavern ahead, and she shimmied towards it. Once she was inside the larger hollow, she was able to stand again if she ducked her head.

Sabrina scanned the chamber, her narrow beam of light piercing the darkness. There was a pile of shiny rocks, a small pyramid of collected stones of various colors, shapes, and sizes. Next to the rocks was an assemblage of assorted animal bones. They had been pulled apart, cleaned, and reassembled, a macabre diorama of mythical creatures on display, complete with insect wings that were stuck to the brittle bones with smashed berries. There was kindling and strips of birch bark in a corner, the beginnings of another cross.

Against the back wall of the cave was something small, wrapped in a blanket. Sabrina crouched down, unwrapping the blanket slowly. Henry's ivory skull stared up at her. Two black stones had been placed inside the eye sockets. The rest of his body was a pile of loose bones beneath disintegrating clothes.

The buzzing in Sabrina's ears was a swarm of bees, and she had trouble catching her breath. She made her way back out of the cave. As she neared the entrance, she heard voices outside. She crawled faster back into the daylight.

"You just couldn't let it go." Beau stared down at Sabrina, wheezing hard, a shotgun in his hand. A massive bruise bloomed on the side of his face, and stale whiskey oozed from his pores, poisoning the air between them.

Rose was on her knees, her hands in the air. "Is he in there?" Sabrina nodded. Rose lowered her head.

"Shut up!" Beau snarled. "It was an accident! He shouldn't have been in the damn road!"

"What are you going to do now?" Sabrina asked. "Shove two more bodies in there?"

Beau smashed Sabrina in the face with the stock of his shotgun. Sabrina dropped her head, spitting blood in the snow and scanning the ground for a rock, a branch, anything she could use as a weapon.

A shadow moved across the ground between them. Snow dropped from the trees, landing on Beau's head. He looked up. A pair of black eyes stared down at him.

Henry scurried between the branches, making his way down the trunk of the tree.

Beau staggered backwards, dropping his gun. "No, no!" Henry hit the ground, as Beau turned and ran. He made it ten yards before a guttural cry escaped his lips. Beau clutched his chest and collapsed into the snow.

Sabrina ran to him, blood still dripping from her split lip. She flipped Beau over onto his back. He was pale, sweating, clutching at his chest.

"Step aside." Rose was behind her with Henry at her side.

Sabrina did what she was told.

Henry approached Beau slowly and knelt. Beau tried to crawl away, but he could only cower, gasping for air. "I didn't see you, I…"

Henry leaned forward, brushing the white hair from Beau's brow. He slowly unbuttoned Beau's shirt, and slipped his hand inside. As Henry's hand sliced through his flesh, he leaned closer, kissing Beau gently on his forehead.

Beau's body tightened, and then went slack.

Henry's body rippled with pain. His eyes grew murkier and black tears formed. He pulled Beau's still beating heart from his chest. It dripped blood between his fingers. He held it out for his mother, attempting a crooked smile.

With great effort, Henry spoke, his voice choked sandpaper. "I'm sorry, mom." He looked down, ashamed. "You told me never to go on the highway. I shouldn't have…"

Rose scooped him up in her arms, burying his face in her chest. "My poor baby. You have nothing to be sorry for!"

Sabrina walked away then, and let them be alone. They spoke for several minutes before Rose finally let Henry go. After a final embrace, Henry turned and walked slowly into the forest. After a few steps, he disappeared into the trees. Rose never told Sabrina what was said between them, and Sabrina never asked.

There was a whoosh above them, and a massive grey owl swooped down, landing on a branch. It stared down at Sabrina, then hooted its displeasure, a rebuke of her presence.

HALF THE TOWN attended Henry's funeral, and the other half attended Beau's. New wounds were opened by the revelations, and festering animosities resurfaced. Some residents simply refused to believe their beloved Sheriff could have had anything to do with Henry's death.

Over time, Granite Falls slowly healed. As did the Lost River forest. Insects, birds, and animals poured back into its hills and valleys, filling every nook, cranny, and tree branch with boisterous wildlife. Even the cave that once held Henry's remains welcomed a black bear and her cubs.

The pine trees in the valley especially seemed to flourish, growing taller and stronger, their needles a shimmering ocean of lush green, sheltering the life that dwelled beneath them.

ALWAYS PREPARED

JONAH BUCK

Dmitry vanished on the third day of the expedition.

It wasn't the first time Dmitry had disappeared. He was the group's geologist. And like every geologist Yulia had ever known, Dmitry would scamper off the trail to collect a cool rock, wade out into chest-deep freezing water to collect a cool rock, or climb to a roughly neck-snapping height up a moss-slick, uneven ravine to collect a cool rock. Yulia had tolerated his antics because he was experienced. Except this time, Dmitry didn't come back to camp.

Yulia stood by her tent, satellite phone in her hand. She stared at the little screen as she dialed the number for Dmitry's phone again.

"Come on," she muttered to herself as she stabbed the number into the phone's keypad for what felt like the hundredth time. She held the phone to her ear. It rang. And rang. And rang. Yulia disconnected the call.

She eyed Dmitry's tent. The geologist's day pack was gone, and he'd been wearing his bright red jacket when he set out. His sleeping bag and personal items were still scattered near the tent though, including the little sandwich bag of sweets he liked to snack on while working. It looked like Dmitry intended to come right back. He probably *had* intended to come right back.

"Dmitry!" Nikolai shouted into the forest. His voice was hoarse from overuse. Nikolai cupped his hands to his mouth and yelled Dmitry's name again. His voice didn't even echo back to him. The forest simply swallowed it.

Russia's Kamchatka Peninsula was one of the most isolated locations on Earth. Even at the height of Stalin's paranoia, when the Soviet Union planted gulags and work camps all over the most remote stretches of Siberia, no major prisons were created in Kamchatka due to the lack of infrastructure. The land was so dismally remote, Lenin himself once offered to lease the territory to the United States as a sort of new Alaska.

Decades later, when the USSR needed an entire secret city to build its nuclear submarine fleet, the Politburo looked to Kamchatka and founded Vilyuchinsk. Even today, well after the demise of the Soviet Union, Vilyuchinsk remained a closed city, requiring special permission from the Russian government and a scourge of security clearances to live or visit there.

Thick with coniferous forests and studded with the slumbering peaks of inactive volcanoes, Kamchatka was a primeval world. Further north, after the forest gave way to tundra and permafrost, lay Wrangel Island. The world's last wooly mammoths finally went extinct there, centuries after the pyramids were already raided by generations of tomb robbers. To the east lay the frigid expanse of the Bering Sea. The land was harsh and unforgiving, the taiga only grudgingly allowing human settlement.

Yulia, Dmitry, and Nikolai had been helicoptered in to scout for potential deposits of oil and natural gas. Dmitry, as the geologist, had planted seismometers and taken soil samples, testing potential extraction sites for traces of past volcanic eruptions, tsunamis, earthquakes, and other catastrophes.

Nikolai was the group anthropologist. Before Russian settlement in the area, the region had been home to the Koryak and Itelmen peoples. Extracting natural resources from the area would become more complicated if there were sites of cultural significance that needed to be surreptitiously bulldozed.

Yulia was the group's petrochemical engineer and official leader. She was a different type of animal from Dmitry. She wasn't interested in pretty rocks. She was here to analyze data and scout out the best site for exploratory drilling.

Yulia would have preferred to go on the expedition alone. But the insurance underwriters demanded a team. And Dmitry and Nikolai had their uses. Until Dmitry wandered into the damned forest alone and got lost.

With her luck, Dmitry had been eaten by one of Kamchatka's thousands of bears. That would certainly delay the expedition. It might even force her to turn back, and if that happened, she could kiss this paycheck goodbye.

Yulia was personally prepared for anything. The forest offered few challenges for her. If need be, she could live out here for weeks. It was the unpreparedness of others that bothered her.

She'd been a mere wisp of a teenage girl when the Soviet Union collapsed. At the time, she'd been one of the Young Pioneers, the main compulsory youth organization. "Always prepared," the motto went. Well, they weren't very prepared for the implosion of communist society.

Yulia learned her most basic survival skills from the Young Pioneers. She learned the value of cold, hard cash in those lost years after the system disintegrated.

It was those lean years that taught her true survival skills. How to thrive on scraps and shelter from the coldest nights. How to make do on her own when her friends abandoned her. How to make new friends fast. How to know when it was time to abandon those friends.

Unlike so many of the older generation, she figured out how to adapt to capitalism. She learned to follow the money, to know the right people, and to learn skills that would let her escape her tenuous existence on Moscow's periphery. Russia's oil and natural gas companies had done very well for themselves in the new order, so they were a natural place to plant her flag.

Dmitry's disappearance reminded her of old girlfriends. Fellow Young Pioneers. They hadn't taken the old motto to heart, though. They weren't prepared.

She thought of Anna and her sweet smile. She and Yulia had been friends since childhood and remained in the same Young Pioneers troop together. They found Anna in an alley, her throat slashed and her purse gone.

Yulia thought of Katerina, who had been a few years older, and Yulia always thought she was so beautiful. They said Katerina had been the fifth of the Gagarin Park Strangler's twelve victims. But they never found Katerina's head, and the Gagarin Park Strangler didn't take anyone else's head. Most likely, blaming a few extra murders on the Strangler was a good way to clean up the police record and "solve" a few closed cases.

And then, there was Sasha. Everyone thought Sasha had it made when that big, black car began picking her up every night, and she began to wear new fur coats from Western brands. But one night, Sasha went away in that big, black car, and she never came home. Yulia still didn't know if Sasha was still out there somewhere, or if her bones were in a jumble at the bottom of Moscow's landfill.

The streets had been so cold. So dangerous. Yulia's friends hadn't adapted. They hadn't bent themselves to the rules of that jungle of vandalized Lenin statues and faded posters promising utopia.

So, she studied. And she stole. And she banished pity from her heart. She aced every exam at the crumbling university. She shook hands with bureaucrats and mobsters, when they weren't the same person, because she already knew the deals they wanted to make. She led expeditions into Siberia and north of the Arctic Circle across hinterlands administered through the barrel of an AK-47. And she managed it all because she was always prepared for the task in front of her.

Kamchatka's bears and wolves didn't frighten Yulia. She had known worse when the Moscow police could still be bought for bread and vodka.

It was her goal in life that she would never be so desperately poor again. Never unprepared again. It was just one of life's ironies that all her effort to make sure she was never cold and hungry again often meant she was cold and hungry out in places like Kamchatka.

Always prepared, the Young Pioneers said. Yulia was always prepared. It was fools like Dmitry who slowed her down.

"Dammit, Dmitry," she muttered. She punched a new number into her satellite phone. After a few rings, the voice of the helicopter pilot who had flown them into this godforsaken taiga answered.

"Expedition One? You haven't been out there very long. Forget your toothbrush?"

"It's Yulia. One of my team's gotten himself lost. He left before breakfast and hasn't returned to camp. I'm going to need extraction and a search party." She said the words with the enthusiasm of a child forced to apologize to a bratty sibling upon threat of the strap.

"No can do. There's a weather system coming in. Visibility is crap already.

It'll hit you soon. I'll get word to the locals to put together a search team, but you're going to have to hunker down for a while."

Yulia gritted her teeth. "I'm not going to sit out here and twiddle my thumbs while the bears finish picking the meat off my geologist. I'm going back to civilization and analyzing what data I have until the Natural Resources Committee sends me another rock jockey. And you're going to fly me out of here."

"It's out of my hands. Air traffic control is grounding everyone. Half the air crews already left for the bars, since nobody's going up in the air. With this fog and that terrain, I'd be flying blind. Just sit tight. This should pass in a few days. I'll put in the calls for a search team."

"A few days?" Yulia asked the question more loudly than she intended. The weather this time of year was supposed to be comparatively balmy for Kamchatka. Her pilot had already hung up, though. Grimacing, Yulia put the phone away to conserve its battery.

A few days. She had the supplies. She had the gumption. She was prepared.

"Dmitry?" Nikolai called. His words were lost to the forest.

FOG ROLLED THROUGH the endless lines of conifers like muddy water through the gills of deep-sea fish. To Yulia's eyes, it seemed like the trees ought to tear the fog apart, to shred it like claws through cloth. But the fog simply drifted onward, unperturbed and impenetrable.

It had been two days since Dmitry disappeared and Yulia learned she was effectively stranded here. In that time, there had been no sign of the geologist.

Nikolai had stopped shouting into the woods for Dmitry. He'd found something else to occupy his time instead.

"Fifty thousand years old," Nikolai said.

"Run your tests again," Yulia said, not because she wanted to confirm the results but because it would keep Nikolai occupied for several more hours.

"I've already run them. Twice. The pigments are fifty thousand years old."

"Run the tests again," Yulia commanded.

They'd found the small cave yesterday afternoon. Yulia had urged Nikolai to help explore the area around camp to look for Dmitry. And she had looked for Dmitry. She'd also checked some of her equipment and gathered a few essential readings. Might as well get some work done while she was stuck out here.

The small cave had been an unexpected find. Yulia only noticed it because it was tucked behind a copse of truly massive, hollowed-out trees. Animals of some kind had used the hollows as nests. They were full of leaf litter, bits of bone, and clumps of fur. Their massive roots all clawed their way toward the cave entrance like gnarled medical forceps holding open a wound in the Earth.

Nikolai had been interested in the cave. Moreso by the ochre drawings dabbed on the cavern walls. He thought they might be signs of a Paleolithic culture. Yulia thought they would be a pain in the ass, since they would complicate any effort to sink test wells in the area. She and Nikolai also found bits of chipped obsidian and splinters of old bone. And a single, tattered patch of bright red fabric.

The scrap definitely belonged to Dmitry's jacket. No other hikers would have come to this godforsaken corner of the forest, miles and miles from any real trail. The geologist had seen the cave, decided to check it out and either gotten hopelessly lost inside the labyrinth or plunged to his death down an unexpected fissure. Yulia didn't care which outcome was correct, but she wasn't about to make the same idiot mistake following Dmitry's trail into the cave.

Mystery solved. Yulia would have been content to wait for rescue except that now Nikolai was obsessed with the cave paintings.

Nikolai had scraped off a small amount of pigment from the cave paintings to run tests. The paintings themselves were essentially abstract. A few of them showed simple stick figures hunting something. Others were just handprints. Well, modified handprints. The fingers were too long. Maybe three times longer than normal digits.

The paintings were no more than an idle curiosity to Yulia, but Nikolai was fascinated by them. They didn't truly grab Yulia's attention until Nikolai told her they were fifty thousand years old. And the only reason that interested her was because it told her Nikolai was incompetent.

Fifty thousand years ago, there was no forest in Kamchatka. The region would have been deep in the Ice Age and buried under an ice sheet half the height of Mount Everest. In the doubtful event that any human beings had been in the region at the time, they would have been miles up, picking their way across the endless glaciers. The only alternative was somebody living under the ice, inside the cave, so deep down that the sunlight would never reach them.

Ridiculous. The paintings were more recent. Nikolai was simply misinterpreting his readings.

Nikolai had of course wanted to further explore the cavern, but it led downward into the Earth. Yulia didn't want the cave paintings documented further, and she had no interest in risking her own life in some dark pit to recover Dmitry's body.

Yulia was no fool. She briefly remembered those girlfriends in Moscow who disappeared without a trace. Poor Anna, cold and bloodied in that dark alley. Poor Katerina, her head perhaps lovingly preserved in some Moscow basement's freezer even now. Poor Sasha, who could be living on a beach somewhere, but was probably a collection of musty, fox-gnawed bones in a trash-lined ditch.

Better not to go looking for them. Better not to know. Even when there was an answer to be found, it didn't change anything. Not in those days. All she could do was move forward and take what precautions she could. Dmitry was no different. Let a recovery team pull his remains out of that cave.

Enough thinking about Dmitry. Enough thinking about caverns that led beneath the root-bound forest floor. Enough about impossibly old cave paintings from a culture that would predate the woods.

Yulia pulled herself to her feet and grabbed her rucksack. She could tell that Nikolai was on edge. She'd been harsh with him. That part didn't matter. She would treat her team in whatever way got her the results she wanted. But she had miscalculated. Dmitry had been the class clown type who needed to be brought to heel sometimes for his own sake. Nikolai was more sensitive. He would mope like a kicked dog if she was gruff with him. An act of contrition would make him more loyal in the short-term, which was as long as Yulia needed his services. The anthropologist had brought not one but two novels with him to read on the expedition, taking up valuable space among his equipment. What was she to expect from such a soft and impractical man?

She rooted around in her own rucksack until she located the chocolate bar she had carefully hidden. She had intended to save it for herself if their supplies ran low, but she could claim she suddenly remembered it and share a few bites with Nikolai to earn back some of his trust. Holding the brightly colored foil like a diplomat about to present a peace treaty, she walked over to Nikolai's tent.

"Nikolai?" The sound of a battery-powered spectrometer whirred inside the tent. Running his tests again. "Nikolai?" Yulia asked louder.

The trees rustled. The sound was like a giant snake moving somewhere nearby, scales sliding over stone. But there was another sound, too. Something so faint Yulia almost missed it. A footstep on a bed on pine needles.

Yulia looked up in time to see a bolt of red. The figure was wearing Dmitry's jacket. For an instant, she thought it was Dmitry, holding Nikolai's limp form in his arms like they'd stepped off the cover of a cheap romance story. But Nikolai's face was coated in red where his head had been struck with a rock.

It wasn't Dmitry. It had been, but not anymore. Dmitry's jaw had been removed, and there was a ragged gash down his neck and chest, as if hacked with a badly made hatchet. Eyes stared out at Yulia from Dmitry's gaping mouth wound. The eyes were bulging black pools, spider's eyes.

Yulia's brain misfired for a second, trying to figure out what she was looking at. It all clicked a second too late. Something was wearing Dmitry like a parka. Something with eyes as black and reflective as her phone screen.

Then the figure was gone, disappearing in the fog in the direction of the cavern. It moved with jerking, twitching movements, like someone who had entered a race in a poorly tailored suit. The thing carried Nikolai's limp form along as it vanished from sight.

YULIA HAD BEEN ON THE MOVE for almost twenty-four hours now. She had taken nothing with her except for her rucksack and the satellite phone.

The helicopter pilot still refused to fly in the fog. Yulia hoped the devil took him. She'd told him that Nikolai was also gone. At least she'd had the presence of mind to not go into very many details. When the pilot asked what happened, she simply cursed him out and demanded an extraction. But still he refused to come in such treacherous weather.

The fog had not cleared. Yulia had stumbled eastward for miles, heading generally for the coast of Kamchatka where it would be easier to collect her. But for all the ground she'd covered, it all looked the same. She would trudge forward, and another conifer would loom out of the fog. And another. And another.

The forest here knew no tracks. It was virtually unexplored. Yulia had to eye the slow course of the sun to make sure she wasn't simply walking in circles through the seemingly endless wilderness.

It felt like she was back in Moscow, passing another identical row of concrete, brutalist apartment towers on every street. Where the world had fallen apart and all that remained was a vestige of bureaucracy. Where her friends died or vanished or were simply swallowed whole by the night.

Yulia had been at the bottom of the food chain before, and she had clawed her way upward. She was tough. She was resourceful. She was prepared.

But she hadn't been prepared for this, now had she? She'd been caught as flat-footed as the Central Planning Committee when the Berlin Wall came down. Doubts buzzed around her like a cloud of flies. She was always prepared, dammit. And who could have possibly been prepared for this? Something had taken Dmitry and Nikolai, something that no doubt lived in the cave.

Were there more caverns winding beneath the forest? Dark tunnels hewn out of black rock and wet earth? She didn't know, and the feeling of not knowing was insufferable. But she'd found more hollowed out trees, like the ones near the cave. Some of them were also filled with forest detritus, like chewed bones and sodden leaves. Others dropped away into blackness, leaving the tree suspended above a void, clinging to the surface by its roots.

Yulia believed the cave paintings might be fifty thousand years old now. She believed that whatever took Dmitry and Nikolai, it did not belong to this era. It was something older than the forest. Something that had adapted when the world changed and the ice went away, just as Yulia had once adapted to a new world.

Her blistered feet throbbed in her boots. Her legs burned with exhaustion from hours navigating over the craggy landscape. Cuts and scrapes marked every inch of exposed skin where she had shoved her way through thickets of trees and brambles.

Yulia ignored all the pain, though. She had to assume that creature was following her after taking Dmitry and Nikolai. Were there more of them? How far would she need to run to be safe? The uncertainty clawed at her, and it stung far worse than the forest's thorns and nettles.

Yulia had only gotten the briefest glimpse of the thing that took Nikolai, since it had been wearing Dmitry like one of Sasha's Western brand fur coats. But Yulia knew she could beat the damnable thing. She had the best hiking boots money could buy. She had a good head start. She had a satellite phone to summon her pilot once she reached the coast. Was the fog beginning to thin out? Was it brighter, or was it merely her imagination? She could do this.

A branch snapped somewhere behind her. Yulia spun around. The trees whispered in the breeze.

Yulia paused for a moment, listening. The forest was not quiet, exactly. There was the low, steady hush of leaves, the occasional creak of a heavy bough, and the crunch of pine needles underfoot as Yulia shifted her weight. But the birds were silent. And she didn't hear the steady buzz and hum of insects.

Yulia turned around and stopped dead. Nikolai stood directly in front of her, his form hunched and bloodied. A furious, red slit ran from his throat to his groin. His jaw had been ripped away, leaving a yawning, red void. His body was not packed with pink and red innards, though. Those had been scooped away. No, Nikolai had been hollowed out, transformed into an empty vessel, and refilled with something dark and squirming, twitching and repulsive. Black, bulging eyes, far too many eyes, peered out at Yulia from beneath Nikolai's upper row of teeth, like hungry baby birds peering out of the nest for the first time.

Yulia took a step backward and bumped into something. Dmitry's cold, blood-caked hands came up and grabbed her arms.

The thing wearing Nikolai pulled out a lump of black obsidian, one side chipped down into a crude, jagged blade. Yulia screamed once. And then the forests of Kamchatka grew quiet once more.

THE FIRE POPPED and sizzled as occasional droplets of fat dribbled down and teased the embers. It was tempting to gobble up the strange meat right now. But, no. No. Better to wait. Wait until the cold times. Smoke the meat. Keep it ready for the days of ice and snow that would surely come. Better to be prepared.

Smoke billowed through the dark cavern. The tiny flames illuminated hundreds of paintings carved and painted onto the stone. They showed a variety of images, interspersed with handprints to indicate pathways through the warren of caves and tunnels beneath the forest.

The paintings depicted many scenes. Hunting beasts both familiar and strange. Hiding deep down when the cold seeped in from above. Exploring the world of burning sunlight during the warm times. The paintings were a map. And a history.

Once, ice had blocked all access to the world above. Creaking, grinding, groaning ice. Until the ice melted. And the world above was revealed.

The cold times still came. Every winter, the cold crashed over Kamchatka. That was why it was so important to be prepared. To save the meat from the three strange creatures, to preserve their pelts for the coming cold times, to use and savor every single scrap.

Because the creatures were warm. So very warm. Their brightly colored hides were thick and unpleasant to chew, but the meat inside was sweet and succulent. And those hides would protect against the cold times.

Once, the ice had prevented the cave's inhabitants from ever going to the surface. Now, the warm times allowed them to hunt for meat under the trees that had sprung up since the great ice melted. But the cold times had always been hard. Always scarce. Always hungry.

But if they could find more of these warm, unwary creatures, if they could harvest more pelts, the forest would be open to them even during the cold times.

Already, many hands had daubed crimson images on the cavern walls deeper in the earth. Pictures of the ungainly, strange creatures that had set up a camp so close to the cavern entrance. The others would know what to look for as they explored the woods during the waning warm times. They would find more of these creatures.

Because more hides meant hunting parties even during the cold times. More pelts meant there would be meat even during the hungry season. With a stockpile of food, they'd be prepared for the cold. Soon, they'd always be ready. Always prepared.

WALDEINSAMKEIT

AIRIC FENN

Moats of dust float in the sunlight that filters through the grimy windowpanes over the kitchen sink. You watch them drift from your seat on your bed, warm mug in your hands. The coffee is fresh, the earthy scent of the instant grounds lingering in the air, but you can smell the damp seeping through the bad seals around the windows.

Coffee, petrichor, and green. That is how you've come to recognize the smell of the old, rotting logs of the lookout tower. It's always stronger after a rain—a thing which the roof has long since given way to. A steady *drip, drip, drip* splashes in a puddle by the front door. Moss has crept in between the cracks separating the floorboards, nourished by the rainwater and undisturbed by your hand for years now. You gradually finish your coffee, one sip at a time.

A cloud passes, turning the tower grey. You close your eyes. Your ears strain to listen beyond the tinnitus-filled silence, as though the dead radio sitting on the counter across from you might crackle back to life. Of course, there's nothing. The radio's been mute for a decade or more. You haven't used your voice in nearly as long, your vocal cords as dry and dusty as the unused fire finder in the middle of the room. You probably wouldn't know what you'd do if you had a visitor, but those stopped coming not long after the calls did.

You let out a sigh and leave your empty cup at the table.

There is no need for you. There hasn't been, not since the machines reached their hands into the forest service. First it was the optical sensors and cameras. Then the satellites, then the drones. With each one, you heard from fellow lookouts less and less, as they each left at the end of their seasons and never returned for the next. Until, one day, communications stopped entirely.

You could have left then. You should have. Yet. For some reason you remain. You've stayed in your tower, eyes always scanning the horizon, the trees. Watching. Perhaps it's all you know how to do. Perhaps you know there would be nothing for you if you returned to your kind. Or perhaps... you still watch because you've seen. On those long, cloudless days that draw into sleepless nights, you've seen what's watching back. You've felt your gaze drawn in by the unblinking eyes lurking through the pines. They reflect on all the windows, the tower exposing your every movement.

You sit so high above the forest canopy, but you were wrong to think there was privacy so far out here. And when you meet their gazes on those sleepless nights, when your heart tells you to leave, to pack your bag and hike for civilization—

You cannot look away.

Come mornings, you often wake on the floor. A stiff back greets you, sharp pains in your neck. Boots still on, you stumble down to the outhouse for a piss. You stop and check the generator after. Always. You must wonder how it still works. You pause, scan the surrounding tree line, then climb back into your tower to make your coffee. You don't like the taste—you make a face every time. But you drink it, because it's what you know. Then you set your empty mug on the counter.

You eat your breakfast—granola, stolen from unsuspecting campers who never notice you or scavenged from what's been left behind. Other times it's fish caught from the lake. That's where you bathe, too, on the days you dare venture out that far. Those are the days you can pretend the Eyes don't exist. There's a scar scorching the land there, just across the cold water. Shadows of blackened trees grasp towards the lake's murky depths. The ashen landscape screams whenever you watch for just a little too long... An echo from before. You seem to have noticed the Eyes don't like to look there, either.

But most often you stay in sight of your tower.

You head out after your breakfasts and make your rounds through the forest. You clean up empty bottles that campers failed to pack out, make sure their fire pits are good and dead. You keep yourself busy. You know that if you didn't, you'd spot the movement in the trees. Their trunks creaking, shifting places out the corner of your vision.

The first time you saw it, you thought you had finally lost your mind: a lone ponderosa suddenly ten yards off from where you had left it. You tried to tell yourself the sun was playing tricks on you, and you guzzled down your water, poured the rest on your head. But when you looked back at it, it was the same tree. You knew because it had the same head-height knot that looked almost like a face. Too much like a face. When you retraced your path to where the tree should have been, there remained only earth, and bone. Only worms and beetles writhing among ivory in a gaping hollow left by the ponderosa's roots.

You ignore every hole you find. You keep your eyes trained ahead. That is, until nightfall, and your blinders fall away. Your curiosity gets the better of you. Every time. The floorboards creak as you pace your self-inflicted cage, biting your nails, muttering like a restless animal. Your wild thoughts are almost visible through your skull. And you watch and you watch and you watch.

But you never dare to venture out searching, no matter how hypnotizing those Eyes in the trees. Though you've come close, once or twice. Both times, you started to leave, but your feet stopped you at the top of the wooden stairs, your hand still on the door. Then like a spell being broken, you shook your head and hid back in your tower.

But not this morning.

Now, you stand from your cramped little bed shoved far into the corner and your eyes scan beyond the lookout windows again. The sun has returned. It's time for your rounds. You should go on them. Instead, you hesitate. You look over your belongings—the fire finder, the silent radio. There is no need for them, anymore.

Crossing your cage, you instead unfold a brown, threadbare shawl from atop a pile of boxes, and pull it over your arms. It, too, smells of green, and though you can't quite remember, it was not always that color.

Your pack rests at the base of the fire finder, and for a moment you consider it. In it still waits your map, your compass, your water, your first aid. You bring them with you everywhere. Always. But not this morning.

You leave them.

You remove your hiking pole from its resting place by the front door. The mosses between the floorboards reach out to greet your boots as you cross over them. They remain undisturbed.

A breeze blows through the tower when you open the door. Your feet pause at the top of the stairs. You observe the forest, then the grassy clearing far below the tower and the rock it's built on top of. You have no need for this place. You have no need to let your body remain a relic inside it. Perhaps that's why you do it. Why you shut the door and continue slowly down the lookout steps. Perhaps you've grown tired. Tired of watching, of waiting for another fire that you can call no one for. Tired of yearning. Or perhaps, your curiosity has just become too much.

You unhook the generator on your way out.

You don't hesitate as the green labyrinth unfurls before you. You take a step, and then another. The forest engulfs you eagerly, and you let it. You tread deeper, deeper into the undergrowth, the bed of damp pine needles softly crunching beneath your boots. And your tower fades from your sight. From your mind. In the end, you leave that cage behind so easily, as though you had never lived there at all.

A campsite passes at the edge of your vision. Just as soon as you notice it, it folds into the trees, a cluster of spruces growing up from within and hiding it from view. The forest calls you beyond it, so you follow. Deep silence falls across the canopy as you pass below it, birds hushing their songs. You glance around, but though you feel them at your back, it's not the Eyes the birds quiet for.

A breeze urges you to march on, the trail ahead sprouting from nothing. White flecks float through the air. You pause a moment to observe them as they blow free from your shirt. When you pinch the hem, the piece crumbles to ash in the wind and smears between your thumb and finger. You wipe it off on a patch of moss and keep walking. You don't need it.

The path meanders, the forest growing older and wilder the further you descend. You don't know where it's leading you. You would never be able to tell if you've been this way before, all the familiar landmarks growing where they shouldn't be. You could be wandering in circles for all you truly know. But you follow all the same, trusting the forest to guide you. Sometimes you look back and spot the hollows in the ground trailing behind you, or ahead, right before the earth or another tree fills them in. You don't avoid them now—You rush to them. You peer into each one, searching perhaps, before continuing on to the next.

You must know you're close now because you pick up your pace. Branches crack and snap under your feet. Ahead, you spot that ponderosa with the knot that looks too much like a face. You run to greet it, not even using your hiking pole now. You embrace it and let out a sob. The surrounding pines and firs groan and creak. Their needles whisper in your ear. You pull away. As you peer between their branches, you spy the lake, the shore only yards ahead.

At the corner of your vision, the ponderosa shifts, and you look back, a hole opening up in the ground. In it, only dirt and ivory. Worms and beetles. You glance again through the trees toward the lake, the glistening water reflecting the sun too brightly to see the wounded forest beyond it. You turn your back to it and look down into the hollow.

Needles poke into your skin as you kneel in front of it. Delicate mycelium threads are woven between the clumps of moist earth and rotting wood. You reach down, digging a hand into the side. Worms writhe between your fingers. Your hiking pole falls beside you as you plunge in your other hand. Beetles pinch at your skin and nails. You hiss quietly and pull your hands from the hole. The beetles scurry up your arms.

And you stare at your hands, flesh stained dark, white bone at your fingertips stained green. You raise them to your face and inhale. You breathe in the smell, that scent that had overtaken your cage. The beetles crawl from your fingers to your face. They skitter over your lips, into your mouth, over your eyes.

You let them.

You half crawl, half slide into the hollow. Your clothes dissolve when they meet the damp earth, leaving your side smeared with wet ash. Roots tangle in your matted hair. The beetles climb your legs, and you sit to let them eat up along your torso. They crawl inside your stomach. Your curious eyes watch them open up your chest to the air. The pair of pink sponges within your ribs expand and contract, and that red, wet thing behind them continues to pump even as the beetles swarm inside.

You cough, losing your breath to the wind. You turn your gaze outside the hollow, to the sky, and to the trees, closer now, encircling the hole. The ponderosa looms directly above you, its face meeting Eyes with yours. Its roots creep into the hollow with you, curling in next to your bones.

Around you, the birds begin their song again.

A final sigh escapes your lips, and you lay down to be buried at our feet.

DESECRATIONS

BRIAN ROWE

Come join me, Daphne.

The words wove into the sound of the wind, only slightly louder than the creaking of branches and the rustle of pine needles. I'd been pretending not to hear them all day, and I did so again, even though that didn't seem to be helping. I kept my focus on the faint trail that the blowing snow worked diligently to obscure.

Behind me, Cornelius, my mule, snorted, as if he heard the voice too. It was more likely that he was annoyed by the cold, but I took some comfort in the thought that perhaps I wasn't slipping back into madness.

I'd first heard the voice early that morning, as I was investigating the desecrated shrine to the Visage of the Creator. In happier days, the repurposed barn had been a place of worship for the folk from the small hamlet that hired me. It had also served as an overnight waystation for travelers making the difficult trip between Fort Implacable and Fort Determination.

Now, though, the shrine sat in ruins. The doors had been torn from their hinges, the benches smashed to splinters, and the pillows and cushions ripped apart. Piles of dirty snow accumulated atop charred scraps of burnt cloth: the only remnants of tapestries that once depicted the Visage bringing peace between the Gahe and Keshi peoples.

The centerpiece of the shrine was a painted wooden statue of the Visage of the Creator herself, in the older style still favored by rural folk and those on the edges of the empire. Their version of the Visage was a human woman with rainbow-feathered wings whose lower half was that of an enormous multi-colored snake. Her scales were now painted black with the ashes of the tapestries, her wings torn off and cast aside, and her serene eyes cut out, leaving behind only deep, jagged gouges.

The shrine's attendant priest was the first person to vanish.

Despite the time between the desecration and my arrival, I'd managed to make out a faint set of tracks leading away from the shrine and deeper into the forest. The story they told was not one of panic and pursuit, but of someone unhurried and meandering, as if simply setting out to take a recreational walk.

That was when the voice first spoke.

Come witness my splendor, Daphne.

While its words varied throughout the trek, the theme remained the same, and it always addressed me by name. But I'd learned long ago never to respond to exhortations spoken by invisible mouths. It didn't matter if they were evil spirits or phantoms conjured by my mind: giving them any kind of attention gave them power. You couldn't argue them away; you couldn't shout them away; you couldn't reason them away; you couldn't bargain them away. Their only bane was indifference.

The next villager to vanish after the shrine priest had been the town drunk. Many people noticed, I was told, but few attributed any significance to it. Then the tanner's apprentice had gone missing. Then the barkeep's daughter. Then the weaver. Then the mason's brother. Finally, the praefectus minor's bed was found unused and empty after she was absent for a town meeting, and that was when a messenger was sent to Fort Determination.

The other trackers at the fort had refused to come out to look for the missing villagers. The vandalism of a holy place cast a pall of superstitious fear over the whole affair, bad weather would be crossing the mountains soon, and the village wasn't able to pay much. In the end, the messenger was desperate enough to ignore the rumors and come to me.

He was desperate enough to ignore that all of my hair was bone-white before I'd seen my fortieth summer. He was desperate enough to ignore the unsettling, angled lines and interlocked shapes scarred into the flesh down my spine. He was even desperate enough to ignore it when I consulted my mule for advice on the case.

That's when I was sure he was serious. I set out that very day.

I will not reject you, Daphne.

The snow had started to fall before noon, and it continued to dog our steps as Cornelius and I moved farther from the shrine. The wind made the tall pines nod their heads in time with its rhythm, and regularly kicked up puffs of powder, which took on shapes like white, feral beasts creeping through the trees alongside us.

Fortunately, the person I followed was not especially wood-wise, or was at least unconcerned about hiding the signs of their passage. The path continued uphill, and the terrain became rockier as I followed my quarry out of the valley and into the forested foothills. I stopped long enough to take an extra furred cloak from Cornelius's packs and slipped it on over my bulky coat, pulling up the deep hood to try to keep the snow out of my eyes. As I made a note of a cliff overhang that would make a good campsite when darkness fell, a flash of red screamed out against the white-blue-gray of my surroundings.

I cued Cornelius to stay put and left the trail to investigate. Low to the ground and fluttering in the clutches of a wickedly thorned bush was a scrap of dyed cloth. I took off one of my thick gloves and grasped it between my fingers; the smooth texture and the way it warmed quickly to my touch proved that it had come from a garment of high quality.

A quick investigation of the area confirmed my suspicions: the scrap had not come from the person I was following. Their trail was more recent, and it had come from a different direction, but it intersected the path I was on and continued along with it. It wasn't long before evidence of a third traveler appeared, and then a fourth. Following their route became easy; the falling snow could hide their footprints, but not the clumsy way they blundered through the terrain.

You will never be abandoned again, Daphne.

A woman in red was waiting for me just a few minutes farther down the path from where the last of the trails met. She was dressed far too lightly for the weather. Her crimson over-cloak was her only protection from the frigid wind, though it had handled the journey into the woods better than I would have expected.

If I had encountered her in a warm tavern, I would have probably bought her a drink and hoped I was as attractive to her as she was to me. I judged her to be no more than five or so years younger than me and clearly of Keshi ancestry: tall, with dark-brown skin, an angular face, and light brown hair. Her eyes, originally a deep blue or light violet, were now clouded over with a thin, white film.

I made no attempt to hide my approach. "Are you Praefectus Minor Alana?" I called out. "I'm Daphne the Determined, I've been hired to find you and the others. Are you hurt?"

Her frosted-over eyes met mine, and it was clear that there was nothing wrong with her vision. She smiled. "I've been waiting for you, Daphne," she said, and her voice sounded hollow, like wind through a rotten log. "You're the last to arrive."

Cornelius stopped several strides from the woman. His nostrils flared, and his ears flattened.

"Stop being such a coward," I said. He snorted indignantly, but he refused to get any closer. I shrugged and approached Alana alone.

"Where are the others?" I asked.

"In the sacred grove just ahead," she said. "We were waiting for you. Now that you're here, we can begin the ceremony. We know all about you, Daphne."

"Yeah, so do I," I said dismissively. I had a lot of experience recognizing the signs: her eyes, her voice, and Cornelius's unhappiness all combined to tell me that Alana was possessed by a spirit of some kind. It was a bit of a relief, actually; it allowed me to be a little more certain that the voice I'd been hearing was coming from outside my head.

"Who recruited you into this?" I asked.

Not-Alana ignored my question. "Do you know what they call you behind your back? Daphne the Demented. Daphne the Damned."

I rolled my eyes at the insult. As if I was that poor a tracker to not hear what my neighbors said in front of their hearth fires, behind their barred doors. "Yeah, I know," I said. "What kind of focus object did they force you to swear over?"

"The Huntress calls you Daphne the Dejected," Not-Alana continued.

"Daphne the Discharged. Daphne the Dismissed."

I reached out and grabbed Not-Alana roughly by the arm. She didn't resist as I turned her hand palm-up and pushed the sleeve of her cloak up to her elbow. The dark skin of her forearm was pristine and unblemished.

"You haven't taken its Mark yet," I said, "unless it's on your back. That means you can still fight this. You must fight this. Whatever it's offering you is false."

"The Visage of the Creator is false!" Not-Alana shouted suddenly, her face distorting in anger. "The Church of the Creator is false! The Kesh–Gahe Empire is built on a lie! All of civilization is false!"

"Yeah, I know that, too." I dropped her arm and turned away to continue down the path, clicking again for Cornelius to follow me. When faced with the choice between being obedient or being left alone with a possessed woman, he chose obedience, and he apprehensively trotted past her. We left her there, ranting into the wind behind us. She would either find the will to fight or she wouldn't. There was nothing Cornelius or I could say that could make the weak strong.

Nobody had a deeper understanding of that than I did, though, by this time, Cornelius must have had some idea, too. He'd listened to me babble about it enough, during the late nights when the moon hid her face from the sky and the alchemist's herbs were insufficiently fresh.

The walk to the "sacred grove" was longer than Not-Alana had made it seem. The afternoon sky began to dim, and I retrieved a torch from Cornelius's saddlebag. There was no point in stealth, and the lack of light would slow me down. It would be rude to keep everyone waiting, and I was, apparently, already late.

As the sun set, the storm worsened. The trees bent against the wind, and my furs did little to protect me against its bite. The snow fell in thick sheets, reflecting the torchlight into a million tiny motes and keeping me from seeing more than a few feet ahead. I followed the path more by feel than sight; some power emanated from the land, and it urged me forward even as it made the long-faded scars on my back burn with an all-too-familiar heat.

Submit to me, Daphne, and you will never be spurned again.

The voice was much stronger now, but I continued to ignore it, even though I was finally sure that Cornelius was also hearing it. Every time it spoke, he shied and balked, but I walked without considering his discomfort, forcing him to follow me or be left behind in the darkness.

The space between the trees widened, and suddenly the snow ceased falling. The light from my torch expanded to fill the opening, and I saw that I was inside a ring of people. I had stumbled into the "sacred grove" without even knowing it.

The ring was about sixty feet across, and the robed figures moved to close it behind me as soon as I passed the edge. Each of the former townsfolk I'd been sent to find was present, along with at least a dozen others, probably from other villages in the region. They all wore cloaks that were the same crimson as Not-Alana's, and, as they lifted their arms to the sky, their sleeves fell, revealing lines of ancient runes branded into the flesh of their forearms that glowed with a faint, green light.

The priest from the desecrated shrine stood in the center of the circle. He had obviously been the first to succumb to whatever primal spirit inhabited this place; his eyes were black pools in his head, and the tips of his fingers sported thick, black claws. He smiled at me, showing a mouth full of flesh-tearing teeth.

Next to the priest was a small, dead tree. It was no more than four feet tall, twisted and blackened, with a network of tough roots that lifted the bole off the ground, forming a hollow underneath. Inside that hollow was a freshly extracted human heart. As I watched, it beat once, forcefully, accompanied by a sound like that of an echoing bass drum.

Welcome, Daphne.

The priest's lips pulled back into a deranged rictus as he spoke. "Now, we can begin," he said.

"Glory to the Huntress," the cultists intoned in unison. "Behold her mighty works."

"You are all here because you know a horrible truth," the priest continued. Even possessed, it was obvious that he'd retained the oration skills necessary for his former station. His voice easily reached the edges of the circle with all the emotion and fire necessary for a good sermon. "The god you have put your faith in is a lie. There is no Creator. The Visage is a deceiver. A fraud.

It did not save you from the monsters of the mountain; it enslaved you. It enslaved you to labor. It enslaved you with houses of stone, and it enslaved you with tools of iron. Tools with which you have built your own shackles. But, in beholding the Huntress, you will be freed."

"Behold the resplendence of the Huntress," the others chanted. "Behold her power. Behold her grace."

The priest turned fully to face me. "Poor Daphne," he said. "You know best the gnawing of those chains. You, alone among us, have something to compare them to."

Come forward and behold me, Daphne.

Above me, in the tops of the trees, the wind still howled, and I could see the blizzard filling the sky with its fury. Down in the grove, however, the air was still, and not a single snowflake dared defy the creature that spoke to me. To all of us.

I hesitated, then took a step forward.

"The pain you must feel," the priest went on, trying and failing to make his horrific smile look sympathetic. "You were cruelly rejected, cast aside… found wanting. You were given a taste of freedom once before, but have been shackled again. Forced to live alone, after so deeply connecting with a kindred spirit. Forced to face the terror of indecision, of doubt, of purposelessness. Tell me now if I speak falsely! Tell us: is this true?"

"It's true," I said in a strained monotone as I slowly walked closer to the center of the ring.

The cultists gave a unified, theatrical gasp, as if in a stage play.

The priest let out a deep, sad sigh. "Alas. Your old master abandoned you. His standards were too high. But the Huntress is kinder! The Huntress is freer with her love!"

"Submit to the Huntress," the cultists recited together. "Submit to the command of nature."

You will never be alone again, Daphne.

The priest gestured to the twisted little tree beside him. "Come forth, Daphne. Do not resist the call of freedom. You deserve to be free once more. Bow to the Huntress; swear yourself over her holy heart."

I took a step towards the tree, conscious that my feet were moving without my full consent. The heart beneath it beat again, and the drumbeat echoed through the forest.

"Come forth and bow before the Huntress!" the priest shouted.

Bow to me, Daphne.

I stopped in front of the tree. I stared at it, at its charred branches, at its tangled roots, and at the heart stored safely inside it.

Bow to me, Daphne!

An enormous weight slammed down onto my shoulders, and my knees bent, but I forced myself to remain standing. With a great effort, I straightened my legs again and stared at the tree in defiance.

Bow to me, Daphne!

A disc of green light exploded from the tree, radiating out like waves in a disturbed pond. It washed over me, commanding me to submit, but I kept my feet. It traveled to the edge of the ring, and the cultists fell to their knees when it touched them, their chants giving way to frightened wailing.

Daphne, you will bow to me!

Another burst of power rushed from the tree, and, again, I resisted. Behind me, Cornelius trembled, then bent his front legs, putting his knees to the earth and lowering his head.

"Traitor," I grumbled. He didn't respond.

BOW TO ME!

The power crashed over me like a waterfall, followed by the horrific sound of creaking wood. From the corner of my eye, I could see the trees in the grove warp, their trunks slowly moving into graceful sideways-U-shaped curves at the base, lowering their boles to the ground in supplication.

The heart in the tree beat again, even more loudly than before, and the Mark of the Exiled Prince on my spine felt like it had been written in acid.

I closed my eyes.

Then I knelt.

The priest smiled. "See? Once Marked, the craving for freedom will overcome any stubbornness. Now, swear yourself to the Huntress."

I turned my head to look at him.

"My old master didn't reject me," I said, with long-practiced impassivity. "I kicked him out."

The priest's eyebrows lowered as he tried to understand where I was going with this. I gripped the torch in both hands and brought it close to my face.

"And a noble of the House of the Velveteen Darkness is much more powerful than some commoner forest spirit ."

I thrust the torch into the hollow underneath the blackened tree. The priest lunged forward to stop me, but he was too late; the heart inside beat rapidly, in panic, before being engulfed in fire. A hideous shriek rose from the tree, an unceasing sound that carried far into the night, far enough to echo back from the mountain peaks.

The priest's black eyes burst into flames. Then the eyes of the cultists, each in turn, did the same. Their agonized howls joined the tree's in a cacophony of noise. The priest fell into the snow, his body consumed from the inside out; I watched as the flames tore him apart from within, licking from his mouth and ears. His hair burned, and his skin blackened like paper as the flames spread across his body.

I watched the weak-willed reverend and his weak-willed flock burn until they were nothing more than piles of ash.

And I felt nothing.

I had a lot of practice in feeling nothing. It was the only way to overcome the fear and the doubt, the hope and the anger. It was the only way to overcome the lies.

The heart gave one last, faint throb, and the green light pulsed again, this time into the sky. The blizzard above me absorbed it, and the storm weakened as if mollified by the sacrifice.

Only when the flames were finished dining on their unworldly and mortal fuels did I stand again. The trees remained bent, though their heads hung in shame at their deeds, and falling snow finally began to penetrate the grove. I walked over to Cornelius and gave him a sharp upward tug on his bridle. He got to his feet, looking properly chagrined, or at least as chagrined as a mule could look.

"Come on, scaredy cat," I said. "It's a good thing I didn't expect you to have my back."

Cornelius snorted and pawed at the ground.

"Apology accepted. I'm sure you'll do better next time."

I was pretty sure he wouldn't. But I didn't keep him around for his bravery.

I lit another torch, and we left the sacred grove. The going was slower on the way out now that no local spirits were drawing me forward. I was exhausted, and I hoped to find another overhang, or something similar, to serve as the night's shelter. I was just about to leave the path to check the cliffs for caves when I heard a pathetic cry for help. It was the voice of Not-Alana, now properly Praefectus Minor Alana again.

I adjusted my course to meet her, and I found her clinging to a tree, blood flowing freely from the places in her skull where her eyes used to be. Her skin was hot and blistered, but she had survived the burning of the spirit inside her, though she would never again see the moon's light.

"Help me…" she croaked, her throat and tongue raw.

"You wouldn't help yourself when you had the chance," I said indifferently. "Why should anyone help you now?"

I turned away from her and resumed my walk, then noticed that Cornelius wasn't following. I looked over my shoulder at him, and he met my eyes with a stern glare.

"No," I said. "I don't care. Don't look at me like that."

Cornelius stamped the ground and shook his head. He snorted loudly, then walked over to Alana and gently leaned against her. Alana released the tree and carefully gripped his coat before lowering her burned face into his mane and sobbing.

"Fine," I sighed. "Fine."

I didn't keep Cornelius around for his bravery; I kept him around for his ability to display compassion. An ability that had been stolen from me long ago.

Listen to the mule, Daphne.

Did that voice come from my mind? Or from the remnants of the Huntress? For all I knew, it had come from Cornelius; it was impossible to be sure. A decade of possession meant those lines would never become unblurred.

I returned to Alana and gently lifted her onto Cornelius's back.

PRACTICAL APPLICATIONS OF FUNGAL BIOREMEDIATION

H.V. PATTERSON

"Bioremediation!" Paul enthused, waving his arms and almost hitting a tree. "It will save us all."

I should have my phone out to record everything this wide-eyed idealist was telling me like a good journalist. But I hadn't slept in almost twenty hours, and between the bumpy landing in Fairbanks and the lurching jeep ride which had dumped us in the heart of the taiga, I could barely plod along, dodging spruce trees, wondering idly about ticks as I brushed past horsetails.

As I'd assured my worried mom, the boreal forest in late spring wasn't like the bleak winter of the Arctic circle, that place which had swallowed countless, foolhardy explorers. All this growth, all this life, all this sunlight—it was surreal. Birdsong flitted from the trees—mostly spruce mixed with birch, horsetails, and riots of bushes and plants I didn't recognize.

"Look!" Paul stopped so abruptly that I ran into him.

I rubbed my cheek and looked where he pointed. A small copse of dirty-white birch trees stood out like ghosts against the blue sky. Paul gestured above our heads at a blackened growth protruding from one birch's trunk. I knew that trees could get cancer and infections, but I'd never seen anything like this. It looked like burnt charcoal.

"*Inonotus obliquus*, more commonly known as the chaga mushroom," he said.

I'd researched fungi before this job. It'd been surprisingly interesting—and complicated. I'd learned that fungi weren't just the mushrooms you found at the grocery store. They ranged in size from microscopic molds to the humongous honey mushroom in the Malheur National Forest in Oregon, thought to be the largest living organism in the world. I'd learned how integral fungi, with their mycelial networks, were for plant health and communication. Beneath our feet, fungal hyphae linked together the trees, the bushes, in a single, vast, ecosystem.

But I'd never seen a mushroom that crouched like a blight on a tree.

"Chaga has been used throughout the world— in the Northern climes of North America, Europe, Asia—in medicine," he said. "Isn't that remarkable?"

"Is it hurting the tree?"

"They are parasitic," he conceded. "A lot of fungi are. Some even switch between being parasitic or free living, depending on resource availability. They really are remarkably adaptive."

He started hiking again, expounding about how fungi were responsible for everything good and useful in the world from gourmet dishes to penicillin.

"If fungi are so great, why haven't we already harnessed their power to solve our pollution problems?" I asked. Too pointedly, but I was so, so tired, and the forest seemed to stretch forever.

"It's complicated," Paul said. "Real life doesn't have the controlled, ideal conditions of the lab. But we've had promising results with *Aspergillus plasticophage!*"

He stepped into a boggy clearing. When I followed, my feet sank into moss-covered ground, and I was grateful that Mom had bought me high-quality hiking boots. I saw tents, supplies, boxes of field sampling kits, and sturdy laptops displaying indecipherable columns of numbers piled at the edge of the clearing. We'd finally reached the site.

"Aspergillus…doesn't that infect humans?" I asked. "My mom's friend had some sort of lung infection from aspergillus."

"This species is more interested in synthetic polymers than epithelial lung tissue," said a voice to my left.

I whirred around. Another man stood there, leaning against a trunk, half-hidden by shadow.

"Welcome to camp," he said, unfolding his massive frame. "I'm Dr. Austin Slater. Call me Austin."

"Lex Chambers, call me Lex," I answered.

Paul gestured to the other side of the campsite. "Come see the pit!"

"The Pit. Ominous," I said. "Wait, I should record this. We can do an initial interview." They watched me pull off my backpack and roll out my aching shoulders. I was painfully conscious of every second it took for my exhausted fingers to fumble open my bag and grab my phone.

"No service," I sighed as I unlocked the screen.

"There's a satellite phone," Paul said. "We're not as far from civilization as you'd think."

"Yes, the world is small and growing smaller," Austin agreed, stepping closer to me. Standing too close, looming, shifting restlessly from foot to foot. "We live practically on top of each other, stewing in our own pollution."

I pretended to fiddle with my screen. There was something disconcerting about these men. Paul was intense, and though I'd just met Austin, he seemed on edge. This was the kind of gut feeling my mom always told me to pay attention to. But, even if I could leave without tanking my already precarious career prospects, chances were good I'd lose the trail and wander through the boreal forest, mocked by spruce on all sides.

You're just tired, I told myself.

I hit record and gave the scientists my most professional smile.

"Please introduce yourselves, and tell us about the project," I said.

"I'm Dr. Paul Bone, and I specialize in fungal genomics."

"I'm Dr. Austin Slater, and I study prehistoric fungi," Austin said. "We're founders of Myco Remediation Technologies. Our goal is to reduce waste through fungal bioremediation."

"And can you tell us what fungal bioremediation is?" I asked.

"Bioremediation is the process of using environmentally friendly methods to break down toxins and waste in our environment, as opposed to simply burying them and pretending they aren't there," Paul said. "Fungal bioremediation is simply harnessing the amazing powers of fungi to clean up the planet."

Paul herded me deeper into the boggy clearing.

"Time to see the pit!" he said.

The pit was a twenty-by-ten-foot rectangular hole gouged into the soft soil, filled to the brim with plastic detritus: children's toys, plastic bottles, indiscernible pieces of industry. An unpleasant, musty odor wafted from the pit. I didn't know if it emanated from the old plastic, the *Aspergillus plasticophage*, or the disturbed earth.

I narrated what I saw to my phone, trying not to let unease or judgment filter into my voice, trying to be the neutral observer I'd been trained to be.

"It's only about ten feet deep," Paul said. "With the warming temperatures, the ground isn't stable. There's potential for sinkholes, and our ground engineer advised us not to go deeper."

"These are all different types of plastic," I said. "Are you saying that *Aspergillus plasticophage* eats all of this?"

"I'm not just saying, look!"

Paul pointed at small dots which dusted the plastic. They looked more like dirt than tiny colonies of mold.

"After Austin discovered *Aspergillus plasticophage*, I sequenced its genome, and compared it to species in the GlobalFungi database," Paul said. "It's very similar to a mushroom called *Aspergillus tubingensis*, a strain of which is known to break down polyester polyurethane."

"Which is?" I interjected. "For the average person."

"It's found in a lot of plastics, and it's not readily biodegradable—it doesn't break down naturally in the environment." Paul explained. "So, I took some of the genes from *tubingensis*, as well as genes from other species known to break down different types of synthetic polymers under the right conditions, and I spliced them into the *Aspergillus plasticophage* we recovered from the environment, creating the promising hybrid variant we're currently working with."

He beamed at me.

"Well, that…sounds…" I hesitated. In truth, it sounded bad. I felt the same frisson of unease I'd experienced when Chat GPT started spitting out articles which read like human-written ones. "So, this is a newly discovered mold?"

"Yes," Austin said. "As the permafrost melts, we're discovering all kinds of organisms. We found *Aspergillus plasticophage* on a field expedition three years ago about 250 miles north of here."

"It just seems impossible," I said, "like something out of science fiction."

Austin shrugged. "Science fiction is based on science fact."

"I've read that there are all kinds of potentially dangerous pathogens which might emerge from the permafrost," I said. "Are you concerned about *Aspergillus plasticophage?*"

"Absolutely not," Paul said.

"It's always good to practice caution," Austin hedged. "Global warming could potentially unleash microbes our immune systems have no experience with."

"So, walk us through the process of why we're here, at the edge of a bog in the middle of the boreal forest near Fairbanks?" I asked. "Aren't there easier places to run tests? Places that are more contained. I noticed that you don't have any barriers to prevent the *Aspergillus plasticophage* from spreading."

"It only consumes plastic," Paul said. "I assure you I have complete control. Everything is set up exactly as we want it to be."

"We think this biome, with its moisture and protective tree cover, most closely mimics the environment the unmodified *Aspergillus plasticophage* lived in, tens of thousands of years ago," Austin added. "We're hoping that these conditions will allow it to flourish, as it did in the lab."

"So far, results are promising!" Paul cut in. "If field tests go well, the next challenge will be getting investors onboard for large-scale remediation projects."

"Why would you have trouble getting funding?" I asked. "It seems like an obvious solution."

"Humanity is very short-sighted," Paul said angrily. "We've found plastic at the bottom of the ocean, and microplastics in our blood, so we know the threat is real. But it's always a bureaucratic nightmare to implement widespread changes. If we weren't so hindered by entrenched lobbyists in Congress and corporations only interested in their bottom line, we wouldn't be in such a mess! That's why Austin and I dumped our life savings into this start-up. There simply isn't time to go through all the tiresome hoops and trials and endless, replicable experiments universities and governments require before they'll give you a scrap of funding!"

There was a lot there to dissect in Paul's rant, but I didn't know where to proceed. I glanced at Austin, but he just looked annoyed and restless, like he'd heard this all before. I decided to steer us back to the science.

"Can you tell me a little bit more about the gene-splicing process?" I asked.

Paul complied, and I nodded as if I understood while he blathered away, grateful for my recording app.

After wrapping up the initial interview, the rest of the evening passed quickly. I was briefed about safety: how to bear-proof supplies, use the satellite phone. I asked about protective equipment, but Paul said everything but wearing gloves when directly handling samples was unnecessary. That seemed unsafe, but he was the expert. I decided to take his word for it. We had a mediocre dinner, and I crawled into my tent before ten.

I pulled my sleep mask over my face and fell into a nightmare almost immediately.

I waded through the pit, reaching for spruce branches dancing just out of reach. No matter how much I struggled, pushing past old tires, disposable cups, and children's toys, I never got any closer to the edge. Then something grabbed me, and I was sinking into the mire.

An owl hooted, like the ghost of a dying world. A musty, wet smell crawled into my nostrils, the breath of whatever terrible creature was dragging me into the boggy ground. Plastic closed over my head, blocking out the sky. I scrambled against the darkness, sinking deeper and deeper down—

I awoke and struggled to sit up. The ground had grown lumpy and treacherous. The smell from my dream had followed me into the real world. An owl hooted again: a warning. The hazy light of early dawn surrounded me.

I was lying in the pit.

I'd had a few episodes of sleepwalking as a kid. I thought I'd grown out of it, but how else could I have ended up here? I flexed everything carefully. Apart from some soreness, nothing seemed hurt or broken.

Embarrassment flooded me. I couldn't let the scientists see me like this. This was the sort of unprofessional behavior which tanked a career before it started. And then, I'd have to move back in with Mom and endure her sympathetic I-told-you-sos. Though, maybe it wouldn't be so bad, to be home, sleeping in my childhood bedroom, smelling the safe, comforting smells of aging carpet, cinnamon, and lavender.

I propped myself against the remnants of a kid's slide, the once-vibrant red drained of color by time. My bare hand pressed against something soft. The musty smell intensified. I yanked my hand back with a cry.

The slide was covered in a layer of soft fuzz. *Aspergillus plasticophage.* Before my eyes, the slide sagged inward. Which was impossible. Mold didn't grow that quickly.

I wiped my hand on the thick jacket I'd worn to bed. It tingled. I rubbed again, and a sharp sting cut through the tingling.

A pinkish-red line slashed across my palm. It was shallow, like any of the hundreds of annoying cuts I'd accumulated over my life. Dread fell over me like a pall. A cut in the vulnerable armor of my skin. I inhaled sharply. Was I breathing in spores? Paul had said it was safe, but every instinct in my body was on high alert.

No, I was being ridiculous. It was plastic-eating mold. I worked my way cautiously to the edge. I had to climb on top of the plastic detritus and stretch to reach the edge and pull myself out. It was like the pit had sunk a few feet overnight.

I glanced toward the other tents but saw no sign of movement. The scientists were still sleeping. I crept back to my tent and cleaned my hands aggressively with sanitizer. My face and neck, too, for good measure. I was too keyed up to sleep, and my phone said it was six in the morning anyway, so I pulled on my boots and gloves and wandered over to the cooking supplies with the vague notion of making coffee. Anything to take my mind off the way my hand throbbed, like a brand.

A scream cut through the early morning followed by thrashing sounds. I froze, staring into the forest. The thrashing grew closer. Paul erupted into the clearing, blood streaking his face, eyes wild. Austin followed on his heels, a gun glinting in his hand.

"Lex!" Paul panted when he saw me. "Help! He's crazy!"

Austin looked crazy. His mouth was pulled into a tooth-baring rictus. Utter rage filled every inch of his considerable frame.

My instincts screamed at me to run, to hide, to do something, but I couldn't move.

"Stay there, Lex," Austin said, voice steady. His eyes remained locked on

Paul. "I know how this looks, but he's the dangerous one."

"Liar!" Paul interjected.

"You woke up in the pit, Lex," Austin said, eyes still locked on Paul. It was a statement, not a question. "So did I. He drugged us and put us there. He exposed us to the *Aspergillus plasticophage*."

"It's not like that," Paul said, inching closer to me. "I inoculated you."

"Don't move!" Austin snapped.

Paul froze a few feet away.

"Inoculation?" I muttered. I had a vague sense of the word. Something to do with vaccines and preventive medicine.

"Inoculation!" Austin bit the word out, each syllable a curse. "This isn't inoculation. This is experimentation… infection!"

"We're scientists!" Paul said.

"We were wrong!" Austin's hand shook, and I realized that he wasn't just angry; he was afraid.

"*Aspergillus plasticophage* is the solution to all our problems," Paul said. "It will cleanse the world of its plastic pollutants—and it can cleanse us, too! All those microplastics in our veins, those polymer pollutants offloaded from mothers to their children during breastfeeding… *Aspergillus plasticophage* will consume it all!"

"That's not possible," I said, voice wobbling. I only vaguely understood how plastics were made and broken down, but it only took a quick Google search to realize that there were dozens of plastics, all of them structurally different.

But then I remembered the pit, the way the mold had covered a bewildering variety of waste.

Austin gasped. The hand holding the gun wobbled, then dropped. He clutched his chest and sank, slowly, to his knees. "What…"

"Ah, yes," Paul said, shoulders relaxing. "I wondered how *Aspergillus plasticophage* would react to your pacemaker. They use polyurethane in cardiac leads," he told me as he stepped forward and picked up Austin's gun. "Lex, please get the satellite phone."

"Don't," Austin panted as he slumped forward, body going slack, settling into the muddy, giving earth. "I changed my mind. We can't let it…"

"It's too late. You know that," Paul said, smiling. "It's in the soil, riding the mycorrhizal network through the taiga, and beyond. It's a new dawn, Austin. A beautiful, new dawn." He looked at me again. "The phone, Lex."

The gun twitched in his hand. It grabbed the phone. Its weight was comforting, more solid than my thin smartphone. But its casing was plastic. Would the mold swallow it, too?

Austin moaned, eyes fluttering, chest heaving. Paul stood over him, eyes gleaming. I'd thought he was a bit much when I met him, a zealot for mycology, a scientist treating the world like his lab. But he was far more dangerous than I'd realized.

Austin's pacemaker. The slide in the pit. The satellite phone, the zipper holding my jacket closed—my jacket itself. I squinted down at myself. Were those dots of mold, or dirt? There were synthetic fibers in everything. The world was full of plastics. They kept our machinery running, kept people alive, kept the economy humming along. The cost was terrible, but what would the cost be if *Aspergillus plasticophage* spread? Could we survive having the microplastics eaten out of us? What if it mutated? I wished I'd paid more attention earlier when Paul had yammered away about gene splicing.

"Lex?" Paul held out a hand. "Give it here, please. I'll call for help, and then we'll sit down and have an interview, an exclusive! You'll be famous: the one breaking the story."

"What about Austin?" I asked.

"There are always casualties, aren't there?" Paul said. "And, how much better to suffer in the service of something meaningful! So few people get to do anything meaningful with their lives." He took the phone with his free hand and gestured to my tent with the gun. "Go get your phone for the interview."

My mouth soured with fear, with anger. I felt dizzy. Was that the *Aspergillus plasticophage*, burning through my body, nibbling on all the pollutants it found?

"I lost it," I said.

"What?"

"I sleep with my phone when I'm in the field." The lie unfolded easily. After all, it was what many journalists did, especially in dangerous areas.

"When I woke in the pit, it was gone. It must've fallen out of my pocket."

Paul sighed and shook his head, like I was a child who'd failed a basic assignment.

"Fine. We'll use my phone."

He turned away, and I lunged, knocking him over.

The gun fell from his hand and spun away, over the edge of the pit. The satellite phone fell next to Austin's inert body.

Paul tried to get up, but I jumped on his back, pressing him into the soggy ground.

"Just what do you hope to accomplish with this?" He said as he lurched beneath me. Soon, I was the one on my back, panting, as Paul stared at me with wounded eyes. "Don't you understand?" he asked, sincerely surprised. "Don't you want to be part of something bigger than yourself?"

His hands wrapped around my throat, holding firmly, but not pressing. Not yet. The pit was so close. I could smell the mold, hungrily feasting.

Then Austin rose from the ground like a spirit of vengeance and knocked Paul off.

"You're not a scientist, you're a madman," Austin gasped, face covered in a sheen of sweat. He teetered, barely conscious.

"You—" Before Paul could continue, I shoved him into the pit. I reached out to grab Austin, but before I could, he fainted and toppled in after Paul.

I crawled to the slick edge and looked down. Paul was pinned beneath Austin's dead weight, and the two of them were disappearing into the plastic-riddled mire. As I watched, the whole pit shuddered and sank. I couldn't see individual pieces of plastic waste anymore; there was just a sea of rippling fuzz. Paul called my name and reached for me. I didn't reach back. He sank deeper and deeper as the boggy ground gave out. Five feet, ten feet, twenty feet.

The muddy edge of the pit buckled beneath me. I crept backward on my hands and knees, ignoring Paul's faint sobs, pausing only to grab the satellite phone. I didn't stop until I hit a birch tree. I looked up, and saw a lump of charcoal, bulging tumorlike from the healthy trunk. Chaga. I kicked the tree, imagining the chaga falling to the ground, the birch free of its parasite, thriving. A boreal owl hooted angrily at me and flew away on silent wings.

The chaga didn't budge.

I flopped onto my back, cradling the satellite phone against my chest and staring through the latticework of branches.

This was supposed to be a relatively easy assignment. I'd expected to rough it a little, record scientific ramblings, and write a flattering article filled with hope for the future.

"I'm only twenty-four," I said to the indifferent taiga. "I'm not a scientist! I don't know what to do."

I touched my jacket. It was fuzzy in places. There was a smudge on the smooth casing of the satellite phone. I could try to push back the sour fear, try to deny what was happening, but I'd be lying to myself.

I could sit here and watch the mold eat away my clothes and disintegrate the phone in my hands until only metal remained. I could watch the tents and the majority of our camping gear vanish. It was a seductive idea, doing nothing. After all, if Paul was to be believed, it was already too late. *Aspergillus plasticophage* was loose in the world.

I could try to follow the trail back to the jeep. I could return to Fairbanks and fly home, pretending that everything was fine—until it wasn't. That was how so many horror movies started, wasn't it? Someone in denial, ignoring danger.

Why didn't I listen to Mom? If I'd majored in something like accounting, I wouldn't be here. I pictured another reality where my days were boring, where nothing I did really mattered, where I was completely ignorant of science or ecology.

Above me, the sky grew brighter. Songbirds sang, a riot of melodies. The trees swayed gently, blurring as my vision swam with tears. The crisp scent of spruce cut through the musty, unpleasant smell rising from the pit—and from me.

Maybe no one would believe me. Maybe they would, and the whole world would come together. Maybe it was already too late. But I had to try. I'd call emergency services soon. But first, I dialed a number I'd known by heart since I was five. I held the satellite phone close to my ear and waited, desperately yearning for my mom's voice.

RULES FOR SEEKING ANGELS

LB WALTZ

1. Begin your journey at twilight, when the sky is the color of blood.
They will not demand a sacrifice then.

There is something Pentecostal about the fireflies, their eerie glow and strung suspension.

You have never seen fireflies before. Not live. It has always been too cold. But here they are, here they glimmer: weaving through the spruces like spirits, fading in and out like ghosts. They blaze—brighter, brighter—as the rest of the world fades away, the last of the day's light hemorrhaging along the horizon.

It only occurs to you belatedly that, perhaps, they are not true fireflies.

At least, not as once you knew fireflies to be.

Sunset drips in baptismal scarlet down your temple. Its gore leaves smears across your features, blurring the edges of your lips and the corners of your eyes. Your hands are stained a translucent red.

Praise be to the gloaming. It does well to hide transgressions.

Beyond and above, the treetops sway, a gruesome patina speared to their outermost needles. Their shine reminds you of entrails.

Expressionless, you venture into the darkness that they gatekeep.

2. Your rosary is offensive. Do not wear it.

THERE IS NOT much left to wear.

How strange it is to think, now, about the clothing that once glutted the thrift stores, grime-soft and salt-stained and bunched as closely as intestines. It staggers the mind to remember the outfits displayed in the malls: the flawless tops, the factory-stitched bottoms, the intimates as uniform in their creation as the mannequins that they decorated.

Plastic was supposed to last for centuries. That was the problem with it. Biodegradables were better, everyone said; recyclables would save the world.

Ironic, then, that those synthetic fabrics would be the first to go: to crumble into gray sands and float away on the breeze.

Ashes to ashes, dust to dust. In your nightmares you watch, over and over and over, as everything vanishes in a singular, smoky plume, modernity reduced to nihility by an awesome flash.

Well. The news stations were right about that part, anyway, if not the bit about the mushroom cloud. Or the fallout. They did not guess the enemy correctly, either.

No one guessed the enemy correctly.

Inexpertly cobbled leather sandals are hardly ideal for traipsing through the woods, but they are better than no shoes at all. The wool is cumbersome. Scratchy and heavy, though ultimately preferable to nakedness. Your two-dollar rosary is your second-to-last possession, and the only accessory you had deemed worth saving.

When all of this began, people believed that rosaries would help. What a bizarre fad that had been.

Bizarre and useless.

As they were with the mushroom cloud, and the fallout, and the enemy, the people had been wrong. Frankly, you have started to wonder if it is possible to get anything about this right.

You remember the Rules and you hope so.

3. The stream that you pass has been Blessed.
Resist drinking from its depths.

FOR THE FIRST time in—days? Weeks? Months?—an age, your mind drifts to a secular place.

There is an allusion here, a parallel that you might draw to grim stories of a different ilk. Ancient fables about children and their run-ins with the supernatural. The use of breadcrumbs. Of white pebbles.

Although you know better than to wear your rosary, you do not have the heart to toss it. Instead, you snap its worn thread and gather its beads. They roll in your fist, clicking together, each imperfect dodecahedron made slippery by palm sweat.

Imperfect.

Even now—days, weeks, months, an age later—the condemnation resounds. You hear it echo in a hundred-thousand voices: bouncing against the chambers of your skull, caught within the pores of your skin. *Insulting, pagan ritual. One of many golden calves, oh, ye have all sinned a great sin.*

So.

You know better than to wear your rosary. Much, much better. But this loop of baubles and waxen string was a gift from someone who loved you, someone who thought they were helping. Someone who tried to keep you safe. You want to honor that sentiment, if nothing else.

And in truth, there is nothing else.

Gingerly, carefully, you set a bead atop the serpentine curve of a root. It is but one part of the living nest that has wound itself inextricably together, soundlessly slinking, making a den of the forest floor; you must pick over an endless snarl of ouroboroses before you are able to find a suitable home for the next.

A stump. It seems appropriate. Low to the ground, but still a sort of perch. Its wood is black in a way that the night is not. Victim of a lightning strike, maybe? Luminescent moss reflects the last, plasmatic vestiges of that light, projecting it onto the bottoms of gathered cloudberries. Spores swirl, their starry spangles redolent of what had bedecked the heavens, once upon a time.

There is the thought of thrones as you place the next bead. Thrones, and infernos, and wheels.

And bones.

Children's?

No.

Beyond the stump, you notice the ground slope, pitching downward to meet a winding slip of river. It gurgles, its current mercurial in the gloom. Even from your sanctuary within the trees, you feel the ice that wafts off its waves: the chill that radiates from its silvery surface.

You can see, too, what has been gilded in that silver.

The bone framework of a doe.

Beyond the pure-white gleam of its carcass, there are the perfect, purified remains of a coyote family, a fox. Innumerable rodents. A young bear, its fur and organs gone, but its skeleton pristine.

Mandibles beget ripples where they touch the shallow water.

I will sprinkle clean water on you, you hear again, ringing as tinnitus inside your inner ear, *and you shall be clean from all your uncleannesses, and from all your idols I will cleanse you.*

You wonder how long it took.

You wonder if this is what a miracle looks like.

You wonder about the radiance—the pale, pale haze—that allows you to see any of this at all. The necropolis is ashine with that incandescent miasma; its seeping, evanescent spirals are cold enough to scorch. It floods from the cracks that have exposed the animals' marrow.

You walk on.

4. Should you hear cicadas, join their worshipful song.

IT IS INSTINCT to look up, even when doing so is pointless.

Darkness is consuming the sky, details incinerated like a painting that has been held too close to flames. High above, a swath of luxurious violet curdles into ianthine, blisters into aubergine, before being seared into something richer, deeper, and far more charred than any purple once associated with royalty. Bifurcating branches break the heavens into fractals of color, their tangles forming a tenebrous craquelure.

Amongst those shards, it is impossible to see what clings to the bark.

"Let all mortal flesh keep silence,
and with fear and trembling stand;
ponder nothing earthly-minded,
for with blessing in his hand,
Christ our God to earth descendeth,
our full homage to demand."

You breathe out the lyrics, attempting a vibrato but managing only a quiver. *Embarrassing* is not the word for it. Mortifying? Humbling? Though you are able to carry a tune, you are not nearly so mellifluous as the harmony that hums beneath the canopy, thrumming through its offshoots as blood does through veins.

Egregore, you think before you can stop yourself. A hive, a swarm. Vacated, chitinous husks. Memories scratch at the base of your brainstem, using a hundred-thousand insectoid legs to crawl out of that loose soil.

You force each one back down. Bury them. Or, at least, hide them between the graves. Symbolism is an earthly-minded thought, and dammit, you will ponder no such thing.

"At his feet the six-winged seraph,
cherubim, with sleepless eye,
veil their faces to the presence,
as with ceaseless voice they cry,
'Alleluia, alleluia,
alleluia, Lord Most High…'"

The intensity of the cicadas' performance makes your fingertips buzz, threatening to turn your guts to strings. Foliage claps an accompaniment to the minor chord being played on your ligaments.

What is a group of cicadas called, anyway? A cacophony? A chorale?

A chorus.

Only then does it occur to you to wonder: should you be louder than them? Quieter? Did you choose the right hymn? For how long must you sing? These seem like such obvious questions, in retrospect; how could you forget to ask? Why were the instructions not clearer?

Did you miss something? Part of a rule? A full one, even? You know of eleven, but maybe there are supposed to be twelve. Thirteen? More?

Or maybe—just maybe—there are no rules. Maybe—just maybe— the list relayed to you by the apocalypse's initial survivors is less like the Commandments and more like the rosaries. Human folly: rumors and hearsay and blatant lies all tossed into a trial of fire, and from its tongues came something golden.

Hope.

You do hope.

With every ounce of your being, you hope that you will—

5. If you smell apple blossoms, run.

THE PERFUME REACHES you before the whispers, but only by a moment.

"Yours…?" "Yours…?" "Yours…?"

Soundless, gentle, something collides with your sandal. Had you not already been standing frozen, you would never have noticed. It is small enough to be a pebble. A white pebble. You would have assumed it was exactly that, had its edges not been prismatic.

A rosary bead.

Ommatidial faces glitter, the cheap glass irradiated. It shines, too bright atop the needles carpeting the forest floor, just as you are too exposed betwixt the gnarled, sprawling trees: spruces, firs, pines, larches.

No fruit trees. No apples.

Yet, that floral stench coils into your nostrils like rot, as heady as it is overwhelming. You are submerged in its sweetness, the odor so pervasive that your respiratory system panics, certain that your body is about to drown.

You flounder, gasping.

"Why did you leave it?" "Why did you leave it?" "What was the point?"

Just beyond your periphery comes the sound of something slithering, its velveteen flesh susurrating over decayed leaves. Pollen threatens to suffocate you, to clog up your throat until you choke; the buckling of your knees reminds you that you still have feet and thus a chance, and you throw yourself physically down the wooded path, away from the stink, before you lose all strength to fear.

But still, you hear the quiet Voice reason:

"You know." "You won't." "Go back."

6. You will lose something from your pocket. It is gone forever.

YOU DO NOT INTEND to stop running; the choice is made for you. By what, you are not certain. A stone, a stick. Fate, possibly. It does not really matter.

Not when the full force of gravity rips the air from your lungs.

The poet Rilke once asked if any higher power might hear a person crying out. Your fall provides a definitive answer.

Supine and dazed, you stare up at the Milky Way.

There are no stars anymore. There haven't been, not for some time. Days? Weeks? Months? An age before an age. They had winked slowly out, every last one, like a hundred-thousand eyes drifting to a close.

Once—oh, it feels like eons ago—someone told you the universe was still young, still expanding, and that after an inestimable number of lifetimes, the night sky would be so full of stars, it would appear encrusted with diamonds. You had wondered how anyone would ever be able to sleep.

No one knew what the stars really were back then.

Does anyone know what they really are now?

"At his feet the six-winged seraph, cherubim, with sleepless eye," you mumble, each phrase gossamer-thin and filled with holes. Gaps where oxygen should be. *"Veil their faces to the presence, as with ceaseless voice they cry…"*

Gradually, your breaths grow deeper. Longer. The pain they spark becomes a smolder, guttering in your chest. When able, you shift your attention to your head: throbbing, but uninjured; your bones: jarred, but unbroken; and your skin: bruised, but without abrasions. Good. You try to focus on your relief, rather than the trickling realization that, had you hurt yourself irreparably, you have no idea what you would have done.

Worse yet, you have no idea if it would have mattered.

If you would have cared.

It is not worth lingering on. The damage you suffered is naught but superficial. There is mud down your back, yes, and a twig has clawed a tear into the side of your loose knit sweater, but beyond that—

But—

Oh.

You need not touch your pocket to know what is missing. A photograph might not be heavy, but a hundred memories, a thousand words, still bear weight.

More so, you discover, after all else is gone.

Unbidden, that smoldering in your chest returns. It is followed by a burn, more intense than anything else you have felt, and your poor eyes ache as its smoke begins to blur your vision. A half-hearted dig through the underbrush reveals nothing but dampness, a spider, and a quarter-eaten worm.

The rosary's misshapen crucifix is your sole possession now.

You are not surprised.

That does not mean you are not heartbroken.

7. *They are watching. They are always watching.*

OF COURSE, the reason the sky is empty is that those things that people once called "stars" all decided to move.

Those are the facts of the matter. There is no question about that.

No, the question isn't if the not-stars had moved, but rather, where those galaxies had gone. Had they simply turned away from the world, having grown weary of their millennia-long sentry? Or had they collectively relocated, choosing for themselves new vantage points with improved views?

You cannot say for sure. No one can. And in honesty, you do not think you want to know.

But for better or for worse, you have noticed this: that while there have always been eyes here on Earth—drawn onto the backs of butterfly wings;

delimited by the shadows of ivy-laden tunnels; created by the depths of small, volcanic lakes; grown into the stained-glass hearts of citrus fruits—never before have there been so many on the trees.

Dead foliage loses its grip on your clothes, falling like molt. You keep the splinters.

You wish you could have kept the photograph.

There are knots in the pine bark, as there always have been. They watch you when you hobble past, sniffling, hunched against the pain. They are almond-shaped, these knots: outlined, dotted in the center. They never blink. You want to say they never move, but you are not sure about that.

Larches stare, too. Their sclerae are gray, their pupils cut branches. Something peers through the ligneous lashes of the spruces and the firs, and you believe it to be sentient.

Praise be to the midnight. It does well to hide your tears.

All the same, you grapple with the unpleasant feeling of nakedness, pulling your wool clothing closer, tighter. Like a shroud.

8. The wind through the grass is a homily. Listen.

BEFORE ALL of this began, you did not spend much time in the forest.

Sure, there was the occasional hike, the rare camping trip, but your day-to-day was squandered in the city, where the most nature you encountered were the ants and the cockroaches and the sad little weeds that struggled to push through the fissures in the pavement.

You had seen maps, though. Had even walked this path, once or twice, before the city and the surrounding terrain had been...

Altered.

Here is a meadow. That this meadow had not previously existed should, at this point, hardly be worth noting, but something about its verdancy gives you pause.

It is so lush. Extraordinarily so. Preternaturally so, you presume, given that each stalk is vibrant enough to cut through the eventide without concern for scientific law: undulant and impossibly visible. Like the fireflies, the fireweed blazes.

You think about that moss. You think about that stream. You think about the ocean, glassy and green, as a breeze brushes unseen fingers over a nearby knoll, creating waves.

Motion pulls from the flowers a sirens' melody. The song resonates in the way that all empty things do.

You stuff a fist into your pocket, if only to fill it with something.

With anything.

You ignore the obvious metaphor.

9. When asked a question, do not answer. They already Know.

WHAT YOU CANNOT ignore is the Voice.

Clear the way in the wilderness; make smooth in the desert a highway. Let every valley be lifted up, and every mountain and hill be made low, It booms in the softest of murmurs.

Alarmed, whirling, you choke out a scream, but cannot hear it over whatever has begun to happen inside of your head.

And let the rough ground become a plain, and the rugged terrain a broad valley; and all flesh will see it together, the Voice continues, shouting in a silent sigh. Consonants and grasses crash in tandem, folding one into the other into the next, while vowels wend with the effortlessness of the late-spring currents.

Its smile can be felt in the tube of your spine, skittering up your nerve endings as a millipede might.

Greetings, favored one.

There is, in a burst, the taste of metal on your lips. Hot, salty, familiar. Eventually, it dawns on you that your nose is bleeding, but by the time you figure this out, you have already touched the flow.

We are so proud of you.

Your hands are red. Again. Your hands are red and the blood is seeping, streaming, pouring like wine. Your ears have started to dribble. You feel light-headed. No, light.

No, Light.

Let there be—

Few people make it to this stage, the Voice reveals in a terrible calm. The meadow is vibrating, its grasses bending. *Your family did not. Nor your friends. They did not wish to be reborn, and so reacted in anger, with grief. Some even tried to bargain their way out of conversion,* It tells you, simultaneously sweet and sneering. Syllables echo between the strands of your DNA, in the hollow of the helix that comprises your most basic parts. Suddenly, you are resonant at an atomic level, and you feel it—you feel it—as the reverberation of Its praise threatens to rip your skin clean off your bones.

But here you are. On your own, you have made it to the end. To 'acceptance.'

There is so much blood. So much. Too much. Is it yours? All yours? Probably. Undoubtedly. The spaces between your particles are fast becoming holes. Holy, holy, holy.

That is why you are here, is it not? You have accepted the call to be a Heavenly Host, It says in tones of such benevolence that your heart constricts in terror. For *oh—You have accepted that life is meaningless. That your soul is empty. That you cannot exist in a world where you are so horribly, unbearably lonely.*

Oh.

You have accepted that this is predestined. That you were always meant to come here. To die here.

There is something—

You have accepted Our Lord Your God as your personal savior. And by His Power, you have accepted that you will live again.

There is something coming out of the trees.

*10. To meet an angel is a transformative experience.
You will be changed.*

YOU CANNOT BREATHE.

You cannot move.

You cannot stop your knees from buckling, and so have no choice but to collapse: to kneel in the puddled remnants of your insides-come-out while fresh heat burbles between your teeth.

There is darkness now. The fireweeds have been smothered. The grass, no longer green, lies crushed beneath you. You, too, have been crushed, but beneath a more existential weight: one that leaves your mind in pieces. Pulled apart, like your rosary.

Presence. Mortal flesh. Fear and trembling. Cry. Veil their face. Hope. A hundred-thousand hopes culled brutally down to one:

You hope not to be alone anymore.

Not anymore.

Not anymore.

What you see in the void before you is too vast to be contained within the narrow confines of a human brain; your understanding of the universe expands in an instant—in a flash—in the manner of an explosive, and your sanity reacts in kind.

Alleluia, alleluia.

Your eyes are too wide for their sockets. They ooze. Its eyes—

The eyes—

A hundred-thousand eyes—on butterfly wings down ivy tunnels under volcanic lakes in citrus fruits upon the trees the trees the looming, sleepless, antediluvian trees...

Our full homage to demand.

Do not fear, coos the Voice, brushing your cheek with those same fingers that move the leaves, and the grasses, and the ever-spinning wheel of existence, *for I have redeemed you; I have summoned you by name; you are mine.*

From where Its flesh touches yours, the scent of apple blossoms blooms.

11. We will all become angels, in the end.

HE HAS NOT SEEN A BIRD BEFORE

SJ TOWNEND

One tree, a metal climbing frame, an empty sand box: this is all that stands in the centre of the brick-walled play space which sits in the centre of the housing development. At night, lit by one flood light, the other lights broken and not repaired, the climbing frame casts a monstrous arachnid shadow over the wall of Caledonian Heights - Block B.

Around the small park, a circle of apartment towers stretch up, flat upon flat upon flat, all the way to the sky. Ms. Theroux tells delivery companies she lives on the seventh floor of the "concrete wedding cake". Up there, on the seventh floor of Caledonian Heights - Block E, young Blake lives with his mother, Ms. Theroux.

BLAKE LOOKS out of the reinforced window of his bedroom. The window does not open, has never opened, for fear of someone falling out or something climbing in. With a chubby index finger, he points at the tree. Today, a tattered bird perches on a skeletal, brown branch, and fills the air with a sorrowful tune. Blake smiles; he is elated. He has not seen a bird before other than on the e-screens which line his play-pen.

"Birdie," he says to himself, sounding out the consonants with his tongue. It is the first time the tree has made the boy happy. The tree is the reason Blake, sometimes, cannot sleep. Blake often cries out for his mother in the night, complains through wet eyes that he senses the tree is watching him.

Blake presses his cheek and eye, against the window in attempt to look closer. "Mumma, tree falling," Blake says, and again, louder, as the creek of a heavy branch is audible through the triple glazed glass. Blake's mother runs from the kitchen to Blake at his window and drags her son away. The boy and the woman fall together onto the toddler-sized mattress as the branch looms towards the building.

"Dear God, no," the woman says, wide-eyed, as the bird, pre-empting what is about to occur, screeches, lifts up from the tree and launches in panic, smacking headfirst into the glass. A dark mark, like a ruddy snow angel, now dirties the pane. Neck broken, the bird's soulless vessel falls to the ground sixty feet below.

The woman's hands cover her child's face, protecting his eyes and skull, as the branch, which is larger than the boy, splits away from the trunk of the old Caledonian pine, instructed by gravity and a rot that has come with age, and thwacks into the blood-stained glass. It all happens so fast. The glass splinters into a silver-white-red cobweb, but, thankfully, the window does not shatter inwards.

"Blake, darling, are you okay?"

She soothes her son, finds his favourite comforter, then carries her babe on her hip through to the living room, away from the damaged window. Here, she places him in his interactive play pen, a walled box from which he cannot climb out, and kisses him on the crown of his head. "Watch some cartoons in your holo-den. Mumma needs to make a phone call."

She finds herself drawn back to the boy's bedroom, to inspect, to bear witness to what has just happened, aware of the sheer nightmare that could have unfurled, and she cries. She has hated the tree ever since they moved in. Pulling the door to her son's bedroom closed, she returns to the kitchen to make her urgent call: something must be done about the dangerous pine in the park, before more blood is shed.

With two firm claps of her hands, the apartment operating system greets her with its duteous tone. "*Good evening, Mrs Theroux. How may I be of service?*"

"Call the building manager," she says.

A dial tone pulses out through the speakers built into the ceiling. With deliberately slowed exhalations, she tries to breathe panic out from her chest and into the clinical void of her kitchen. She drums her fingertips on the stainless-steel kitchen work top and waits for the manager to connect.

HARRISON TOSSES his mobile back into his bag. He has had no reception for three hours, not since he'd first stepped out of the car and into the grey container unit hut, his office for the next few months. It hadn't mattered, the lack of connectivity, when he'd been with his team of surveyors and contractors. They'd snaked after each other through the labyrinthine maze of cramped Scots pines following a hired guide.

The guide had handed out to each of them a paper map of the area, warning them all reception would be lost as they ventured deeper into the noir of the woods, but most of the men had left the sheets behind in the hut, smugness and ego splattered on their middle-aged faces, Harrison's included. This was Harrison's project after all, he was self-appointed deputy lead of the board who'd purchased the vast area of woodland. The blue prints for a luxury housing development destined to provide homes for 10,000 new residents are pinned up on the wall in the hut. He'd studied the technical drawings for weeks prior to setting foot in the Scottish Highlands, knew the future layout of his city-to-be like the back of his hand. Soon all these bastard trees would be building timber. Harrison had stopped to take a leak, nipped off the track for a moment, and on returning to the spot in the forest he'd left his team, he's dismayed to find the group gone. He spins round, desperate to find his crew, only to see trees, shrubbery, a solitary deer which scarpers immediately at the sound of his heel turning in leaf litter, and more trees.

He walks in a straight line, hopeful his feet will lead him out of the forest. Some sort of grouse darts out of nowhere, jolts him, and this spurs him into walking faster. He fastens his jacket and pulls the flaps of his hat over his ears. Despite the shelter the trees provide, there's a chill in the air, a mist descending. The rare, small pockets of already bleak sky which break through the canopy grow dimmer as he walks. Night will fall soon. In his hurry, he trips on a tangle of cream-encrusted, rotting tree roots and hits his head.

"Fucking mushrooms," he says to no one and pulls himself up into a seated position.

"Tooth fungi." A voice. The crimp of white fungus he'd tripped over bleeds red, jam oozes from its myriad gaping pores. "You've damaged it."

Harrison looks around. No one. He looks to the fungus then up again. A one-armed woman looms over him. She takes his hand in hers and helps him onto his feet.

"Thank you," he says. "Sorry about the fungus." Harrison rubs his eyes.

The woman smiles at him, softly, with no anger in her jaw.

Through the mist, he studies her. A member of his team? He squints. Through the impending darkness, a slice of light falls. Her eyes sparkle. Flecks of golden light shimmer from them and scatter around her face, like unfurling galaxies birthing new stars. *I have concussion*, Harrison thinks, *the thin strip of light must be reflecting motes of dust.*

"It will survive," she says. Her smile drops. "But as for the forest—" She lifts her palm, gestures at the trees around her and shakes her head.

Harrison's cheeks rouge. He can't tell the woman he is, in part, responsible for the logging on the forest periphery, for the new roads which connect this patch of nature to an adjacent city in preparation for the people who will spill into the apartments his company will erect over the months which follow. She may turn her back on him, and in this moment, he needs her help.

"Could you direct me to the edge of the forest?" he asks. "The grey hut."

She takes his hand in hers, an intimate act Harrison is not prepared for, and as her cool skin brushes against his palm and her fingers knit with his, a longing pulses in his chest. He can't recall the last time a woman has touched him without some sort of financial exchange.

Together, they walk, run, as she leads him over tumultuous ground, through branches and shrubs. Ribbons of her long autumn-red hair bounce as she strides over rocky pockets and mossy tumps. He does not know who she is, but he knows he does not want to let go of her hand when he sees the hut in the clearing on reaching the edge of the forest.

She stands under the shade of a tall pine and says goodbye, says she will not travel with him any further. Harrison thanks her, wishing more than anything he could spend more time with this woman with firefly eyes. He plucks up the courage and asks, "May I take you out, for something to eat this evening, to thank you for your kindness?"

"No," she says and steps back into the forest, hiding herself from the crowd of men who are just out of earshot, all drunk on cheap bourbon, playing cards around a makeshift table. "I cannot leave."

"Will I see you again?"

"Maybe." She beckons him back towards where she stands and Harrison watches as she plucks out a long black feather from what appears to be a skirt, but may also be her flesh, the tip of its quill crimson with fresh blood. "For you, a piece of forest, a keepsake."

"What is it?" Harrison accepts the feather. It has an iridescent shine to the blade of its vanes.

"Tail feather, caipercaillie," she whispers. Her words of nature are a fresh balm to his ears after months of only hearing about spreadsheets and budgets.

Harrison slides the feather in the pocket of his cargo trousers and as he looks up again, she is gone.

IT IS ALL Harrison can do over the days which follow, think about the red-headed woman with celestial eyes who had led him out of the thick tapestry of mist and trees. He dreams of her, sees her face in the faces of strangers, hears her voice in the night. It is as if she is calling to him as he lies in his hotel bedroom in the nearby city, several miles outside of the forest.

A week later, he ventures back into the woods, with his paper map this time, on a quest to find her. It does not take him long, as if she wants to be found. He finds her leaning up against an alder tree. She is wearing, what looks to Harrison, like a black mourning veil over her face.

She tips her head to the tree as he approaches her and tells him, "alder," then plucks and shows him the heart-shaped, leathery leaves the tree wears in its broad green crown.

He identifies each alder proudly as she draws him deeper into the dark forest, the tree branches wavering slightly overhead, as if sentient.

"Correct," she replies each time, and teaches him "hazel," and "birch". As she names plants, she passes him small branches of each, instructs him to cherish them. He takes the gifts from the mysterious woman and places them in his bag.

Minutes become hours as they glide and weave through the woodland. Harrison wishes she'd hold his hand again, as they walk side by side, as the woman points out tracks left by red deer, a pile of leaves she insists is a hedgehog's nest, a cluster of white creeping lady's tresses in bloom. Eventually, he asks her if he may take her hand in his, and she allows this.

Barefoot, she leads him further, further into the forest, her skirt train of black feathers and twigs trailing behind her, her hair streaming out like unfurled, red ghosts. She stops to point out rowan berries. He asks her if he may kiss her, her lips have become his obsession, are as red as the berries she points out. "These are sour berries," she tells him instead of answering his question. "But waxwing adore them." She shows him waxwing birds, how to locate them up above by their distinct high-pitched trilled *bzeee* and their prominent tuft of head feathers. He smiles when he sights his first, unaided, and later, she lets him kiss her.

After their lips press, Harrison touches her eye veil. Up close, he realises the eye covering is stitched from a dark red thread, not black. "Sac spider webbing," she says as he lifts it from her face. He is shocked, gasps audibly. Her eyes do not sparkle like they did on their first encounter, instead, today, they weep slightly, red. "My tears have stained the webbing." Harrison is taken aback by the crimson which drips from her eye ducts, yet he is still overwhelmed by the enchantment of her beauty.

HE VISITS the woman in the forest again and again, each time learning more about the woods, and less about himself, and always departs with a gift from the lady: posies of lesser twayblade, intermediate wintergreen and twinflower, woven baskets of pine cones, dried leaves filled with juniper and crowberries, a pouch of tooth fungi she says can heal memory loss, anxiety, infected wounds. He takes each gift and thanks her, unsure, embarrassed, as to what he might offer from his world of construction and machinery in exchange.

OVER THE NEXT few weeks, more loggers arrive. A metal army of heavy machinery pitches up on the outskirts of the wood. Harrison fears for his forest lover's habitation. He is too heavily invested financially to withdraw from the development, but has fallen in love with this woman with bleeding eyes. Her eyes see into his soul like no lover has before.

One afternoon, loosened by gin and after a long meeting with colleagues, Harrison finds himself again, walking in the woods. He no longer needs a map. The forest has become smaller. He recognises each tree, each shrub, and uses them to guide himself to her. He finds her. With her one arm, she drapes herself around him, pressing her lips on his. Pushing her hair out of the way, he kisses her neck, works kisses down her arm, lifts up her skirt of feathers and presses his lips and tongue in other places. She wails with pleasure, guides his lips back to her mouth, and unbuttons his trousers. "Is this what you want?" he asks.

"More than anything, yes," she replies, "It is what I need," and she takes guides him inside of her body. Each thrust is exhilarating. Locked in desire, they stumble back until pressing against a sturdy pine. Lost in the moment, eyes closed, faces kiss close, he does not see, or feel the rivulets of vermillion which gush down her inner thighs as they make love.

I'd rather die than stop now, he thinks, the friction of his flesh on hers feels like this is all he was ever meant for. His worries and thoughts unravel and his thighs shudder as he comes.

They lie together in the leaf litter afterwards: him propped up against the tree, her curled, with her head on his lap. Red tears follow the line of her nose and drip-drop between his legs, onto the forest floor. Harrison strokes her hair and realises he does not even know her name.

"It's Nàdair," she says, although he is certain he had not asked.

"Harrison," he replies.

"I know."

Harrison gasps. His cargo trousers are stained dark red, too dark a stain to be due to her bleeding eyes. "Your arm, where you had an arm I mean— The stump of it…it's bleeding."

Nàdair shrugs, reaches for a handful of leaves, and wipes her weeping elbow. Blood continues to trickle out. She is unphased. "It appears I am becoming undone."

Harrison clears his throat, swallowing back the impulse to vomit that'd risen in it. "How did you lose it?"

Nàdair drops eye contact. "Once, I tried to leave the forest," she says. "I do not wish to talk about it." She pulls away from him.

Harrison stands, lifts her up only so he can again pull her in close, then kisses her. Her body feels light, too light, weak in his arms, and her kiss tastes of copper.

Harrison asks if there is anything he can do to help her feel better as his heart floods with guilt. He feels, in some way, responsible for her illness, her constant loss of blood.

"I love you," he says.

"It is time for you to go home," she replies.

On their walk back to the edge of the forest, it is dark so he does not see the additional trail of red which leaks from the soles of her naked feet..

They reach the boundary. *She is pale*, he thinks, *perhaps exhausted from the intimacy.*

From the shelter and shadow of the forest canopy, she tells him, "I will go no further," then presents him with a fallen antler. With sixteen tines and covered in ragged velvet, it is a majestic thing of beauty. Harrison thanks her for the gift, kisses her passionately farewell, and wipes away her red tears.

He carries the antler home in his hands, the beautiful souvenir too large to fit in his bag.

HARRISON STRUGGLES to sleep that night, his nightmares haunted by lost limbs, visions of rutting, eyeless monarch stags, and forests drowning in red. As the sun rises, he realises he must try to halt the final stage of the forest clearance, preserve what is left, but he fears it may be too late to stop the project—deep foundations have already been dug over nine tenths of the purchased land.

AT WORK, from the window of his grey hut, he sees giant, robotic cranes lifting girders, long-wheel-based trucks zooming in to deliver bricks by the tonne every hour, machines with steel teeth: angled, poised, ready to bite. The metal and concrete jungle he had stared at in blue print for so long now nears completion. The project has snowballed out of his control.

HE DECIDES he must visit her immediately, the woman of the forest, to tell her to leave the ecosystem she calls home before automated machinery bullies its way in. He will guide her out, bring her to safety, then teach her there is nothing to fear in the modernised world in which he has grown up. He wants to look after her, marry her if she wishes, but today, she must relocate. A convoy is on route to tear down the last cluster of trees. The loggers have refused to delay this, despite his reasoning and offers of cash. But talk of his descent to madness echoes between the workers.

Harrison marches into the forest, which is now no more than a grove, a copse. Light passes through from one edge of it to the other. It is no longer swamped by the thick canopy-cloak of gloom he had grown to love. A few strides in and he reaches the sentinel pine in which he has so often found his lover leaning against. But today, she is not sat at the bottom. He follows the trunk of the tree up and searches for a glimpse of black and red amongst the branches. He steps back, his face contorted.

Nailed to the tree bark, pulsing, pumping in time with his own, a little larger than the size of his balled fist, he sees a heart. Blood dripping from its pierced core, the heart still thrums. It beats faster as he moves closer, as does his in response. He vomits, narrowly missing his shoes. A noise, from above: the sound of a woman crying. He hears her sob over the angry roar of engines revving and other motorised cutting machinery chomping at the bit. She is there, twenty feet up in the tree, her legs hunched up, her face in her hands.

"Please Nàdair, come down. I tried to get them to stop, to leave you time to say goodbye, pack—"

Through a gap in the forest, the first automated tree feller machine bursts. Its sharp blades churn and spin. Harrison screams at it to stop, but it is unstaffed, controlled by a man in the hut, a mile or so away. Harrison scrambles up the tree and pulls Nàdair over his shoulder. She weighs but a feather. *It is as if her bones are hollow,* he thinks, but as he lifts her, he sees her belly is swollen.

"I can't leave," she says, her voice reedy, weak.

He drags her down from the tree. "You have to."

"It's yours," she says as he places her on the ground. Her hand wraps around her belly protectively. "I cannot leave my tree. It is my heart and I, its." She pushes his head hard, his ear turned in, onto her chest. There is no beat, no repeating push of blood coming from behind where he imagines her ribs must sit.

"I'm the father?" he asks. She does not have time to tell him again.

The blade of the chopping vehicle rams through the wood of the heart-tree's trunk, slicing it, pushing it over. "Quick," Harrison says. He lifts his love and runs with her in his arms to an exposed clearing, a spot already logged, where a scattering of thin forest soil and leaf detritus dusts the ground, and there, he places her gently down.

Nàdair screams, crouches . Her face crumples in agony as she lifts her feathered skirt, reaches up, between her legs, inside of herself, and pulls hard, extracting a large brown seed. She places the seed, covered in blood, into Harrison's shaking palm, folds his fingers around it.

"Our child. Nurture her. Keep her out of the harsh, synthetic light of this new world your people are creating," She falls into his arms, scrunches her eyes closed, screams again, and then her body becomes like dust in his hands.

Harrison sinks to the ground and hits at it hard with his fist, the seed still clamped inside. "No. No." But she is gone. He rips open the top layer of soil with his hands and, afraid the seed may suffer a similar fate as his lover, buries their child in the soil.

HARRISON DOES NOT leave his child. He remains, slightly broken, at the location where the seed is buried. He refuses to move on, despite visits from his team, until they agree to alter the blue prints of the city. The contractors begin to build a wall around him and his buried seed: this place will become a play park for the ghost of his dead lover.

He sleeps there each night, guards the place he buried his seed, his progeny , and lets his tears water the ground. His colleagues, scared for his wellbeing, bring him drinks and food which he barely touches.

Weeks pass. The apartments are complete, a climbing frame and sand pit have been installed in the centre, near Harrison's pitch, for the coming residents to use. Harrison sits tight in his spot, mourning for the woman and their seed , until one day, a solitary green shot pokes up through the top layer of soil.

COUNTLESS PLANT POTS, jam jars, small buckets fill every shelf and each spare space in the rooms of the flat on the eighth floor of Caledonian Heights - Block E. Each vessel is filled with red soil, and from most of the containers, green shoots and tempered cuttings sprout out. Some containers show no visible plant growth, and their soil remains bare to the naked eye, but beneath the soil, expectant pine cone seeds lay snug, drinking down the last of the coppery fluid in which they have been bathed.

Grow lamps shouting out blue and red spectra in all directions dangle from the ceiling. The flat stinks of neglect and manure. Half empty bottles of plant feed and discarded, empty beer cans litter the floor of his internal forest.

In a chair, by the window, an old man lies slumped, his heart having given out the moment the bird in the tree had hit the glass pane of the flat below. Catheters, needled into every available varicosed vein, dangle from the old dead man's black-bruised arms. Plastic tubing drains and dispenses the last of his blood into bottles scattered around his feet.

A coffee table is pushed up against a wall, and on it, several razor blades glint in between curled slices of long-yellowed skin—an attempt at grafting his own flesh to the bark of his babies had been the last project he had undertaken. In his lap, a long black feather, posies of dried flowers, and a large antler rest.

Speakers embedded into the ceiling of his luxury flat boom out their message, again and again, "*Ms. Theroux, floor seven, wishes to connect. Do you accept?*" but he is gone, and will not ever answer.

The sound of the operating system requesting connection, on repeat, is driving the angry saplings barmy. Each writhes in its pot. Multitudinous pine plantlets are hungry, and their soil is drying out. The eldest, a mere six-inch sprig of brown and green, dribbling red from each of its leaf buds, leads the objection, with a shrill, eardrum-shattering scream. With all its might, it screeches again, lifts its first shallow root out of the pot, and places its down on the filthy floor.

FOR THE FORESTS WERE MADE OF OUR BONES

SARAH MUSNICKY

With the arrival of spring comes the threat of hope and the promise of fickle heat. The only clock Iosif trusts is the sun's rays trickling through the stoic birch trees overhead. Time in the logging camp moves differently from season to season, but with the arrival of the slow, steady thaw, the pressure to meet quotas breathes down their necks. The city needs to be rebuilt, but for each of his fallen men, he imagines their bones would make a better foundation.

How many bones are broken to build an empire? Iosif wonders while he helps the others pack up the tools for the day. The sun's rays now descend deeper into the forest, where all light goes to die. It is then that nighttime comes hungrily, and with it, the return of the cold desiring the warmth from their bodies. Looking at the state of the men, there's not much more warmth left to give.

Vasily, a big bear of a man, waits for them all to finish before nodding toward the direction of the barracks. It'll take an hour or two to get back, depending on the state of their path. Two other guards flank the group, one on either side, as the collective moves solemnly toward the entrance of the clearing. Like obedient dogs, they will be back in the morning. After three years, there have been few changes in the routine except for those coming to replace the dead.

The dead weigh heavily. When he sleeps at night, Iosif conjures the fallen whispering to him in his cot. They tell him stories of their family:

Naum with his uncle and his big belly laughs at the dinner table. Mikhail with his doch, waiting for her papa to come home. In another life, Iosif could have saved them, could have given them the medicine they needed and the food to warm their bellies.

It is the lost hope in their eyes, the gradual fading out of light as weakness takes hold he can never combat. Without hope, how can the sick persevere?

This thought sweeps into his mind on their way back. The snow-turned mud clings to their boots, drawing tired legs deeper into the ground. The forest and its trees steadily creep closer to the wandering men. Their barren grey trunks soar high into the sky like a fortress. The men cannot leave their path, the forest taunts. The taunts fall on deafened ears. One day, the men will fall these trees, too, all in the name of growth and a better tomorrow, whatever that promise entails.

His thoughts clouded, Iosif doesn't notice Vasily's all-seeing gaze. Nor does he see the man approach him, matching him step for step.

"Where have you wandered off to?"

The man starts, nearly sliding the bag off his shoulders. Vasily catches the strap before gesturing to Iosif to fix himself. Never lose composure, Vasily always says. Never lose face. It was as if they hadn't routinely witnessed their peers losing face the longer their sentences wore on.

"Thinking."

Vasily snorts. "That's dangerous." He soon changes the subject, directing his gaze to the right on a struggling young man. The trees loom over him in shadow, their dark tendrils licking at the worn fabric of his shirt, but they can still make him out in the encroaching darkness. Their eyes have adapted to the dark.

"Tak…skol'ko yemu ostalos'?"

"If we do nothing? Depends on if his mind is playing tricks on him yet." Iosif says.

The silence between them creates distance. Neither of them was willing to admit the truth out loud. Except for the guards, everyone in their group has seen something. As a man of science, Iosif once considered them mere hallucinations. But the winters wore down his resolve. By his logic, they all didn't have much time left.

Neither of them noticed the pathway opening ahead. The forest's trees part their trunks to reveal a sinister secret. It isn't until a guard comes barreling through the group that Iosif and Vasily register the change. They are back at the entrance.

A rumble of curiosity seizes the prisoners as the two guards blunder about. They are as hungry as the workers but less prone to patience. A hungry man makes a dangerous man. What then makes a starving man, Iosif wonders. One of the guards storms up to Vasily, jamming a long, undeservedly arrogant finger in the unreadable man's face.

"Tell me what happened."

Vasily shrugs. He knows no better than the men around him. "We all walk the same path. Just as you do."

The guard's face reddened. These men are beneath him. How dare this criminal say that they are the same? Anger wastes his body's precious warmth, but his emotions are in control here. He jams the finger again, this time into Vasily's cheek. Over and over, he prods, expecting different answers and different outcomes. But like the forest, the big man hasn't wholly yielded. Not yet.

Some illusions need to be broken.

A resounding crack whips through the air, reverberating through the clearing before being swallowed up by the surrounding trees. The guard falls to the side, landing squarely on his butt: his face crumbles, the faux layer of masculinity cracking before tears prick the corners of his eyes. The guard is only a boy now cowering before his overbearing father.

Vasily leans forward until his body dwarfs the guard's entirely.

"That's enough."

The prisoners know to say nothing. The guard whimpers while his colleague can only stare. Iosif shakes his head—the follies of youth. Give the young some power, and they think they own the world. Away from the safety of their superiors, both Iosif and Vasily know there will be no reprimands. Instead, they have other things to worry about.

The sun's rays are all but gone now. They've had enough time standing in the clearing for the cold to sneak in steadily. It quickly burrows under the worn fabric of their layers to nestle into their bones. In better conditions, they would have time. Now, time is fleeting, and the forest rapidly transforms into a different prison.

"We need light. Get the lanterns ready." Vasily turns back to where they had come from. "We will try again." He gives Iosif a strange look, implying he should know his thoughts. But he can't. All Iosif can think of is what the night brings.

With lanterns ready, Vasily directs the group back out, and they move forward. Iosif moves alongside his peers, keeping an eye out on the group. The muddied path hardens with the drop in temperatures, but he knows the frigidness of the dirt is gleefully leeching away at the soles of the men's feet. Frostbite is a common enough mistress in the camps; tonight, she'd revisit the men.

With the dark comes further illusions. The trees move closer to the group, encroaching on the manmade path the soldiers have had to cut back over the months. If Iosif didn't know better, the forest was just as hungry as the men. Coming out of hibernation, it, too, needed more than what the Republic could toss its way. The illness-ridden bodies left to rot in the forests were little more than snacks with no fat to suck on. There is barely any muscle to pick between the teeth.

Or perhaps it was his mind playing tricks on him. The balanda soup had long since made its way through his system. What else could his body do to distract him from hunger rather than conjure silly theories?

"Iosif, come! He's down."

Snapping him out of his thoughts, Iosif directed his attention towards Vasily. In seconds, he knows. His eyes snap around, trying to find the struggling man from earlier. A couple of men had swarm around the fallen comrade, leaving little doubt as to the patient's state. Iosif trudges forward, righting himself as the ground tries to slide out beneath him. Crouching down, he knows by the shallow breathing and the fluttering of eyelids that this is another body to add to his list. Another person he has failed.

The trunks of the trees sway in agreement as an Artic blast of wind whips through. Everyone ducks seemingly to escape it, but it's no use. There's nowhere to hide from the elements at this point.

The untouched guard from earlier pokes his hand down. A gentle tsk

tsk escapes his thin lips. "Kakaya trata. Leave him alone. They'll have us toss him out anyway…"

'Like the trash he is' goes unspoken amongst the group. If the boy isn't healthy enough to contribute to the cause, leave him. That's what they've always done. And failing is all that Iosif has done—first his country, then his family, and now his comrades. What good would he have been if he couldn't even help the few he was able to care for?

He stands up, looking around wild-eyed to see the faces staring at him. Something threatens to crawl out of his throat. Its claws scratch up his esophagus and run its talons against his throat. He wants to cry and scream. He wants to take his bloodied, callous- covered hands, poorly wrapped to stave off the cold and rend his clothes to ribbons. How much more can he mourn? How many more can he continue to watch fall?

The forest joins his comrades, watching, waiting to see what Iosif will do next. Vasily is the only one who looks at him calmly. They share this weight between them. The leader and the healer, failing and surviving in tandem. Vasily moves over and grips Iosif's shoulder like he always does. *Don't let them see you lose face.* Closing his eyes, he swears he can hear the bark crinkle and rustle with mirth. A life for a tree. Is that what this is? Is this the cost after all?

"I am not leaving him. You can go ahead, but I will not leave him." Vasily juts out his jaw and grunts in agreement.

The guard shrugs and gestures to the others. They can choose to stay or go, but the guards would instead select the barracks over the cold. The group murmurs, weighing the pros and cons. Loyalty means nothing in the camps. Iosif doesn't expect the others to stay, and they don't. One by one, the group follows behind the guards. As the light moves further into the forest, the darkness swallows them whole. Only Iosif and Vasily remain with the fallen man.

The two huddle back down, surrounding the young man with their bodies' warmth as best they can. Convulsions wrack his body, and he mumbles incoherently, each breath a waste of what little life operates in his flesh. Iosif can only watch before he feels the lightest touch cover the back of his neck. It tickles like fallen leaves, but it is a deception.

"What would you have me do, Iosif? Talk to me."

The voice is high and sweet; a boy barely of age whispers in his ear. A thin arm wraps around Iosif's neck, bright as day in the pitch blackness of night. Abram. Sweet, young Abram. He was the first to go. His crime? Stealing bread to feed his sister, Yelizaveta. The only thing he now fed was the forest floor.

Iosif tries to focus on the man on the ground. His hands reach downward to try to stabilize his head and keep the youth from injuring himself further. It's better to go peacefully than not.

"There's nothing peaceful about dying out here. You know this."

Brusk and deep, Mikhail, the father, walks out of the tree beside them and squats. Iosif jumps, dropping the man's head slightly. Vasily notices the lapse and quickly catches the head, taking over. He looks at Iosif's face and knows he's lost him. His friend's eyes are too far gone to be genuinely rooted in reality. The ghosts plague the guilty, and guilt is all Iosif can spare.

Mikhail now looks at him, his spirit long since untethered by the body he left behind. The specter reaches forward to pat Iosif's face, smiling that near-toothless smile he was once so ashamed of. Wispy white tendrils flit through the trees one by one, pushing up through the ground and leaving unbroken soil behind. Those left to die in the peak of winter easily slip through. The ground was too frozen for any burial for those fallen.

Scores of dead surround the living men. One barely breathed, the other futilely tried to keep the other alive while simultaneously keeping a watchful eye on his friend, and the third witnessed as he had witnessed so many before.

The forest stands back and watches, parading its ghostly citizens for the living to endure. For each fallen log, it has claimed another and another and another. It shall rebuild its domain with the bones of the Russki, with the bones of anyone who would dare infiltrate and take what wasn't theirs.

The men who had abandoned their comrades, too, greet the dead back in the logging camp. They will watch as the guards are torn apart, doing as they were told and relishing the power. The fallen comrades then turn on their own. They were ripping, peeling, and crushing the ones who barreled ahead, who stepped in place and kept their heads down to survive. Each one has families and friends; none will be spared.

For the forest grows from those left behind. Iosif knows this, and Vasily knows this. They've repeated this cycle again and again. As the man between them expires, his death rattle breaching from his chest, crackling and wet, they know their cycle is soon to reset. Once the man's spirit wanders from the flesh to join the others, their part in this is done until the next, for there will always be someone waiting to die. Someone unable to carry on.

With a final crack of bone and the man's breath finally dispersed, Iosif screams loud and never-ending: Another failure, another ghost, another inevitable outcome. Writhing in the mud and snow, the birch trees almost agree to give him solace. But as the spirits gather around, wrapping the hysterical man in their arms and bodies, whispering the tales of their brethren and fallen dreams, an agreement is shared among the whipping wind tickling the treetops.

To witness is to suffer. To repent is to dream. To dream is to hope. And for Iosif, hope remains forever fleeting.

A CLEARING NEAR VANAVARA

KUZMA MAC

In the railway station at Novosibirsk, you and I wait for the eastern Trans-Siberian line. We stand upon the concrete slab overlooking the tracks. The air is electric. It shimmers with heat from the steel. It buzzes with commerce, with conversation, with the new world overtaking the old.

It is the winter of 1995, and you are an old man. You feel the weight of decades on your bones. Your skin loosens and sags. Your back is hunched, and your nose has grown too fleshy. The cold worsens the ache of your joints. The others awaiting our train ignore us, these two ancient things out of time, as we stand at the precipice of our goodbyes.

You are young in the summer of 1908.

You are living in a house in the south of Yeniseysk Governorate, on the outskirts of the Vanavara Trading Post. Your family are trappers by trade. Your father hunts and brings furs to ship down the Tunguska river to the cities. You are a trapper now. You follow in his footsteps, seeking the skins of forest creatures, seeking the shapes of things hidden amongst the trees. The two of you are up at dawn, seeking your fortunes, and this is how I remember you: in a butterfly-shaped clearing near Vanavara.

In the winter of 1995, the distant whistle of the train pricks our ears.

A new electric model is pulling into the station, and with it, the air turns acrid. I always miss the smell of coal and steam, but you remind me that this is the price of progress. You miss it too, though. More than that, you miss what you were back when you smelled coal and steam.

The station activates around us as the carriage doors open by themselves. Streams of passengers flow and ebb into the metal bellies of the train. They shout over the sizzle of the engine, but their tide grows cautious around us. They bend away, heads bowed. "A sign of respect?" I muse. You remind me we are now fragile cargo.

You move slowly, purposefully, up the steps of the train. Your cane noses each curb as you ascend them. The metal rail sears cold against your wrinkled palm. The people behind us broil at the sudden stymying of their flow. They pull around each other to see the cause. Some find their patience and settle. Others edge around us to pass into the carriage.

You heed one such impatient group more than the rest. They are a particularly loud lot. They bark in English, betraying their origins, while their smells and uneven gaits betray their intoxication. You shrink yourself closer to the railing, but they fall into one another. One throws an elbow. It finds its mark against your shoulder. His body spills over us, breath reeking of cheap vodka. It's a miracle he remains upright—as if the ground itself refuses to indulge this drunken lunacy.

A hand presses you where the elbow struck—this one gentle and helping. The arm folds around you, lifting you back to your feet. The stranger apologizes profusely. His Russian lacks nuance in its pronunciation, but you follow his meaning well enough.

"Are you hurt?" he asks.

You shake your head. His friends are laughing. At us or at him? You wave off the thought, and you try to wave off the young man, but he insists on pursuing us to our cabin.

The sleeper car is quiet, but the reprieve is short-lived. His friends follow us inside. The young American helps you into our berth and asks if he might join us for a spell. You oblige. The view from our window is too lovely to take in alone.

I shrink from him. You can do the talking. I keep still and try to see him through your eyes. You see yourself in him: the son you never had. I admit, he reminds me of you in the summer of '08. But it is a surface familiarity, a shared ancestry and nothing more. He is from somewhere far away. You remember when they were our uneasy allies, then our enemies, and now again, our friends. Is it that I bear the old grudges more than you? You think his family is one of the lucky ones. They were among those who fled as the borders collapsed, who had means to strike out for a life in the west. He is one of the lucky ones by the very fact of his birth. Those who made him survived these many changings of the guard. At the end of it all, he lives, proof that someone like you once existed.

I balk at this notion and turn my thoughts to the man, here and now.

He looks to be in his twenties, little older than you when we first met. His hair is black, like yours once was. It is shaggy and hangs down over his eyes. The whole of him is unkempt. I wonder if these are the trappings of modern youth, or if his travels have taken their toll. He is not as drunk as his friends. The red of his nose and cheeks speaks to a slight tipsiness. Or is that the cold he's not used to, coming from America? He leans his head upon the window, shooting looks of reprimand over your shoulder, at the boys in the berth across the aisle.

"Where are you headed?" he asks as the boarders settle and the din dies down.

You answer, "Home."

The young man nods. "I'm crossing into China," he says. Then he continues, the purpose of his first question growing clear. Of the few Americans we have known, all behave this way. Talking to you is an excuse for them to talk more.

You were right. His ancestors were Russian. The ones who spoke the language were dead before he was born, but he learned what he could in university. Now, he's here to show his friends the sights, though he himself has only ever read about these sights in the guidebooks.

I watch out the window. It is many kilometers to Krasnoyarsk, though fewer than to the border. I think to ask why he takes the train, but you ask for me. They've been traveling since Moscow—because the Trans-Siberian is an experience, and not one to be missed.

You beg that I pay attention. I do. But really, I bide my time until we pass out of the city.

"So, you're heading home?" the young man asks.

I did not expect him to return to the topic of us. He seemed so keen to prattle on about his own travels. Yet, he asks, and you answer, "Yes. To a village called Vanavara."

"I don't know that one," he says. A pause. He squints. "Unless… There is *something* familiar about it…"

I make myself even smaller. His scrutiny is more than I can bear. But you bear it just fine, and answer, "It is remote, but we have had many come through over the years. Thanks to the meteor."

"The meteor?" he asks, the moment before it clicks, then, "*Ah!* The Tunguska Event?"

You nod. I do not like this line of questions.

"You must have–"

He stops himself. No doubt, he thinks himself rude for assuming we could have been alive that long. But you nod again, and his eyes grow wide—with awe, with wonderment of how you came to still be, with even more questions.

The second memory you shared with me was the sky split in two.

In the summer of 1908, you and your father are deep in the boreal forests that engulf the trading post you call home. It is early morning, but you are out as early as you can be to catch what stirs amongst the pines. You follow in his footsteps and you follow the line of his finger as he points to the blue starlight hanging above the treetops. The sky should be too bright to see stars. The blue light streaks downward, growing larger, growing so bright you must shield your eyes. It smears itself against your blue sky. From its body, black storm clouds roil to sully that vast, cloudless blue. There comes a sound like cannon fire and for the moment that follows, you sense nothing. When you come to, the sky is red and broken, and the earth beneath you buckles.

You fall to your knees as fire rains down. The heat of the flames bursts over you, forcing even the great tree trunks around you to bend and nearly splinter. It sears their bark and your skin. You are thrown back and shoved to the shuddering ground. Your father falls on top of you, shielding you from the worst of it, until the shaking ceases and the sky dims.

You learn later, upon returning home, that your windows were shattered and your door flung off its hinges.

The young man listens, enraptured by a story you've told countless times before. Like many others before him, he holds his breath until you've finished.

"We know now what it was," you say, "But when it happened, I thought the world was ending."

"That's astonishing. And this all happened—?"

"The summer of 1908."

The young man whistles. "I can't believe you're still around to talk about it. You might be the oldest person I've ever met." He stops himself, remembering his manners. "I only mean that… you'd be nearing a hundred. A hundred years! How much you must have seen…"

He lets his last word hang, begging you to continue recounting your memories. He expects these stories to fade with age, but I hold them all. You chuckle and silence me.

"I have many stories. Tell me what interests you."

I ask what you are doing. You say, "Indulging the curiosity of youth." I realize he no longer reminds you of yourself.

He asks the typical questions—about the world wars, about Stalin, about the rise and fall of the Union. He has known the Cold War, but only in terrifying concepts – an alien menace meant to corrupt the American ideal. His questions remind me of so many others, but in our twilight moments, they bring me back to 1921, and the first time they interrogated you about me.

"Why are you doing this again?" I ask.

"What again?" you respond. But I know what you are doing. You are suggesting something. It's in the tone of your responses and the way you're looking at him. These subtleties are not for him, but for me. And this isn't the first time you've suggested this.

The first time was in 1921, when the expedition arrived.

They are a survey team out of Leningrad, led by a mineralogist named Kulik. They are here to get eyewitness accounts of the explosion, they say. They tell you it was a meteorite. Kulik's men say many things you don't understand, about epicenters and blast radii and atmospheric transparency. They measure your memory in kilotons.

They ask what you experienced and you tell them everything. They ask what you found and I lie through your teeth.

We are both afraid in the survey of '21. Kulik's men are persistent. I fear what you will say, and I fear that I haven't been you long enough to speak believably in your stead.

You offer me your interrogator, and in that offer, I taste your fear.

He is educated, you say. He is a man of thought, of science. He is worldly and traveled. With him, I would have means far beyond a fur trapper's son. I could go to the city, go beyond the borders even, and seek experience beyond your peasant life. You insist then that you are thinking of me. You do not want me gone, but I know you are lying because you are afraid of what I will make you.

"Do I seem afraid now?" you ask me.

It is hard for me to tell. In the winter of '95, it is hard to tell where I end and you begin.

"I am not trying to get rid of you," you insist, "Not after so long."

"What, then?"

You tell me the same thing you told me back in '21. This young man is a man of the world. Compare the depth of our memories with the breadth of his. Think how rich his must taste. But now, you add—he is young. His muscles are not weak, his joints are not sore. He can move without pain. You ask that I remember what that's like. You tell me I must go on.

"Still pretending to think of me," I hiss.

"No," you say. I am surprised by this response. "I am being selfish. I am thinking of myself, because if you go on, then in whatever small way, so, too, do I."

I banish this thought of yours, like always.

The young man points out the window and finally, I feel peace. The city gives way to our forest. Siberian pine trees tower and spill out over the tracks. I ask that he get the window, and as he does, the breeze carries the familiar scent of their needles in the cold. The young man remarks on the sight, but I close my eyes and take in that smell.

There are still many kilometers to go until the station in Krasnoyarsk. The young man's friends have given up trying to steal his attention. Even now, when I open your eyes, he waits with another question. You tell him another story from your years away from Vanavara. You speak of what you can remember. I do not correct you, though I recall every detail.

You insist your experience is so little, and yet, it is more than you can even hold. We leave in '33 with Kulik's men – now no longer interrogators, but family. We remain us. We remain in Russia. We witness every shift of her political sands and we survive. We do not flee to America like this young man's people. We suffer the bitterness of winter and war. We love and feel the sting of its loss. We wonder together at every lesson learned, every stranger encountered, every new concept and dialogue and sight and smell. We do not need progeny to carry us on.

The young man hears out all your half-recalled tales, and then, at the last of them, he asks, "What brings you home, after all these years?"

You smile that he does not already know. "There is small comfort at the end," you tell him, "so you seek whatever comfort you can find. I am returning to the place I was born."

It sobers the young man and quiets me too. The happiness I feel at our return has clouded the concept, but now it looms again: evergreen and sharp and cold. *The end.*

"Sounds like you've led a good life," the young man offers. He hopes the platitude will add to our comfort, but it stings more than I let on.

In '21, you are not alone in offering your interrogator. But where I refuse, my siblings accept. It is the way of things. We are not meant to keep one skin for long. We are seeds meant to be sown. My siblings drop their bodies for Kulik's men. They bury the old in the dirt behind their shacks, in the darkened recesses below coniferous canopy. To you, my siblings are strangers now. Before, they were friends and neighbors. She was the woman cooking communal dinner every Sunday. He was her son, delivering letters for the post. She was the Evenki fur trapper who traded wares alongside you. They are shed and buried now. No more.

He was your father, asleep in his bed, never waking again.

I do not tell you I am sorry in 1921 because it is the way of things. Your father was an old man who lacked the wanderlust of my sibling's youth. Back then, you understand. You learn this is what will happen to you too, and your offers cease. When they return in '33, and there is nothing for you in Vanavara, you convince me and we leave with them.

The train whistles over our heads. In the summer of '95, the young man wishes us good night. He thanks us for your stories and returns to his berth.

When the sun sets, and you rest, I dream of the days before you. I am a wolf, hunting my prey. Desire alone drives me. My belly hungers, so I hunt. My body grows weary, so I rest. It is a simple existence—a single looping experience -- and though I am only wolf for a few days, I am bored.

In the morning, we are approaching Krasnoyarsk. As the train slows to its stop, you rise and exit the berth. The American stops us.

"Is there anything I can help you with?" he asks. He does not know the journey we yet have ahead of us, nor the inconvenient cost of helping us at all.

"Let him," you say. You are again asking me to consider him. Again, I decline.

You press me. His friends can stay in Krasnoyarsk. There is always drinking to be done. He will join us for the rest of the trip. He will fly with us to the old trading post. He will walk with us to its outskirts, to the place you buried your father, and to the promised place beyond. He will keep me company so that I might not decide now, but at the end, and your thought of the end wounds me once more.

"If you change your mind," you insist, "it will be too late."

But I will not change my mind. When I refuse, the young man shakes his head. "Let me at least help you off the train."

Before I can say anything, you accept.

The young man leads us by the arm down the steps. At the station in Krasnoyarsk, he extolls us with bittersweet goodbyes. He is better for having met us, he claims. You wish him well on his trip, and he wishes you the same.

"I hope you find your comfort," he smiles. The last we see of him, he returns to his seat and the cajoling of his American friends.

I watch the train disappear around the bend. We wait for our taxi, bundled in our winter clothes, watching our breath in the cold. Vanavara is not easy to reach by land. When we left in '33, it was summer and we took a boat down the river to reach the railways. In the winter of '95, we charter a flight from the airport in Krasnoyarsk.

It is another few hours until we land. You have never flown before. You take in the sight of our forest from so high up and I am elated with you. We look for the butterfly-shaped clearing amongst the pines, but we do not find it.

Vanavara has changed much since '33. The airport is tellingly modern but simple: a giant concrete slab two kilometers outside town. The roads remain unpaved, but there are motorized vehicles traveling them now. We walk as we always did. Your house is gone, and has been for a long while. No marker remains to indicate where it once stood. There are other buildings here – a new house, a logging outpost, a parking lot. If your father's grave was still behind that cabin, there is no sign of it now.

"I am sorry about your father."

You do not respond, because you forgave me long ago. You and I remain quiet until we reach the edge of civilization.

The first memory of yours I tasted began with you stepping into these woods.

Three nights have passed since the sky turned red, but for all that time, the night sky glowed as if by day. Your father has had trouble sleeping. Your neighbors, the cook and her boy, think the world truly is ending. Something has come to the forest, they insist. The light from the heavens now roosts deep beyond the trees.

In the summer of '08, the men and women of your village go seeking that light.

You and your father know these woods well. You lead the charge. You are armed, as are your father and the Evenki woman. This is a hunt, after all.

You move through the trees in formation. Though you set out with the rising sun, the forests are dark with places sunlight does not reach. Your eyes adjust and you walk with care. Your steps know the feel of solid ground amidst peat bog. Through fifty kilometers of pine and spruce, you trudge. You seek what you do not know but you will know if when you see it.

By evening, you are getting close. Closer and closer to the blast, the trees shift. Their trunks bend away, as you saw them do that fateful morning. They have frozen so. Continuing, they bend farther and farther still. Many are splintered and charred black, their needles seared from them. The canopy dissipates, opening the forest floor to a sky it hasn't seen in centuries. The charcoaled land still smokes, raw and empty. Further on the blackened trees remain upright, stripped of leaves, branches, and bark. All around this copse of dark spires, their brothers spill broken in unending heaps, felled by the blast. Years later, the scientists will tell you the decimated trees form the shape of a butterfly.

Beyond this clearing, you spot the blue light.

In the winter of '95, you stop walking.

We must have reached the blackened thicket, I think. A hundred years of growth have rendered it unrecognizable. By memory alone, we find the place, where just ahead there once was light.

You are exhausted. We have walked hours already. I tell you it is only a little further, but you sigh and sit down against the nearest tree. Just over that hill, past a young Siberian spruce, is a crater. We're so close, I beg you to get up, to just keep going, just a few steps more. You tell me to give you a minute.

I sit in silence waiting for you. This forest is so changed, and yet unchanged. These trees are not the ones you moved past in the summer of '08, yet they remain in the space of their ancestors, readying the space for their descendants yet to come.

Your village came seeking the light. You found me.

The first memory of yours I taste is the sight of me. I shimmer, because your eyes did not evolve to interpret my shapes. I am crystal and blue, because my true colors cannot be seen in your vision.

I am beautiful until I twist myself out of the shape of wolf.

You think you are dying. You are terrified. How my beauty betrays you. Your friends and neighbors are screaming as my siblings shed their wolf skins to join me. Your father is screaming. You scream at me. I am corrupting you, devouring you. I am a rot consuming your brain. I am a monster visiting upon you the worst violation imaginable.

You tell me, in the winter of '95, to stop thinking myself a monster. You stopped thinking that a long, long time ago.

In the summer eve of '08, I am seeking and consuming your memories. The taste of your mother's love, your father's pride. The taste of first steps and consciousness coming into being. I am your interrogator and you sate my natural born curiosity with the taste of human. Before you, I am so rarely the shape of things with their own thoughts. I am so rarely meat. I taste wolf, ever so briefly. But before that, I was stardust for so long. And before that, long before, in my infancy when even the universe was young, I was so many other things, beings you could never begin to imagine.

But you did imagine them, didn't you? In my dreams.

Because of me, you have existed far beyond yourself and the capabilities of your being. As I sustain myself on your memories, you consume mine incidentally, in fleeting glimpses at our stillness. In my memories of millennia, in my dreams, we are the wolf sprinting through the brush. We are stardust. We are beings of light and liquid and metal. We are an infinitesimal single cell and we are an infinite god.

You cling to my dreams as I cling to yours.

"You are still so young," you say, remembering all these impossible things, "There is so much left to be."

Again, I balk at this notion. "Do you truly wish that I leave?"

You do not answer.

I do not wish to argue with you, but it strikes me. "Is that why you spoke to the American? Because you think the dreams are real?"

"Aren't they?"

"No. They do not live. They are fragments of reality, but they are not real."

"Is there a difference?" you ask.

"It is only through something like you that I can experience anything at all. The remnants I hold from previous shapes are not those shapes. Your memories are not you."

You say nothing.

I continue, "If I become that American, I am that American. If I stop being you, I will never be you again. Can't you see that?"

Again, you don't answer, and I realize why.

For the first time in a hundred years, I am alone.

I move your eyes for the first time without you. I try to breathe, but your chest is so heavy to lift by myself. We did not make it to the butterfly-shaped clearing. It is just beyond that spruce, I think, or maybe many meters more.

"Is this good enough?" I know you won't respond.

I slowly lift your head—no, my head, mine alone. I lift my head to rest my skull against the trunk of the tree. I feel its bark press against my skin, wet my thinning hair against my scalp. I look up into the spiral of its needles. This one is young for a Siberian pine. It grew from the charred ashes of its forebear, burned from this earth at my arrival. It began growing not long after you passed its ancestor's corpse for the light in the woods. It will keep growing, for many years still, barring some unforeseen event burning it from this earth.

I have been many shapes in all these millennia. I do not wish to be more. I want to end with you, yet still I remain and you do not. Yet, you wish to. You are as afraid of death as you were when I became you. How has so little changed?

I think for a good long while in the empty stillness of your shape. I think until it dawns on me. I have been many shapes, but I have never called myself a name. Yours was my first. The millennia of things before you did not share that tradition. The American did. He had a name, and I have forgotten it already. It is useless to me because I do not want it. I will not be the shape of that young man, because I will never have another name.

I will wait until your body breaks down. I will wait until every piece of you returns to soil. I will wait until the roots consume what remains. I was born in the dark void at the beginning of time. It was nothing like this forest. But you were born here. And over that hill, beyond that spruce, I contorted myself into your shape and we were born. This is a good place to be born, and it is a good place to die, though I will not be gone for millennia yet to come.

But until then, I will stay the shape of the Siberian pine, and I will be your name.

ABOUT THE AUTHORS

E.M. ROY is a writer who loves all things weird and dark. Her horror fiction is rooted in queerness, existential anxieties, and New England aesthetics. *Let the Woods Keep Our Bodies* is her debut novel, released October 2023 from Ghoulish Books. She holds a B.A. in English from Boston University and currently resides in Maine with her parents, sibling, and dog, Boo.

AKIS LINARDOS is a shapeshifter disguised as an AI scientist to steal tech secrets from humans, and maybe help them make their innovations less dystopian for everyone. When his mission is complete, he will settle forever in his greek cave where he conjures dark tales and poetry, some of which can be found in *Apex Magazine*, *Strange Horizons*, *Uncharted*, *Heartlines Spec* and other bloodied places. Everyone's invited to his lair: https://linktr.ee/akislinardos.

VINCENT WEST is an emerging trans author with a keen interest in fantasy, horror, and romance. A writer since childhood, Vincent lives in Ontario, Canada, with his partner and pets. He can be found on Twitter as @VWestWrites and Bluesky as @VincentWest.

JON GAUTHIER grew up in the shadows of a pine forest just outside of his small Ontario hometown, where a steady diet of *Unsolved Mysteries*, *Ghostbusters* and *Goosebumps* fueled his love for the dark and macabre. He lives in Ottawa, Ontario, Canada with his wife, daughter, and a couple dozen unfinished and uncooperative stories.

K.L. MASSEY resides in the beautiful city of Nottingham, England. Specialising in weird fiction, she crafts surreal and sensual short stories infused with deep emotions, mundane terrors, and layers of symbolism.

NICOLE LYNN is a New England writer and legal guardian of two amazing kids. Her fiction has appeared in *The Arcanist, Nonbinary Review,* and *Orca, a Literary Journal.* She enjoys hiking mountains with her dogs and reading Kafka to her pet rats.

J.R. SANTOS is a Portuguese author of strange stories. His work was featured in anthologies such as *Archive of the Odd, Escalators from Hell,* and others. You can also read his novella, *Don't Cry For Santos,* or check out the upcoming *Love Aliens.* Find him online as ccskeleton, or customer care skeleton.

NEIL WILLIAMSON lives in Glasgow, Scotland. He writes in a mixture of genres and his work has been shortlisted for British Science Fiction Association, British Fantasy and World Fantasy awards. The Caledonian forest in western Argyll, where *The Family Axe* is set, has been part of the Scottish rural landscape since the last ice age.

MARISCA PICHETTE is a queer author based in Massachusetts, on Pocumtuck and Abenaki land. More of her work appears in *Strange Horizons, Clarkesworld, Vastarien, The Magazine of Fantasy & Science Fiction, Fantasy Magazine, Asimov's, Nightmare Magazine,* and others. Her poetry collection, *Rivers in Your Skin, Sirens in Your Hair,* was a finalist for the Bram Stoker and Elgin Awards. Her first novella, *Every Dark Cloud,* is forthcoming in spring 2025 from Ghost Orchid Press.

REN GRAHAM is an illustrator and fiction writer living in the rainy Pacific Northwest. With a B.A. in Art History and graduate studies in Scientific Illustration, Ren is fascinated by history, biology, and folklore, and especially how these elements can combine to make a spooky story. They are fond of isometric RPGs, their three cats, and a warm cup of tea.

J.S. BETULA is a genderqueer speculative fiction writer from the swamps of rural New York. Xe loves goopy practical effects and unpleasant final girls, and you can find hir work in *Divinations Magazine, Troublemaker Firestarter, Underscore Magazine,* and elsewhere! You can also find hir on twitter @jsbetula.

ALLY WILKES's debut novel, *All the White Spaces*, was a Bram Stoker Award finalist, and her second novel, *Where the Dead Wait*, was one of Esquire's best horror books of 2023. Her short fiction has been published in numerous magazines and anthologies including *Nightmare, Three Crows, FOUND: an anthology of Found Footage Horror,* and *Darkness Beckons.* Ally grew up in a succession of isolated—possibly haunted—country houses and boarding schools. After studying law at Oxford, she went on to spend eleven years as a criminal barrister, learning how extreme situations bring out the best (or worst) in human nature. Ally now lives in Greenwich, London, with an anatomical human skeleton, and far too many books about Polar exploration. Whatever the time of year, she can't wait for Halloween.

DAPHNE FAUBER (she/her) is a queer writer, Best of the Net nominated artist, and microbiologist based out of Boston. When not reading books or agar plates, she can be found playing too many video games. Her work has been published in the *Brave New Girls Anthology, Permafrost Magazine, Diet Milk Magazine, and Pile Press,* among others. She can be found on Instagram at @daphne.writes or at her website www.dank.pizza.

BRYAN HOLM grew up in Minnesota and lives there with his wife and dog. He is a photographer by day who spends his nights writing and consuming all things horror. His short fiction has been published in anthologies by *Sinister Smile Press, Eerie River Publishing*, and *HellBound Books.* His debut novella will be released in 2025 with Anuci Press. Website: www. bryanholm.com.

JONAH BUCK wanted to study eldritch knowledge and commune with pale, semi-human creatures that flit across the sunless landscape to terrorize the living, so he became an attorney in Oregon. His interests include history, professional stage magic, paleontology, and exotic poultry. He is the author of several novels, including *Carrion Safari* and *Substratum*, as well as a bunch of short stories.

AIRIC FENN is a child of the Rocky Mountains and spends more of their time in their own vivid imaginings than perhaps is proper (but who really cares about proper?). Their writing currently focuses on fantasy and horror told through a Queer lens, and they've been known to pen the occasional poem. When they aren't writing, you can find them making art or dabbling in one of their many other hobbies, from leathercraft and bookbinding to exploring the outdoors and attending renfaires.

BRIAN ROWE spent most of his life working as a truck driver and equipment operator. After suffering injuries that limited his mobility, he went back to college and earned a degree in English from Kent State University in 2022. He is ace-spec and neurodivergent. He can occasionally be spotted on Bluesky at @brianedits.bsky.social.

H.V. PATTERSON (she/her) lives in Oklahoma and writes speculative fiction, poetry, and plays. Recent publications include *Haven Speculative, hex literary*, and *Flash Fiction Online*, as well as anthologies from Sliced Up Press, Flame Tree, Eerie River, Creature Publishing, and Black Spot Books. H.V. loves fungi and hopes fungal bioremediation will help reduce pollutants and plastic waste in the future. She's a cofounder of *Horns and Rattles Press*, and you can find her on X @ScaryShelley, on Instagram @hvpattersonwriter, or at hvpatterson.com

LB WALTZ has been publishing creative works for over 20 years under various pseudonyms. They enjoy taking walks, biblically accurate depictions of angels, and reading about botanical folklore. Find them on Twitter @balmroomdance, or hiding *UNDERNEATH THE PERSIMMON TREE.*

SJ TOWNEND, an author of dark fiction, has stories published with *Vastarien, Ghost Orchid Press, Gravely Unusual Magazine, Dark Matter Magazine*, and *Timber Ghost Press*. Her first horror collection, *Sick Girl Screams*, is out Oct' 2024 (Brigid's Gate Press) and her second horror collection, *Your Final Sunset*, is coming in 2025 (Sley House Press). Twitter: @SJTownend

SARAH MUSNICKY (she/they) is the author of *"For The Forests Were Made Of Our Bones,"* a story loosely inspired by familial stories as told by her otchim. In these stories, memories are like ghosts. When we look back far enough, they come back to haunt us. When she's not last-minute conjuring up stories, she can be found working one of her many other jobs. If you're looking for more of her writing, check out her contributions to Ghost

Orchid Press's *Rewired* and Third Estate Books' *Spectrum*. Follow them on Instagram at @sarahmusnicky.

KUZMA MAC is a video game designer by day, writer, artist, and horror enthusiast by night. He has been telling stories in one form or another since he could pick up a pencil. In art school, he discovered a particular passion for horror and never looked back. His writing centers the beauty of the grotesque and the unusual, drawing inspiration from cosmic horror, stop motion animation, and the Ukrainian folk tales of his grandmother. He currently resides in Los Angeles with his partner and their two cats.

ABOUT THE EDITOR

KATHERINE SILVA is an ace Maine horror author, a connoisseur of coffee, and victim of cat shenanigans. Her favorite flavors of the genre mix grief and existentialism which she combines with her love of the New England wilderness in her works. She is a three-time Maine Literary Award finalist for speculative fiction. Katherine is also editor-in-chief of Strange Wilds Press. You can find out all about her work at katherinesilvaauthor.com.

CONTENT WARNINGS

CABIN CREATURES - gore, death

EVERY MASK, ANOTHER CASK - none

GATHERING OF THE DEAD - off-screen femicide, implied gender-based violence, body horror

NIGHTMARE IN KETTLE PARK - violence, blood, cannibalism, death

TRUE NORTH - child neglect, abuse, and murder

COLD WHITE TEETH - frozen human remains, death

THE FAMILY AXE - death of a parent/family member, body horror

SOFT FIRE - trauma, attempted murder, burn scars, death

THE BANNIK - death, implied abuse

HALLOWED GROUND - description of animal injury, graphic description of a dead animal, implied attempted suicide

IN THE HIGH PLACES - none

PATRIMONY - implied child neglect, burning, death of a parent

ROADSIDE CROSS - animal death, child death, organs, death, skeletons

ALWAYS PREPARED - blood, death, violence against women, gore

WALDEINSAMKEIT - bones, death and decay, and body horror

DESECRATIONS - fire/burning, eye trauma, implied gore, organs, religious themes (fantasy possession)

PRACTICAL APPLICATIONS OF FUNGAL BIOREMEDIATION - Death, failure of medical devices

RULES FOR SEEKING ANGELS - existentialism, dead animals, body horror, religious themes

HE HAS NOT SEEN A BIRD BEFORE - blood, body horror, death, sexual intimacy, animal death

FOR THE FORESTS WERE MADE OF OUR BONES - death, grief

A CLEARING NEAR VANAVARA - harm to people and animals, body snatching, loss of a loved one, natural disasters, and allusions to alcohol consumption

SPECIAL THANKS

A special thanks Red Lagoe for her insight while putting together this anthology. Since this is the first anthology from Strange Wilds Press, I was out of my depth and needed expertise from someone who knew better than I did. If you haven't read any anthologies edited by Red or put out by her small press, Death Knell, be sure to check them out.

Thank you also to authors Amanda Headlee and L.P. Hernandez for their early blurbs for the book. You two rock.

OTHER WORKS
FROM
STRANGE WILDS PRESS

THE DEADLANDS SERIES

UNDEAD FOLK
DEAD FOLK
NOTHINGLAND

THE WILD OBLIVION

THE WILD DARK
THE WILD FALL
HALLOWED OBLIVION
LOST OBLIVION
ORCHARDS
DAN & ANDY'S SCARY-OKE HOLIDAY

THE MONSTRUM CHRONICLES

VOX
AEQUITAS
MEMENTO MORI
ACQUOLINA

OTHER TITLES

VULPINE CURSE
THE COLLECTION: A NOVELLA
NIGHT TIME, DOTTED LINE